SOLACE

S.L. SCOTT

Dreams Are Free!
S.L. Scott
x

S.L. SCOTT

Happy Camping [illegible]

[illegible] x [illegible]

Editing:

Marion Archer, Making Manuscripts

Karen Lawson, The Proof Is in the Reading

Marla Esposito, Proofing Style

Kristen Johnson, Proofreader

ISBN: 978-1-940071-57-2

Nothing heals a broken soul like the love of a true heart.

ALSO BY S.L. SCOTT

The Kingwood Duet

SAVAGE

SAVIOR

Hard to Resist Series

The Resistance

The Reckoning

The Redemption

The Revolution

The Rebellion

Talk to Me Duet

Sweet Talk

Dirty Talk

Welcome to Paradise Series

Good Vibrations

Good Intentions

Good Sensations

Happy Endings

Welcome to Paradise Series Set

From the Inside Out Series

Scorned

Jealousy

Dylan

Austin

From the Inside Out Compilation

Stand Alone Books

Missing Grace

Until I Met You

Drunk on Love

Naturally, Charlie

A Prior Engagement

Lost in Translation

Sleeping with Mr. Sexy

Morning Glory

To keep up to date with her writing and more, her website is www.slscottauthor.com to receive her newsletter with all of her publishing adventures and giveaways, sign up for her newsletter: http://bit.ly/SLSNewsletter

Join S.L.'s Facebook group here: S.L. Scott Books

SYNOPSIS

A second chance never tasted so sweet

He puts the Bad in bad boy.

She puts the Sweet in sweetheart.

When a hired gun burns out from the life he's been living, he returns to the small country town where rumors run rampant and everyone goes to church on Sunday.

With sins and secrets trailing *Jason Koster* home, he is searching for redemption in hopes of living a life less complicated. He didn't expect to find the only girl he ever loved now a recently single woman running her family farm.

Delilah Noelle never needed much, but she wanted Jason Koster—one time love of her life. When misunderstandings tear the former beauty queen and quarterback apart, can a second chance heal their broken hearts?

Will the years and circumstances that have passed be too much to bridge the distance to a future together?

Solace is a heartwarming small town romance with plenty of action and swoons that will have this hometown hero vying for the affections of his high school sweetheart.

SOLACE

Noun

Comfort or consolation in a time of distress or sadness.

Verb

Give solace to.

There is no comfort to be given from one who knows no comfort.

Can I be a man who provides solace when I can't find my own?

PROLOGUE

It's pouring rain, but I don't care. I can't look away from my past.

God, she's beautiful.

We shared so many shameless kisses. Our bodies covered in the slick love we'd made. Carefree hair blowing in the wind. A sunset captured on the back of a fishing boat.

Yeah, we were wild and in love back then with no cares in the world. But something I've learned is all good things must come to an end, whether by choice or circumstance. Nothing good can last.

And it didn't.

A love so pure, so innocent in its faith—like ours—could never survive.

Didn't survive.

We were young.

We were naïve.

We were so damn in love.

And then apparently, we weren't.

The motorcycle's too loud to be considered stealth. A

bike like this, even custom and almost costing as much as a small house, will never impress her.

How do I know that? Because *I* never impressed her.

Guess that's why she left me.

Or did I leave her?

I know the truth, but sometimes I pretend the facts are fuzzy. Hazy facts or not, four years is a lot of time to pass without living with your other half—your better half.

She'd called us soul mates at one time. Maybe she was right, and it's half my soul I've been living without all this time. I'm back in the same town I once hated, sitting in front of the same house I once visited regularly, not thinking clearly, much like a night I'd like to forget.

This time she's standing on that front porch.

I don't know what I was thinking coming back here. I don't know what to think at all.

Maybe . . .

No. She's not an option—she's married. She's off limits.

It didn't stop *him* back then, but it should stop me now. But then wild memories fill my brain—holding her in my arms and making her promises I intended to keep.

So young.

So naïve.

So damn in love.

Rumor is he hits her.

Rumor is she visits my mom on occasion to reminisce.

Rumor is she misses me.

Fuck.

Rumors. Fucking rumors.

Looking at her on that front porch now, she's still so damn beautiful. I see that same look in her eyes I remember from back then. It's the one that brought me to my knees the first time I ever laid eyes on her.

I scrub my hands through my soaked hair and question everything I'm about to do. *What am I doing here?*

Her smile, her small wave . . . two things I've craved. *Missed.*

My choice is made.

I swing my leg off the bike and cut the engine to the black Harley to find out. I shove my hands into the pockets of my wet leather jacket and start walking across the lawn I've walked a million times.

I grab the railing that wobbles and is covered in chipped paint, prop one foot up on the bottom step, and stare at her.

Life brings many things that catch us, distract us, keep us. I'm not one easily caught, though. But the one thing I never seemed to be able to get *uncaught* in is Delilah Noelle.

It's been too long since I've laid eyes on the beauty standing before me. "Hi."

Her shoulders drop, the tension falling away as if she's been waiting for this day, and it's finally come. "What took you so long?"

1

Jason Koster

New York is always an option. I hate Manhattan, but I could live in a borough. I could blend into city life and disappear among all the other ghosts donning black clothes that inhabit the area. I pass the exit, the city no longer a choice, and keep driving south.

I never felt like I belonged there anyway.

I've traveled this country from Maine to Los Angeles, Alaska to Key West. I stayed a few days in a motel outside of Atlanta. Swam in the gulf along the Mississippi coast. Drank whiskey in the freedom of Joshua Tree, and slept under a blanket of stars in Texas.

~~I lived.~~

I survived.

Yet, all roads seem to lead me here.

My jersey number still graces the beat-up old sign along the highway. The billboard is just before the exit that leads you to a one-traffic-light town with a pharmacy that still serves ice cream at the counter and Wilbur Macy still sits in a rocking chair at the corner of Main and First Street.

It's the kind of place where you'll find the whole town at the stadium on Friday night and then in church on Sunday morning, not leaving much time to sin. Although we always managed to squeeze a little in.

I laugh when I spot the sign I use to shoot my BB gun at while driving by: *This is God's country. Don't drive through it like hell.*

This time I actually slow down. Might be the first time. I don't want the attention, much less Jeffrey Whaley, the town deputy, pulling me over. I've managed to avoid the law for some time now, so there's no need to cause trouble in my hometown, especially when I've earned a few new scars and inked my skin. I know he'll have a problem with a tattoo. He'll judge me from that alone, but I also have a backpack full of memorabilia. I don't want to explain, much less talk about where I've been the last three years.

Unfortunately, I have to cruise down Main to get home.

Home.

My home was never a place, but a person. It's funny how time changes things. I don't think about Delilah as much anymore. I'm really good at pocketing those disconcerting feelings away, but damn if being here doesn't drag them all back to the surface.

As familiar as this place feels, it doesn't feel like home.

Glancing down First when I pass under the green light, I'm tempted to cruise by her house. I wave to Wilbur instead—glad to see he's alive and still rocking on that corner—and keep driving. I should really say hi to my mom, but my throat is dry, so I pull into a parking spot a few down from Red River—the main bar here. Don't want to see anybody I know, but I will, so I might as well get it over with.

I pull open the door and walk inside. It's dark and my eyes aren't adjusted, but I know this place by heart so I keep walking until everything comes into view.

Front door. Top half glass.

Back door through the small kitchen in the left corner. One large window.

One window in the men's and two smaller windows in the women's restroom.

Five booths.

Six people.

Ten barstools.

Five taken.

Nodding to the bartender standing by the far end near the three beer taps, I take the one vacant place at the end of a row of occupied barstools. Looking down, four guys stare back at me.

"Daryl and Billy. Should have guessed you'd be taking up space here."

The bartender, McGilley, swings his towel over his shoulder and rests two hands on the bar top in front of me. "Well, look what the cat dragged in. If it's not Mr. Eight himself, Jason Koster. What do we owe the pleasure, your high and mighty-ness?"

"I haven't been that number or guy in a long time. How about a Heineken?" That entertains the guys, and they start laughing, mocking me. "Never mind. How about a Budweiser?"

McGilley asks, "You sure about that? That's a working man's beer. Might be hard on your stomach."

"Serve the fu—" I catch myself. I can't talk like that around here. I'll end up in a fight and spending the night in jail. "I think I can handle it." I put a ten on the counter. "Keep the change."

"Big spender. So where've you been that you decided to come home and spend money like it doesn't matter?" Daryl asks.

Daryl Satters—grew up down the road from me. One year ahead of me in school. Got a job at the plant out of high school. All-around asshole. I'm not surprised to see him here. I figure his ass is parked on a barstool at Red River by five each night, drinking his sorrows away just like his dad. Once dreamed of being a pro-baseball player, but that took a dedication he never had for the game. Ironic how he's worked at the same industrial plant for eight years. *That* takes dedication.

My beer is set down, the money swiped from the bar. I take a long pull before answering. "All over."

Billy lines up and fires his question next, "What have you been doing for work?"

I always liked Billy Langston. A tick older than me, we were in the same grade. At one time, I called him one of my best friends. He always had my back.

"It's good to see you, Billy."

"You too, Koster. Rumors have been flying for years about what happened to you. Did you return to put 'em to rest?"

"Nah. Let them gossip." I down my beer and set the empty down when I stand up. Not looking to entertain an interrogation, I'm ready to go. This might be a record. Ten minutes and I've already had my fill of this town. Or maybe it's these two in front of me. They look the same, talk the same, give shit the same. But I know I'm not that same guy they used to know. The darkness I carry hangs heavy over my head. My carefree football days are long gone. I don't need to be here any longer. "I'm heading out."

McGilley asks, "Going to see your ma?"

"Heading there now." I tap the bar top and head for the door. "See you around, gentlemen."

The sun is setting when I head down Main Street and take the curve out to the house where I grew up. It's dark when I pull up the dirt drive and cut the engine. I'm surprised the sound of the Harley didn't drag my mom to the window. The lights are on inside, a few of the shades still open. The TV is muffled but heard through the thin walls of the old house. It needs some care. If I stay more than a day or two, I can help her around the house, make sure things are in good working order.

I think about walking in the back door like I always have, but decide against it. She hasn't heard from me in a few months, much less seen me for years, so I head to the front and knock.

The door opens and she pushes the screen door with her hand before leaning against the frame. A mischievous smile appears, tipping up one side. I've been told I smile the same way. Guess I learned from the best. Her hair is pinned back but some strands from a long day of work have fallen. She's dressed like she has someplace to go, but I know better. She's a homebody by choice. Meredith Koster just likes to look good. She crosses her arms, and says, "Well, if it isn't my long-lost son. What brings you to town, kid?"

The kid reference makes me smile. Also makes me miss the innocence that the name suggests. "Just thought it was time for a visit."

She drops the hard-ass act and opens her arms. "Come here." Hugging me tight, she adds, "I have missed you so much. I don't know why you like to worry me like you do."

One front door. Two deadbolts. One chain. A screen door.

Back door. Three small windows. Two locks. A screen door.

Fourteen windows total.

It feels good to hug her again. I'm way bigger than she is, outgrowing her by eighth grade, but she still hugs me like I'm her baby. Backing into the house, she says, "Get on in here and close the door behind you. You're letting bugs in."

The screen door screeches closed and I shut the front door, locking it behind me, even though I've never considered myself the paranoid type. I probably should be, considering what I've been up to, but I never felt unsafe at home.

She moves into the kitchen as I drop my backpack on the floor. Peeking out, she says, "You sure are traveling light these days."

"A few changes of clothes. The basics are all I need." I start for the kitchen but get sidetracked by the framed photos on a bookcase. My graduation photo is too large to enjoy. No one needs to see an eight-by-ten in a cheap brass frame, highlighting a bad haircut. There's a photo of me as quarterback senior year of high school and one from my little league days. The baby pic of me with my face covered in cake is humiliating, so I don't linger too long on that one. That seems like a lifetime ago, and a broken arm in college ended my glory days.

Bending down, there's a smaller five-by-seven from prom night. Delilah Noelle. The belle of the ball. The queen of my heart. The town darling. We made a good-looking couple, a match in every way. The head cheerleader who fell for the football star. *So unoriginal.* People said we were so sweet we gave them a toothache.

It was real.

We were real.

Looking over my shoulder, my mom says, "I can't seem to pack it away."

A lot like my feelings for Delilah, despite how hard I've tried.

I stand up and turn to my mom. I take the offered mug of tea, not wanting to talk about the girl in the photo or the woman across town.

Sitting on the couch, Mom asks, "How long are you staying?"

"How long will you have me?"

"As long as you need."

"I'm not hiding out."

"Okay, as long as you want then." She sips her tea and I do the same. "I've cleaned your room, and you have plenty of clothes in the closet and the dresser. I can take you out shopping tomorrow for anything else you might need."

"I don't need you to buy me things. I can afford what I need."

"How is that exactly? What do you do, Jason?"

"Odd jobs. Here and there."

She knows when to stop pushing for answers I'm not going to give her. Standing, she asks, "Are you hungry? I was just about to make grilled cheese sandwiches with tomato soup."

"That sounds incredible."

"You go settle in and clean up, and I'll make dinner."

I grab my bag and head down to the hall but stop when she adds, "It's good to have you home, son."

Home.

There's that word again. It's a word I haven't known in some time. Am I home? I'm not really sure anymore, but my mom has always been a haven, so she deserves to hear that from me. I smile and say, "It's good to be home."

2

Jason

MY CHILDHOOD BEDROOM is a memorial to my golden years —the football star, devoted son, all-around favorite. I was the envy of this town.

The fall from grace was inevitable. I was set up for it with every win, trophy, and accolade I received.

Looking around the room, I take off my shoes and clothes, leaving my briefs on as I make my way down the hall to the one bathroom the whole house shares. It takes a week for the water to warm up, but when it does, I let it pound the stiffness from my shoulders. One hand on the tile, and my head lowered, I wonder why I came back. Why do I bother?

My mom?

Sure. It's always good to see her. Doesn't matter what I've done or how long it's been since we talked, she's open arms, all smiles, and still proud of me. She's a good woman who works too hard.

No one else in this town mat—

I can't complete that thought.

I know it's a lie. Everyone knows it's a lie. I saw it in their faces down at Red River. They can see through me when it comes to Delilah.

My only true weakness. *Even after all this time.*

The one weakness I can hide when I'm *not* here.

Married.

I push the thoughts of how I got my feelings all fucked up back to the dark compartment I keep them buried in. I think that's my heart, but I'm not sure anymore.

Can a man that's killed another man really have a heart? It's a mystery, even to me, if I'm allowed to feel anything other than remorse, and I just can't reason that emotion into my psyche. Not when that same man wanted to kill the people I care about. I remind myself that it was part of the job, but not the job I signed up for. Who did I become once I left home? And is that guy truly gone forever?

The water rains down, and I hope to have some sense of myself once the wicked is washed away, if it can be washed away. I have my doubts.

After showering, I wrap the towel around my waist and head to my room. I dig through old drawers until I find some boxers and flip through the hangers, choosing a black T-shirt that's not too faded. Grabbing a pair of black jeans from a stack on top of a crate in the closet, I pull those on too.

The leather of my shoes is wet from the road, so I grab socks and head out to the living the room. My mom is setting down two mugs of soup and two plates with the hot sandwiches on top. She made me two and browned the edges making them extra crispy how I like them. They're better for dipping in the soup that way. Less soggy when you pull them out.

She smiles, looking surprised. "And here I thought that dirt was freckles."

"Ha. Ha." Sitting on the couch, I lean forward over the coffee table, my stomach growling. "This looks good. Thanks, Ma."

"It feels good to cook for someone else again."

Despite the distraction of dinner and *Wheel of Fortune* playing on the TV, I can feel the slight tension in the room. I take one of the sandwich triangles and dip it in the soup before taking a bite that almost finishes off half of it. We're casual people, the kind that manners matter, but when we slip up, we're forgiven. So I keep eating and glance over at her. "What's on your mind?"

That catches her attention and gives her the opening she's been waiting for since I showed up on her front porch. "You going to tell me why you're home and why I didn't get a heads-up?"

"Can't a son visit his mom?"

"Any time, any day. You're always welcome. I haven't seen you in a long time, so I didn't know if I should be worried or not."

I take a sip of my tea, the ice crashing around the glass. "No need to worry. Just stopping by on my way through."

"Through to where?"

"Not sure. I've got no plans right now."

Reaching over, she pats my leg. "Then stay a while."

"I might. Not sure yet."

She sits back with her mug of soup, sipping it quietly and staring at the TV. "Aurora Borealis."

"What?"

"The puzzle. It's Aurora Borealis."

I smile. "Sure is. Good job."

An hour passes with ease, but my body is starting to give up the fight to stay awake. I'm road weary and the thought of that bed in there is heaven. I gather our dishes and clean up the trash. I refill Mom's glass and get her the blanket from the couch, helping her settle in for the night. "You staying up?" I ask.

"There's an old Cary Grant movie coming on I want to watch, and I'm halfway through a very intriguing book. Are you going to bed?"

"I am. I'm tired."

"Tomorrow's Saturday."

"You don't work. Anything I can do around here for you?"

"I have a whole list we can start on if you don't mind."

Walking toward the hall, I reply, "I don't mind."

"Maybe we can talk about the subject you're so eager to avoid, too."

Maybe not. I'm not used to having anyone care about my thoughts. That probably won't or shouldn't change while I'm here.

"Yeah, maybe. Night, Ma."

"Good night, Jase."

After readying for bed, I climb under the covers and let my body sink into the mattress. It's a cheap bed, but it's worn in all the right spots to fit my body. Delilah used to complain about rolling into the middle. Secretly, I loved it. I loved holding her close like that, my lips against the back of her neck, my nose full of her scent—vanilla with a hint of oranges—my arms cradled around her with no space left between us.

I didn't expect to have such a visceral reaction to being

home again, especially while lying in this bed alone. It almost feels like I never left.

Almost. Until I remember what I've been doing the last three years, what I've done . . . It's a life I can never drag anyone into much less my mom *or* Delilah. Not like she's an option anyway, considering she's married.

I get up and squat down next to the mattress. Lifting it, I dig around a few dirty magazines until I find what I'm looking for. The blinds are cracked open enough to let a little moonlight drift inside the small room. I lie back down and hold the photo above me. Those little summer dresses Delilah wore back then drove me wild.

Easy access is the term that comes to mind, but it wasn't like that with us. She was never easy in my eyes . . .

Every day our sophomore year Cole, Billy, Daryl, and I followed the Noelle sisters and the other cheerleaders from the high school to the diner downtown. We never talked to them as we ate burgers and drank milkshakes, but boy, they were pretty. Easy on the eyes was an understatement. The brightest star in our country corner of heaven was Delilah Rae Noelle.

I'd catch her eyes on me when she thought I wasn't looking. She was a straight-up distraction during football season, but man, she did that short skirt justice.

. . . By seventeen we were having sex, but every time I lay down with her, I felt air leave my lungs and my heart beat faster. She took my breath away.

I'm not sure how it got out of hand so fast. Four years, almost to the day we started dating, we were breaking up. Junior year in high school to junior year in college. Football season. One minute we were fighting about me getting a full ride scholarship to a state university and transferring the next semester, and then she was walking back to town with me driving behind her, begging her to get back in the truck.

She never did.

That whole situation was a clusterfuck. It didn't matter how many times I called her, texted, or stopped by her house; she shut me out. As a last resort, I poured my heart into a letter I never had the fucking nerve to send. Billy brought the beers. The letter became a part of the night when I poured beer on it and threw a match on top. I watched it burn, like I was watching my heart catch fire. The ashes floated toward the sky, and I wished the pain I felt inside would go along with it.

I was almost convinced I could move on from loving her, but four years isn't easily forgotten, especially in a small town where everything held a memory of happier times.

On a cold day just before New Year's Eve, almost three months after the worst day of my life, I detoured by her daddy's farm in one last sad attempt to talk to her.

I then realized why my best friend had been too busy to hang out. Cole Cutler's truck was parked proudly in front of her house. I'd been wondering why he hadn't returned my calls, and why he wasn't hanging out with the guys when we went out. He never showed up for our Sunday fishing trips. It was all too clear. Cutler also got called out in football practice for unnecessary roughness against the quarterback—aka me.

Every guy loved the Noelle girls. By our junior year, Daryl had the gumption to ask one out every day on that walk from the diner before we all split off in different directions to head home. "Might today be the day that the beautiful Delilah Rae will accept my offer of a movie and a drive over to Kerbyville?"

Every day the girls giggled. Shelby Noelle was never shy and was happy to smart back. "You know, Daryl, if you put this much effort into playing football as you do begging my sister to go out with you, you might make first string."

Cole hit his shoulder. "She's got your number, Satters. Step aside and watch the master."

. . . I never confronted him. I didn't get the chance. They made *their* couple debut on a Friday night at Red River, even though we had told each other how much we loved each other and would *always* love each other. Even though she never allowed me to see her and apologize and sort out what-the-fuck ever happened that night. There she was. Forget Cole and him fucking over his best friend while trying to fuck his girlfriend. Despite *all that*, she walked into Red River with him. Her eyes found mine the minute she showed up and mine found Cole's. McGilley is strict on the no-fighting rule, but I was the only one thrown out that night.

My best frie—*former* best friend—stood there with blood running from his nose and a new black eye to match his dirty deeds. I sat in my truck parked across the street for thirty minutes, watching him and Delilah argue on the sidewalk. Guess the honeymoon phase of their courtship had already worn off.

From what I heard from Billy the next day, she walked home from the bar that night. But Cole's truck was back on that farm the next night when I drove by as if I had business out in the middle of nowhere.

It was strange to think about us graduating high school together and starting college as a solid group of friends. Now as juniors we were divided and broken beyond repair. I headed off to college a few days later, ready to start training with my new team and determined to forget how good she felt in my arms. I tried to forget how my sheets used to smell of her and how our bodies were made for each other.

But coming back that next summer was tough. My mom needed help around the house with a new fence, so I came home. It was the longest summer of my life. I became a pro at avoiding all the places we'd frequented as a couple and adding the loss of one of my friends into the mix didn't help matters. Our friends felt divided, so I bowed out most of the time to make it easier on them. For the life of me I couldn't understand how Daryl and others took Cole's side on this. They knew how much Delilah meant to me. They knew better than to touch another man's girl.

Billy remained by my side, the only one I trusted. He hung out with me all summer. He didn't talk about Delilah, but let me when I felt the need. Made me realize that it wasn't about the quantity of friends I had, but the quality that mattered. We built my mom's new fence with all the spare time we had to burn before I returned to college in the fall.

I said goodbye to my mom and almost took the long route out of town, passing by the Noelle farm. *Almost.*

Instead, I took Main and hit the highway. I was gone and had no plans of coming back. I would play college football on a scholarship and then get drafted into the NFL.

Sometimes life doesn't go as planned.

Sometimes you don't end up playing pro ball.

Sometimes you don't get the girl.

I drop the photo on the nightstand, giving it more respect than being buried among my old stash of magazines. Maybe I should stop by the farm while I'm in town. Maybe I shouldn't. I scrub my hands over my face and get up to check the window.

The moon is bright, lighting the backyard. I scan the area, and my gaze lands on the swing I use to sit on with Delilah late into the night. Sometimes you find yourself living a life you never expected.

Sometimes you wish you could go back and change the things that you regret the most.

I wiggle the lock on the window, testing its strength. The blinds are bent, but the seal is solid around the glass. The house is safe, but I'll double-check it once my mom goes to bed.

Because sometimes you become a man who has an exit plan at all times to escape the life you've created.

3

Jason

ROOSTERS CROW in the distance as I walk around the back of my mom's house inspecting it. She's almost paid it off, and it's going to be the place she lives for the rest of her life. I need to make sure it's in good shape for the long haul. She'll be fifty this year, and hopefully has another forty or fifty ahead of her.

My mom's been the one constant in my life. When I graduated from college, though, I didn't look back. Well, didn't look back until thirty-six hours ago. I drove away from the Kingwood Manor at peace with my role in that situation. And I don't really know what made me come back, not even after a good night's sleep, which was one of the better nights I've had for a while.

I don't understand why, but I'll take it.

Kicking a loose board on the side of the house with the toe of my boot, I mark it to replace and move to the front. I'm wondering how long I can keep my mind occupied on tasks to do and not on the woman that's lingering at the back of my mind.

Not long apparently. There's a honeysuckle bush growing wild at the corner of the porch. Honeysuckle.

The flowers are wrapped in a band around her head. Delilah has spent the better part of an hour creating her floral halo and it was worth it. She's beautiful. Hovering above my head, she's upside down and smiling at me. "What are you doing, Jason?"

"Watching you." While lying down, I reach up. "C'mere."

She moves around and kneels next to me. Plucking a flower from the wreath in her hair, she says, "Want some nectar?"

"Thought you'd never offer."

The flower is between her fingers when she starts to gently pull it away from the stem. I lift up and rest on my elbow and watch the satisfied smile appear. But when she offers the nectar to me, I say, "You taste it first and then I'll taste you."

My favorite pink—Delilah blush—covers her cheeks. She's so enticing. I watch as the nectar touches her tongue and then she teases, her eyes on me, her lips tantalizing. I sit up and run my hand through the back of her hair and kiss her, tasting her honey mixed with the flower's sweetness.

. . . The screech of the screen door cuts through the mire of my thoughts. "Are you hungry?" my mom calls.

"Sure am."

"C'mon. I've made you some eggs and bacon."

I add the front steps to my list. They need replacing before I leave again. Inside, I wash my hands and sit at the table in the kitchen. I'm served a glass of apple juice, which makes me smile. I could really use a cup of coffee but don't ask for it. My mom wants to serve her son, and I'm happy to play that part for a few days.

She sits down after setting a plate in front of me. I take a big bite and then look up. "Are you not eating?"

"I ate while I was cooking." She smiles.

I'm about to take another bite, but it's time. I set my fork down and swallow some juice. "Let's do this so we can get past it."

She's always direct. I like it. I've been called direct. Guess I got it from her. "Are you going to see her?"

"You want me to drive over to the farm and just walk up those steps like I have business there? Ma, she's married."

"She's not married."

"What?" My neck jerks back.

"She's not married, Jason."

"But you told me once—"

"Well," she starts while fiddling with the loose threads of the placemat, "she was then. Now she's not."

I get up for coffee. Apple juice isn't strong enough for this conversation. After filling a mug, I lean on the counter, my palms pressing into the tile as I stare down at the stained grout. Mentally, I add this to the list of things to fix, right after I add Delilah Noelle. I don't think that can be fixed by a visit to the hardware store, but it's tempting to find out.

Looking back at my mom, I ask, "They're separated?"

"No, divorced. Finalized two months back. She's out on that farm by herself. He moved across town to a rental on the east side behind The BBQ Shack."

"Why are you telling me this? I'm not going to be here long enough to spend my time thinking about the past."

"I think you already are. I also think she might be the reason for this spontaneous visit."

"She's not." I cross my arms over my chest and lean my ass against the counter, facing her. "I thought she was married."

My mom shrugs. "Call it kismet. I think something inside you was unsettled, and we both know the best way to get settled is to visit the one that caused the uproar in the first place."

"I'm not visiting her. We left on bad terms." No, that's not how it went down. She left me. She left me with no explanation.

"*You* left on bad terms. She's been here all along, and if I know her at all, which I feel I know her pretty well after all these years, I think she's been waiting for you to return."

"Why fill my head with this nonsense? We both know I won't be home long and adding that crazy back into my life won't turn out good for anybody."

She stands and walks around the table. With her mug in hand, she heads for the back door. Before she leaves, I ask, "What about kids?"

Looking back at me, she smiles. "What about them?"

"Rumors had it she had one with him."

"No," she replies, shaking her head. "No kids either." Pushing the screen door open, she leaves, the door slamming shut behind her.

Delilah Rae Noelle isn't married and has no kids. Despite the adrenaline rushing through my veins in an attempt to move my feet toward that door and drive out to the farm, my grip on the counter tightens. "No. I can't get tangled up when I'm here to untangle some of the mess I've made of my life."

Why am I talking to myself? Fuck. This town is already messing with my head. I grab a few more bites of breakfast, shove my list into my back pocket, and head out to the bike.

My mom is checking out the bike. "Looks expensive."

"I've done okay the last couple of years. You've been getting the money I sent, right?"

"Yes, and about that . . . I have it saved in a box hidden in the house. It's yours."

"No, it's yours. That's why I sent it." I swing my leg over the seat and settle into the leather while righting the bike.

"Honey, I don't need your money."

"Save it for retirement then. I'm heading down to General Hardware to get a few things."

"You might want to take the truck then." She walks to the garage and pushes a code in. The door slides up and there's my old truck. "You're not going to be able haul more than a few nails on that motorcycle."

She's right. I move it to the side and get off, out of the way. Tossing me the keys, she says, "You can charge everything to my account there. I'm sure Fred will remember you."

He'll remember me all right. He busted Cole, Billy, and me stealing a tractor to joyride through the fields one night. Deputy Whaley let us go after a few hours, saying he was tired of our laughing. We were disturbing the peace of the jail. Coach came down to haul us to the field that night and worked us hard until the sun hit high noon. We'd dropped and lay there until my mom and Delilah showed up with turkey sandwiches and water, giving us just enough energy to get our sorry asses home. I pulled the drunk card.

Bad move on my part.

I was grounded for a week—no after-school fun, no phone, and no Delilah. I learned my lesson. Don't be a dick and don't screw up. Stay on the right side of the law, although that one might not have sunk in the way it should have when I reflect on the last few years of my life.

An hour later, I have everything loaded into the back of the truck and pay Mr. Carver for the supplies, because there's no way in hell I'm sticking my mom with this bill. "Say hi to your mom."

I give him a glare similar to the one I've used with the

guys right before they were fucked up for whatever offense they committed against my clients. Getting into the truck, I'm about to leave when Billy shows up in a beat-up old Dodge truck and parks. With my window down, I roll up behind him. "You still driving that old clunker?"

He leans against the trunk and nods. "Yeah, she's sweet when she wants to be."

"Sounds a lot like Lou. How is Lorraine these days?"

"Married to some accountant two towns over."

Shaking my head, I drop my hands from the steering wheel but keep my foot on the brake. "I always thought you guys would make it."

"Some could say the same about you and Delilah."

"Yeah, some could, but we all know how that turned out."

He comes over, resting his arms on the door of my truck and looks inside the cab. "She's in good shape."

"Delilah?" I ask, wide-eyed.

He laughs. "No, the truck. Your mom's kept her in good shape."

"Oh yeah. She keeps her in the garage." Silence slips in, an awkwardness that never used to exist back in high school. "Guess I should get back."

Looking up at the sky, he says, "Yeah, it's gonna rain. You need help getting that wood covered?"

"Nah. I got it."

He backs up, and says, "We should grab a beer sometime before you leave."

"Maybe."

"Yeah, I get it."

Considering I have no idea how long I'm staying, it's probably best if I keep the people at a distance. But I hear the hurt in his tone, and guilt starts to sink in, so I offer, "You should come by."

"Maybe I will. You're drinking the fancy stuff these days? Heineken, huh?"

"I don't know about fancy. I'll drink a Pabst or Bud with you if you prefer."

His keys jingle as he shoves them in his pocket. "I'll bring some by later or tomorrow."

"Sure. See you around, Billy."

"See ya round."

Eyeing those gray clouds in the sky, I should just head straight back, but my better senses seemed to have left me and I take the scenic route. There's a shiny white truck parked out in front of the Noelle house when I drive by the farm. It's not practical in color, and the rain is going to ruin that just washed shine, but if that truck's hers, I like that she's damning the elements of this town. If it's not . . . I swallow hard, my ego caught like a lump in my throat.

4

Jason

AFTER UNLOADING the back of the truck and covering everything with a tarp, Billy pulls up. He's got a six-pack of Heineken in one hand and a bouquet of flowers in the other. "If you're looking to get laid, you came to the wrong house."

"Brought your mother some flowers."

Standing up, I cross my arms over my chest defensively. "Umm, back up there. Why?"

He starts laughing. "I'm not hitting on your mom, dude. She may be pretty, but yeah, not my speed." He hands me the beer. "Brought your girly beer for you. The flowers are for the last time I was here. I ran over her flowerbed and she was pissed."

Chuckling, I say, "I remember that now."

"Figured I'd try to make amends."

Amends. Can a sinner of my stature make amends, or am I a boot too deep into hell already? I stop thinking about that other stuff and return my thoughts to the here and now. "Come on."

After he schmoozes my mom with the flowers, we pop the top on two beers and grab a seat where we can. He sits on the back steps, and I sit on the rusting swing where I used to sit with Delilah. Her fingerprints are still on every part of my old life. It's only a dumb swing from my childhood, but the only memories I seem to recall are the ones where I pushed her on it or sat next to her. She would hold the chains, leaning her cheek against the cold metal and smile at me, the tips of her sneakers dug into the dirt.

She'd been the only one who could get me to open up about my feelings. I shared so much with her—my fears about football, the loss of my father, my worries about my mom. We saw shooting stars sitting on this swing. We laughed and we fell in love. I thought those times mattered to her like they did me, but I guess that's a part of growing up—having your first love break your heart.

One good thing about Billy is he never needed to fill the quiet. I didn't either. We talk when we have something worth mentioning. Other than that, it's just good to have the company. I finally ask, "What are you doing these days?"

"I'm coaching out at the high school. Assistant for the offensive line."

"No shit."

He laughs. "Yeah, no shit. Saved my parents' place."

"What's going on with the farm?"

"They were turned down a few years back for an extension on a loan. I was already full-time at the plant in Cedars, so I sold my shit, moved back home, and added coach onto the résumé."

"Sorry to hear about your folks. How's everything now?"

"I coach part-time and still work full-time at the plant, but moved to supervisor."

"That's good. Congrats."

"Thanks. I work the farm in my spare time. We've changed crops. We used to be straight corn. Now it's all about the soybean. At least this year."

"Wow, that is a big change."

"Corn syrup's out. Soy milk's in."

"We do what we have to do to survive." I know this better than anyone. Like I do with my thoughts of Delilah, I'm an expert at compartmentalizing the things that fuck with my head . . . and my conscience if I let them.

I'll never forget finding that sweet girl I met in the mountains and how she lay curled on the gravel, on the paler side of death. Any innocence she'd managed to hold on to was gone as she gasped for life. And then I was confronted with *him.* He and his partner did that to her. Stole her innocence. Nearly her life. He slept with his arm stretched toward the nightstand. I could put money down that his gun was in the top drawer. Sick. Fuck. Took the shot. No, I'll never forget, but I refuse to sink into the abyss of guilt or remorse. He deserved neither.

That fucker got what he deserved. I'm starting to think I lost more than him. Now I wonder if surviving was only something I did physically. Is my soul too far gone to find at this point?

He finishes that beer and grabs another. "So what have you been doing?"

For anyone else, this would be an easy question to answer, but for me, it's one I'm always thinking about how I'll answer. I give him the rehearsed response, "Odd jobs here and there. Worked on a fishing boat in Alaska and a mini-mart in the Northeast. Hauled lumber in Northern California, and worked on a cattle farm in Oklahoma."

"Never used your business degree?"

"You know," I say, thinking about this harder than I should, "I kind of use it all the time. I just don't get the bragging rights around the office water cooler."

"Ah." He drinks more and lies back, resting on his elbows.

I dig my heels in, starting to slowly rock back and forth. "What happened with you and Lou?"

"Too much to remember. It's just easier to say we were together too young, and I couldn't give her the life she wanted or deserved." He doesn't sound as regretful as I feel over my screwed-up relationship with Delilah.

"Yeah, sometimes I wonder . . . fuck it. It's not worth the effort to worry about what could've been."

"That's for sure." He tosses the first can toward a bin a little ways away from where he's sitting, but misses. "I still see Cole every now and again." His humorless laugh leaves me curious, but he adds, "Not by choice."

I toss my can from across the yard and make it in the bin. "What a fucking asshole." I laugh. I thought I could hide my disdain better. Guess not.

"Every time I see him I wanna punch his fucking lights out. Hands up." He tosses me a beer.

"You should, the fucking wife beater. If I'd been around —" *Fuck.* I crack it open and chug the first half, tamping down the anger growing inside thinking about that fucker.

He lifts his hat and scratches his head. "I hear ya. I paid him a visit two times to make sure the shit would stop."

"Apparently it didn't work either time."

His eyes hit mine. "She was good at hiding behind lies."

"Can't hide bruises," I snap back.

"She wasn't my wife, and I wasn't inspecting her body. You got a problem with me, Koster?"

My hand starts crushing the can. I've learned what I'm capable of. I've learned that it's hard to come back from the darkness once it gets its grip on you. Anger is a surefire way to get me seeing red, to dig deep and let that darkness back in. That red will turn to gray and the whole wide fucking world will fade away, except for one thing—my target.

Cole Cutler.

My former best fucking friend.

He saw his chance to take my place and took it.

I may not have had many years with my dad, but his life always revolved around my mom, me, and his love of sports. From coaching me in T-ball at three to tackle football at five right before he died, he told me to always work hard and to do my best, but if you're not having fun it's not worth it.

When he died, I did my best. It helped that playing sports was the only fun I had left. It became my escape, and I became even better. Thinking back on all those sports and every team I played on, Cole had always been right there next to me. Football was an escape for Cole. My house. Our friendship. He'd made for a good partner, a great teammate. He'd been someone I counted on. His father had been an asshole, but we'd been like brothers. Why the fuck he went after Delilah . . . *Can't go there.*

We make a beer run just after eight, and keep driving like the days he might recall as the good old days. I'm not feeling nostalgic quite yet, but I can get onboard with a few good times we had. I look over at Billy and suddenly I feel like I'm eighteen again with the world at my feet. "Remember when used to go fishing every Sunday? The sun hadn't even come up and we'd be heading out."

"We were still drunk."

"Were we ever sober?"

"I don't know," he replies. "I was too drunk to remember."

His Dodge slows to a crawl and the headlights are turned off. I don't have to look out across that field to know where we are. I know this route like the back of my hand. The truck stops, and he turns off the engine. I take a long pull of my beer before I turn my attention to the farmhouse. The living room and kitchen lights are on, the TV casting a blue tint across the corner windows.

I let my gaze wander up a story to the second floor and see her bedroom light on and the bathroom connected to it lit up. She owns that farm now, her parents long passed. Does she still sleep in that room? The one with pink striped wallpaper and a full-sized bed atop a squeaky metal frame? I can't see the side of the house where I used to climb up the trellis to the roof and run across to sneak into her bedroom. Wonder if that trellis is still there?

He looks at me, his jovial mood wiped from his eyes. "I'm sorry."

"Why?"

"I took her to the emergency room once."

I'm not ready to dig this deep into the past, but since he's brought it up . . . "Why?" My stomach tenses, my grip around the can tightening, the aluminum giving in before I toss it out the window because I already know why.

"I should have stopped him."

"Were you there?"

"No, but my warnings weren't enough. I knew he had a drinking problem. He'd picked a fight with me earlier that night outside Red River. She'd just gotten back into town, so I guess he decided to take it out on her later."

Staring out the window, I avoid looking at him. I don't

want to hear his confession. I don't want to see his guilt. It becomes mine, and I don't owe anybody anything.

Lies.

Lies.

Lies.

I owe her. I owe her better than she got. I was across the country when I first heard the rumor—*Cutler hit his wife*—the same girl he claimed to want enough to screw me over.

Cole never struggled to get a girl's attention if he wanted it. He'd tell everyone how he hooked up with the popular girls and then ventured across county lines for what he called fresh meat. He was the guy who bragged in the locker rooms and teased you relentlessly if you didn't score with a girl.

Except for me.

There was a silent agreement—the bullshit put on for others didn't fly between us. I knew beneath that attitude he was a good guy. He'd only slept with two girls, but I kept his secret safe to protect his rep.

On that *day I was uneasy with his confidence. I didn't want him talking to Delilah. He knew better. He was crossing a line and for what? To score with her or to look like a bigshot for the guys?*

He knew I liked her, but his arrogance blinded him that day as he ran ahead of us and cut the girls off on their path home. He got down on two knees and with hands like he held in church, he said, "Please, will you go out with me, Miss Noelle? I'm begging you with my hands and on my knees with my three best friends as witnesses and half the cheerleading squad staring at me. Please don't let this be the most embarrassing thing I've ever done."

Now maybe that worked with most girls—on bended knees, pleading to save his pride—but it didn't with Delilah.

Despite her being a cheerleader, her voice was soft that day.

"I'm sorry, Cole. I like our friendship too much to ruin it." She let him down in a way that wasn't embarrassing him, but kind.

. . . Delilah was good inside. He knew. Somehow he knew we had fought. He was waiting for that moment. He went after her. Pursued her. But after kicking my heart to the sidelines, why did she want him?

She still owns parts of me that others will never see, and I'm left wondering why. Why him over me? Why didn't she fight for us? Those are the questions that were packed away with the baggage I carried with me. The details weighing down my rucksack with emotional bullshit I've tried to shed across the miles.

Billy says, "The night he hit her, he only spent one night in jail for it."

"One night," I repeat. One fucking night for hitting the love of my life.

Why'd she fucking stay?

She had eight hours to get the fuck out of there, but she stayed. I rub my fingers over my forehead in frustration. Why the fuck didn't Billy get her away from Cutler? "Can't fucking understand why you didn't get her out. He hit the woman I love."

He glances my way but then turns toward the steering wheel. "Love?"

"Huh?"

"You said the woman you love."

Love. *Present tense.* Shit. "Loved. Anyway, this is about you. He hit a woman you've been friends with for years."

"Delilah's forgiven me."

"I haven't."

"Join the club, because I haven't either."

The car's now too quiet and the memories too strong. "We should go."

5

Jason

The love of my life has bounced around my head since the errant thought last night. *The love of my life. The love of my life.*

What the . . . *No.*

It makes no sense. I loved Delilah, but the love of my life? I'm twenty-five. I have a lot of life left to live. Am I sure that the love of my life is the same girl I started dating when I was seventeen? That seems like a stretch to my more logical side. Was my *love* for Delilah just teenage lust mixed with hormones? That makes more sense. Was she never meant to be my *one*? Surely a man as cold and ruthless as I am now doesn't get to have a *one.*

That thought mixed with the pouring rain has really put a damper on my day.

Sundays are supposed to be lazy days, but I'm not used to sitting around. I only bought supplies to fix the issues out back, so by four o'clock I'm going stir-crazy. Standing abruptly, I accidentally scare my mom in the process. She jumps, her book flying from her hands. "What are you doing?" she asks, holding her heart.

"I'm going for a ride."

Turning behind her, she looks out the window, then turns back. "It's pouring out there."

"I'm used to riding in all kinds of weather."

"I don't want you getting sick, Jason."

"I won't. I just need to burn off some of this energy. I'm not used to sitting around doing nothing."

She's staring at me with concern written through the soft lines of her face. "You can relax here, son."

My shoulders drop some of the burden they were holding. "I know. I'm just going to go for a ride." Working all those years for my last boss, hanging around, watching, you would think I got used to being still. Patient. But not here. My mind is active. On alert like I'm still on someone's payroll. I don't feel like I'm *home*. Not like I used to. I need something to alleviate the restlessness in my veins. I need out. Fresh air. Space.

"Okay. Will you be home for dinner?"

"I'm not sure. Don't wait for me. I can always make a sandwich when I'm back."

"All right." She's done trying to convince me, and I appreciate the space she's giving. Kicking her feet on the coffee table, she opens her book again. "Be careful. Those curves get dangerous when wet."

"I will be."

I slip on my leather jacket and tighten the laces on my black shoes before starting the Harley. The loud muffler is a musical masterpiece, owning the chorus of the road while I ride.

The thing about small towns is they're small. There

aren't a lot of places to get away from it all unless you find a cranny down by the river to hide inside. Or you own property that doesn't back up to the main roads. No, privacy isn't a specialty of small towns, so I decide it's time to stop hiding and show up to make my presence known. With my chest puffed out and my emotional armor in place, I drive straight to the Noelle farm.

I even rev the engine when I drive up the dirt driveway as if to prove some point I've already forgotten.

Never expected her to be outside. I should have. She always loved rainy days. The bike is stopped before I take a good long look at her on that front porch.

Delilah Rae Noelle looks younger than her years. Always did, but damn, if seeing her now doesn't make a million memories come back as if they were yesterday.

Her hair is twisted on top of her head, but that strawberry-blond hair still shines. She moves to the railing, leaning against it as if she sees me every damn day. Even from here I can see that sparkle in her blue eyes, an expectation I always hoped I could fulfill when she looked at me. I would have done anything for her.

Except the one time I didn't think twice, never thought of her or how my choices would affect us. I was selfish, but I've learned a lot since then. I'm curious if she still smells of vanilla, so I run my fingers through my hair hoping to tame what must look a mess from the rain and riding.

I take a deep breath when I see her smile and wave at me like we're old friends. Not what I expected.

I cut the engine and swing my leg off the bike. I shove my hands into the pockets of my wet leather jacket and start walking. When I reach the bottom of her steps, just four dividing us, I grab the railing. It needs a good paint job and it's unstable. I add it to my list of tasks to take care of, though I know good and well taking care of her isn't my job any longer.

Three years is a long damn time not to see the beauty that stands before me. Not even knowing why I'm here, I say, "Hi," to see where it leads.

She rocks back on her bare feet, and smiles so wide the rain has trouble hiding her sunshine. "What took you so long?"

"I got here as fast as I could." I take another step up and she turns as if I'm welcome on that rickety old porch of hers. "With a few minor detours along the way."

"I'd say."

I cover the last two steps, which leaves only a few feet between us. Leaning against the railing, she says, "I never thought I'd see you again, but here you are looking like all sorts of trouble in all black."

"I like your dress."

Her cheeks pinken like the color of my mom's roses in her backyard. "Well, are you gonna give me a proper hello, Jason Koster, or are we going to pretend like we never danced in the moonlight?"

There's my Delilah.

He didn't destroy her.

"No pretending over here." I go to her and wrap my arms around her, my eyes closing, my senses on high alert. She always awakened all of me, my whole body responding to her. Vanilla with a hint of orange.

Damn, she smells good. Like home.

She's just not my home to lay claim to anymore.

I feel her cheek rub against my neck before she lowers back on her feet and our arms return to our sides. Her eyes are cast down when she steps back. I want to lift her chin, to touch her again just to feel the surge through my body, but I don't.

When she finally looks up, she asks, "I heard you were back. What brings you around?"

Gossip. It spreads as fast as a phone call in this town.

I rest my shoulder against the column. "Figured I should since rumors were going to be spread anyway."

"So you came by to nip it in the bud or to start the mill spinning?"

The right side of my mouth lifts. "Maybe a little of both."

She smiles, but it falls quicker than it appeared. Her eyes are set on her toes, a dark pink dotting the nails of each. "You know, Cole's going to hear about this." The change is fast, her sunshine gone. Does she fear Cutler finding out that I visited?

"Not if you don't tell him."

Her gaze flashes to mine. "I don't talk to him unless I'm court ordered."

"What kind of court is ordering you to talk to him?"

The rain has become the most fascinating thing again when she turns away and reaches out to catch a few drops. "You've been gone a long time. I think you've forgotten what it's like living here."

"Yeah. Maybe." I reach out and take her hand in mine, bringing it under the shelter of the roof. Tapping the water that pooled in her palm, I say, "Maybe you can remind me."

She pulls her hand away, the rain falling to the wood floor. As if she caught herself in a compromising position, she backs away from me and gives me a cold shoulder. "You know," she starts, staring out over the long drive up to the house. "It was good to see you, Jason, but I think it's best if you go."

One second.

Two.

Three.

"Why?" What just happened?

Her smile is gone and an unfamiliar sadness creeps onto her face. She lowers her head for the third time in the last few minutes and it's wrong. All wrong on her. She moves across the porch, opens the screen door, and steps inside. "It's getting late."

Before it has a chance to slam closed, I catch it. "Talk to me, Delilah."

I see her chest rise and fall with a heaviness that wasn't there in the lighthearted moment shared a minute earlier. "Don't say my name like that, Jason."

"Like what?"

"Like you still care."

"I do," I reply too quick to replace it with the lie I should have told.

"Then don't." She tugs the screen door and I let go, letting it slam shut. "I think it's best if you don't visit me again." She moves into the darkness of her house and the front door is closed.

One lock.

Two locks.

One chain slides into place.

I'm tempted to ring the doorbell, but I'm in so much shock by the turn in her demeanor.

I mount my bike and start it, but before I drive away, I glance back at the house. She's quick to hide to the side of the window, but not before I caught her spying on me. What's going on? *Why the sudden change?*

Per her request, I leave. I'm over being wet and the path to her farmhouse will become a mud pit if I don't get out of here soon. I maneuver around the watery potholes on my way to the street. Once I'm on pavement again, I take off like I have someplace I'm supposed to be. I don't. I have nowhere.

I think it's time to start mapping out a plan. I have about a week's worth of stuff to do around my mom's house and then what? Where do I want to go? What do I want to do?

Jobs found me during the last three years. After landing in LA, I was spotted by a scout at the beach working out. Boom. I was hired for stunt work. Then an actor I met on set. We grabbed a few beers, and partied together on the regular. He made a few headlines around Hollywood and asked me to cover him. The money was good, but then I was a free agent and scooped up by referral by a visiting dignitary.

I liked working in the private sector with my last boss, but almost getting killed several times over wasn't fantastic. It's not bad to just hang around a bit and work on things that don't have me sleeping with one eye open.

Skidding to a stop to test the brakes of this bike, I arrive at my mom's still hell-bent out of shape over that farewell. I dash inside and shake my jacket off just inside the kitchen door. My mom comes around the corner with two towels. "Looks like the rain won this round."

"I wasn't in the mood to fight." With Delilah, but I let it reside as if that response fits her comment.

"Take your shoes off and let them dry out here. I'll hang your jacket in the laundry room. Go change and bring me these wet clothes. I'll wash them."

Toeing off one of my shoes, I look up at her. "You don't have to wait on me like I'm a kid."

"You don't have to be so resistant to help. We all need it every now and again."

"Is this really about clothes? I have a feeling it's not."

She takes my shoes and moves them off to the side of the door. "Everything I say doesn't have to mean more than the words I choose."

"Fine." I strip off my wet shirt and cut through the kitchen to the laundry room to dump it into the washer. "You were actually talking to me about wet clothes." I strip off my soaked socks and add them in too. I pass back through the kitchen and head for my room.

"Jason? What's wrong?"

I shut my door and strip the rest of my wet clothes off and pull on some pajama pants and a T-shirt I yank from the closet. When I return to put the rest of my wet clothes in the laundry room, I pass my mom as she sips a glass of tea. Her eyes follow me, but she doesn't say another word.

When I return, I do. "She told me not to come visit her anymore and shut the door in my face. Is that what you want to hear?"

Her glass is set down and she looks at me. Really looks at me—right in the eyes. "No, that makes me sad to hear. I'm sorry."

Leaning back against the opposite counter, I sigh. "You don't have to be. I wasn't planning on staying long. Just long enough to help you out, and then I'll be out of your hair again. Delilah obviously wants nothing to do with me now, so she can go about her life like I never stopped by."

She crosses the small kitchen and hugs me, resting her head on my shoulder. "I don't want you out of my hair, Jason. I like you being home. I miss you and wish I saw you more, not less."

I lean down and look at my mom. She's always been so strong—a single mother since my dad died when I was five. Working full-time, even if it took two jobs to get the hours.

Never missed a Friday night game of mine—whether home or away.

She's the one person who would be most disappointed to know the depths I've sunk during the time away. Somehow, even with mother's intuition, she hasn't seen the black of my soul. She's looked past the dead in my eyes, in my heart, that allowed me to do my job—*and do it well*—for the last few years.

Detachment was key. When I finally thought I could befriend someone, it put them at risk. Is it safe to attach myself now—to her again, to this town and the people here with so much unsettled? "I'm not running out the door. Not yet anyway. But I'm not feeling like I can stay much longer either."

"I'll take what I can get. Or I'll bake your favorite cake to tempt you to stay."

Embracing her again, I say, "I never could resist your chocolate cake."

"Good. Now that it's settled and you're going to stick around a bit, can I get you something to eat?"

"I'd like that."

"Head into the living room and find us something to watch tonight."

I do as I'm told and settle on the couch. As I flip through the stations, my eyes keep shifting to the right, straight to that prom picture. When everyone looks dated and awful, there's Delilah Noelle looking gorgeous even in her sister's hand-me-down prom dress. I get up and set the frame face down and return to the couch. Continuing through the channels, I stop when I reach a Marvel movie.

The problem is I'm still too distracted. I'd like to blame the frame but I know it doesn't matter whether I can see the photo or not; that woman is ingrained in my brain.

I get up once more and position the frame the way it was before and return to the couch just as my mom comes in with a plate of snacks. Glancing between the photo and me, she's about to say something, but I cut her off before she has a chance, "Just let it go, okay?"

She sets the plate down on the coffee table, and says, "I wasn't going to say anything."

I look up with raised eyebrows, contesting that last statement with just a look.

Rolling her eyes, she confesses, "Fine. But I'll wait until tomorrow."

"Thank you."

"You're welcome."

"I'm talking about the snacks."

"Oh," she says, then laughs. "You're welcome for that, too."

God, I love my mom.

6

Jason

FIVE DAYS after being back and I'm already feeling like I could hang around a little longer. Sure, Delilah has kept her distance, and I've kept mine, but it's been nice working around the house during the day and kicking it at night with Billy. I haven't felt as restless. Working with my hands has been calming on my mind. It keeps my attention focused on the task at hand instead of the million angles that someone might be playing to feed their greed.

I've managed to avoid Cole Cutler, thank fuck, our schedules running opposite so far. The evening starts off easy—catching up with McGilley while Billy keeps the tab open. I've never been one for loose lips, but the easy nature of being parked on a barstool like the guys have for the last four or five years, I find myself talking about some of my adventures, leaving the illegal parts out.

The door swings open, and I hear a few guys call his name, "Cutler."

I'm tempted to turn and look when the conversation goes quiet, but I keep my focus on the half-full pint glass in front of me. One by one, he greets the guys and then he's behind me. Billy says, "There's a free stool at the other end of the bar. I reckon it would be best if you take a seat down there, Cutler."

Cutler ignores him, his eyes already burning a hole in the back of my head. "Well. Well. Wellllll. If it ain't the great number eight himself, Jason Koster." His hand lands hard on my shoulder, and he squeezes.

Cracking my neck to the opposite side, I pick up my glass and down a swig or two before turning and looking back over my shoulder. "Cutler. It's been a while."

"Sure has." He slides in on the other side of me and pats the bar. McGilley already has a pint ready and sets it down. "On them," he tells him. With a fake smile plastered on his face, he leans closer. "Here to visit your mom? Your girl? What dragged your sorry ass back to town?"

"Here we go," Billy says. "Cool it, Cutler. We're just catching up on old times here."

Bopping his head, he adds. "Oh, that's right. You don't have the girl. She's mine."

"Not from what I've gathered."

Cutler asks, "What did you say, Koster?"

Turning to Cutler for the first time, I look him dead in the eyes. "I said, not from what I've gathered."

My shoulder is shoved, but I catch myself before I fall. Billy is on his feet and pushing Cutler back against his protests. "Get off me. Fucking assholes." He shrugs out of Billy's hold, giving up the fight before it ever really began. Sneering at him, he spits, "Where's your loyalty, Langston? Or are you brainwashed into bowing down to this fucker, too?"

His insults don't hurt me. Him breaking bro code pisses me off. "Loyalty. What do you know about loyalty?"

"Let's take this outside, Koster."

McGilley adds, "Yes, take it outside, boys."

After finishing my beer, I slide off the barstool and head for the door. The bell above the door rings as I walk out. Moving down the sidewalk, I hear them behind me but move to the corner before turning around. A calm I've come to expect washes through me. My hands fist and release. Fist and release. I've wondered many times if I've become desensitized to violence, almost looking forward to it. Release.

I have to remind myself where I am and who I'm with. These are my friends.

Well, not so much Cutler. *Fuck him.*

But the others . . . I look up just as Billy comes toward me. "Walk away, Jason. He's drunk."

Cutler comes toward me, his fists raised as if he'll intimidate me by holding that ridiculous position. I stare at him, crossing my arms over my chest. "You're fucking sad, you know that?"

McGilley demands, "Get him outta here, Langston."

Billy wrangles Cutler backward as he yells, "Fuck off, Billy. This is a long time coming. Let me just kick his ass and get it over with tonight."

I don't lose my temper easily, but he manages to push all my anger buttons. "Fuck you."

He comes flying around Billy. Just when he's about to hit me, I have him by the throat and slam him to the ground. His face turns red, the veins in his neck beginning to bulge. His pulse is pounding against two of my fingers. I could end him. Right here. I could look into his eyes and watch life leave them. This asshole doesn't deserve death. If this piece of shit doesn't get out of my sight, he's going to find it though, so I whisper, "The more you fight the more your throat will close on you. Relax if you want to live."

Pushing off him, I back away and tell Billy, "I'll see you tomorrow."

Cutler is gasping for air while Billy stands there in shock. My buzz is dead and I go around to the side of the bar and get on my bike.

I take the long way home.

Cutler's not the guy I knew growing up. Something's changed him over the years. Jealousy that grew into anger that expanded into hate? Hitting women? He's become his father, who he regularly saw hit his mother.

Some fucking example he was.

Everyone knew what happened behind closed doors, yet his mom stayed. My mother was the only one who reached out—*repeatedly*—to his. Eventually that relationship ended when his father decided he didn't care for people knowing his business. *God, no wonder he's so fucked up.*

I need the dark of the night to relieve the aggression I found too easily tonight. I left that behind. Or so I thought. The cool night air clears my head, giving me the space to figure out what I'm doing because I'm not so sure anymore.

By the time I step into the house, I know I want to see Delilah again. Doesn't have to be a big deal, just to talk, to settle the wild thundering of my heart. To put this issue with her behind us once and for all. I need to understand why she left me without any explanation. Was it for Cutler? The why. That's what I need in order to move on. She wasn't meant to be a part of my future, I get that. Even though she seems content to leave things be, I can't seem to let it go. And I need to. I know I do. We're not those same kids in love. We're adults with problems to match.

My mom's bedroom door cracks open, and she says, "You okay, Jase?"

"Yeah, I'm fine. Go back to bed."

"Just checking on you. And hey, I want you to come to church with me in the morning."

"I don't think that's a good idea, Ma. Jesus and I aren't that tight these days."

"That's exactly why you should come with me."

She's tired and I'm not looking to argue over this. "I'll go. Now go back to bed."

With a smile, she says, "Good night. Love you."

"Love you. Good night."

~

WE CATCH the only light in town, and I come to a stop at the red. I tug at my tie, which is feeling too tight. I haven't worn a tie in a long time. My mom is talking about what she calls the gossip girls and how they are going to lose their minds when I walk into that church. But I'm looking at this tired town, the streets nearly empty on a Sunday morning. Glancing into the rearview mirror, a familiar white pickup pulls up behind me. I know she recognizes my mom's car. I know she's looking everywhere to avoid looking at me or catching a glimpse of my eyes staring back at her.

I see that smile that threatens to break the frown right off her face. Delilah might have broken my heart, but sitting here, I'm wondering if she'll do it twice. Am I willing to risk it?

I used to think she couldn't resist me, but she had no problem earlier this week. Let's see if she still can. I've got a few tricks up my sleeve when it comes to Ms. Noelle. "I'll be right back."

"What?" my mom asks, watching me get out of the car. "Where are you going? The light's going to turn green any second."

I keep walking.

She sees me. Even though her pretty eyes are hidden behind big sunglasses, I figure they're probably damn wide right now. Reaching for the truck door lock, her finger pushes it down as I arrive. She can kid herself like that. She knows deep down I'll never hurt her, but I might pressure her into giving me a little of her time.

Standing on the other side of her door, I knock. Delilah finally looks up and points at the light. It's green. I shrug. I make the lame twist of the wrist roll-down-your-window motion with my hand because I have a feeling she might not understand if I pretend to push a button to roll it down.

"Get back in your car, Jason," she says through the glass.

"No. Roll down your window." To sugarcoat it, I add, "Please."

"Why?"

"What do you mean why? I want to talk to you, and I don't want to shout through the glass."

Huffing, the glass slides down slowly. "What is it?" She keeps her hands on the steering wheel and her grip seems to tighten just a bit.

She glances my way, so I say, "I want to see you."

"You're seeing me, Jason, so if that's all there is, I'll be going no—"

The glass starts to roll up, but I clamp my palm over it. She releases the button and looks up at me. "I don't know what happened the other day, what turned your mood so quickly, but I'd like another chance to talk."

"It's not a good idea."

"It's a great idea, actually. All you have to say is yes."

"No."

My smile tilts into a smirk. "You haven't changed much."

"Then you haven't been paying attention." She sighs. "Red light."

"I've got three minutes to change your mind."

"Why do you want to, Jason? Just let things lie the way they're meant to be."

Meant to be . . .

She and I were once *meant to be*. Maybe that's why I can't give up this notion of at least seeing if anything's still there between us. "I want to come by this afternoon. I'll bring you lunch."

Shaking her head, she looks down at her lap. "I can't."

"Delilah." Just me saying her name draws her attention back to me. That glass was leveled with the car again, and I rest my hands on the door. Leaning down, I say, "Let me see your eyes."

Another car pulls up behind her car. I wave. Seems like the courteous thing to do.

Her body gives her debate away, her chest rising and lowering—her breath deepening. She gives in and moves her sunglasses to the top of her head and looks into my eyes. "What are you doing, Jason?" she whispers.

"Is that you, Jason Koster?" a woman calls, sticking her head out her car window.

"It is. Good morning, Mrs. Robertson."

"You're going to make us late for church if you don't get a move on."

"I'd love to get a move on and not be late for the Lord, but Ms. Noelle has refused me the pleasure of her company, so I thought I'd see if I could change her mind."

Delilah's blush spreads across her face and starts down her delicate neck. I know where it's heading and the memories of her bare chest against mine cause me to shift. "Jason, please?"

"Please what, honeysuckle?"

"I've not been your honeysuckle in a long time."

"But it was so good when you were." She stares ahead, trying to pretend that her whole body isn't reacting to me like mine is reacting from the close proximity to hers. Leaning even closer, I rest my arms on the door. "We can play games all damn day, but you and I have unfinished business to tend to. So how about that lunch or better yet, dinner tonight?" A car horn blares and I look back. Mrs. Robertson shrugs, but it wasn't her honking.

A woman behind her hits her horn again and I'm surprised when I hear my mom yell, "Cool it, Karen. You'll survive if you don't get there in time to flirt with the choir director."

With that out in the open, I have to look to see this Karen person. I recognize her the minute I see her. She's one of the gossip girls my mom was talking about. When I turn back to Delilah, she looks anxious. A finger taps on her thigh.

"We've got quite the lineup of anxious churchgoers."

She looks into her rearview mirror then back to me and asks, "You're not going to give up, are you?"

"Nope." I tap my watch. "The sermon starts in two minutes. Do you really want to be the cause of a church delay?"

Sighing loudly, she gives me a glare. "Dinner. One less thing I'll have to worry about if you're bringing it over. Seven o'clock and don't be late."

She should know me better than that. I've never been late when it came to her. Tapping the roof of the truck lightly, I smile from ear to ear. "You got it. See you at seven, *honeysuckle.*"

I return to my mom's car to the sound of applause. When I sink into the seat, I check the mirror again and see Delilah smiling.

My mom says, "You sure know how to give them something to talk about. You've stirred up all kinds of trouble."

She's totally worth it. *I hope.*

All the cars pulling into the church parking lot late causes quite the stir. Grumbles are heard as a large part of the congregation finds seats. It's really quite amusing. Even my mom thinks so. She struggles to hold in her laughter. At one point, she leans over and whispers, "It's good to have you home."

The moment Delilah walks in, the sun shines a little brighter through the stained-glass windows that line the sides of the church. I watch her move down a row and sit between two families. I can't imagine she doesn't know them since everyone knows everyone in this town, but she keeps to herself.

Being here in a holy place makes me recount my sins. I don't have as many as I carry the burden of, but the few I have are major. When everyone lowers their heads to pray, I don't. Instead, my eyes find the only other person who remains the same.

Delilah turns and looks at me across the church. A little line forms between her eyes as if I'm a puzzle she can't figure out. Just as I raise my hand to wave to her, the minister's throat is cleared harshly and my eyes meet his irritated ones. "Amen," we say in unison.

Fully delighted, Delilah finally lets that beautiful smile show. With everyone listening to the minister, I lower my head this time and chuckle. After the service, I get tired of nodding, shaking hands, updating what feels like the whole town on what I've been up to. I toss out my regular spiel—traveling around the country working odd jobs.

Since sinning sends you to hell, sinning in church must get you a fast pass. I tell my mom I'll meet her at the car and walk out the wide-open double doors into the sunshine. I veer left when I spot the minister ahead, but I'm not stealth enough because I hear, "So glad you could join us today, Mr. Koster."

I stop and turn around. "I am too. How are you, Minister Polk?"

He pats me on the back as he turns us toward the church. "You can call me Stephen. You're not a kid whose mother forced him to Sunday school anymore."

"All right. Stephen."

"I've been good, son. How about you?"

"Good."

"We've seem to have lost touch with you for a few years. I'm hoping you carried God with you on your journeys."

Anger feeds the finger that pulls the trigger. One shot to the head and I know he's dead without having to shoot again. God wouldn't have wanted to see that in my journey, but it was too late now.

The bodies differ in size and shape, their souls long gone. One was a friend and deserved a different ending. The other deserved worse. I don't think. I just act. I grab the black plastic from the trunk and get to work.

Another body to hide—when did I become the expert in cleaning scenes? I need to get out of here, to leave this city, leave this life. Just because I can stomach the work doesn't mean I should do it. It's messing with my mind. The guilt digging deep, creating crevices in my soul. I need to leave before my soul becomes so blackened from the depravity of my actions. Maybe I'm too late.

"Jason?"

My eyes lift to find the concerned gaze of the minister. I reply, "Yeah. God." Knowing the crimes against God I've committed, I can't honestly say I carried him with me.

He pats me on the back again and says, "We should talk sometime."

"Okay."

"Good to have you back."

"Thanks. It's good to be back." I'm an expert at giving the appropriate responses. Although this time, I've already found some peace being here. I'm not sure if this is where I belong, but I'm beginning to want to stay.

We go in opposite directions. Cutting through cars in the parking lot to get to my mom's, I spy Delilah getting in her truck a few down the line. Seeing her, I'm reminded how we're divided on opposite ends of the spectrum. She wants to leave things the way they are, and I need understanding, closure. Maybe we can meet in the middle. Guess I'll find out in a few hours.

7

Delilah Rae Noelle

JASON KOSTER ROLLED into town like he still owned it. He just might, considering he's only been back one week and he's the talk of the town.

Just like old times.

It's not like the locals have anything better to gossip about, but I don't like being thrown into the mix. I've managed to keep most of my drama at bay despite Cole's best efforts. But here I am at the center of everyone's chatter because I once dated the hometown hero.

And then he broke my heart.

When I first got wind he was back, I felt a surge of giddiness. That flew out the window as I started to worry how Cole would take the news. I've finally found a peaceful coexistence with him in this godforsaken town, but now this will stir everything right back up. Cole won't be happy. Hopefully the gossip girls don't mosey this way tonight.

From the time they were five and catching tadpoles out

on the shores of the lake, Jason and Cole had been best friends.

They were best friends up until I came between them. Insecurity and immaturity sent me into the arms of someone who should have never been more than a friend.

Among other hard lessons, I've learned the word catastrophe is also spelled C-O-L-E C-U-T-L-E-R.

I've made amends with myself over my role in that relationship and marriage. Amends with lingering regrets. I made things as right as I could with the people I hurt—the people I always loved and who cared about me. Like Meredith Koster. She'd been like a second mother to me when my mother passed away. My sister, who'd endured snide comments about what a whore I was. *Endured*, minus the time she knocked Sabrina Smith right in the kisser for calling me a slut. Shelby Noelle had never been in a fight prior, much less clocked someone, but everyone had their limits, and Sabrina Smith pushed my sister's that day. Sabrina still crosses the street when she sees the Noelle sisters. She was a mean girl all through school so it's not a loss to us.

Billy Langston is one of my constants. If you would have asked me at fifteen if the geeky kid who had lanky legs and a really bad sense of humor would one day be the only man I relied on, I would have laughed all night. Now I know better. Sometimes it's the underdogs who become the true heroes.

He's been there more times than I can count and has stood by me. I've never asked him why. I often wonder what his answer will be, but I'm afraid to ask in case it changes things. Both he and Daryl were caught in the middle of this ugly triangle back in the day, but while Daryl firmly took Cole's side against Jason, Billy is a trusted ally to me, and it seems Jason, even to this day. He's a good guy.

I've dropped more than a few hints to my sister about possibly hooking them up. Billy's outgrown those gangly legs, and his sense of humor is better than I remembered. He has made me laugh more than I imagined possible. But Jason's back, so I'm curious how that might affect my relationship with Billy. He doesn't come by all the time, but Billy's not been hanging out as much as usual this week. I've noticed, but I don't say anything. Jason is one of his best friends. I imagine they've picked up like no time has passed at all.

I set the prom pic back in the shoebox and put the lid on. Tucking it in the back of my closet, I shake my head at myself. That I'm nervous over Jason Koster being back is completely ridiculous. I don't know why he is or why he wants to see me, but I intend to find out what he's up to. I just wish it wasn't over dinner.

While slipping on a pair of flats, I stop to check my outfit in the mirror and dab a bit more gloss on my lips. My makeup is light but pretty, my dress cotton and cool for the warm day, and my legs freshly shaven.

Wait, what?

I roll my eyes and walk away from the mirror. There's no justifying how I spent the last hour getting ready for a man who is forcing me to have dinner with him when all I want to do is try to push away the heartbreak his presence has brought back.

Visions of his face that day all those years ago come back like a torpedo. If I'd really looked at him, I could've seen how broken he was too. He'd said it was for us. Promised me we'd be fine. But that was a lie. Jason had no way of keeping that promise, much less making it. I thought he loved me as much as I loved him. Clearly, I was wrong. Someone who loves you wouldn't make a decision about your future without consulting his or her partner.

Partner.

That's the problem. I wasn't a partner in that relationship. I was only a girl holding him back. Taking a deep breath, I try to rid my mind of that memory and the pain I still feel to this day. I grab my phone, head out onto the front porch, and call my sister. Shelby answers right away, "Hey, sis."

"Why do you have to live so far away?"

She laughs, but it's light, both of us well aware of the reason why. "Are you nervous or excited?"

"My emotions are undecided how to feel about him. On the one hand—"

"Oh, here we go."

"Hush. It's true. He hurt me, and that pain is tangible even now four years later."

"But?"

"I'm getting there. But he does look good, even better than I remember, and more charming if that's even possible." Smelled amazing too, just like he used to. I was tempted to touch that clean-shaven jaw of his, to run the tips of my fingers over the veins in his hands as he gripped my door like I'd escape if he didn't. He was intense. Determined. On a mission. Powerful. I struggle to swallow, remembering how imposing his body was, how he leaned in, leaving me no room to say no. God, it was hot. I start fanning myself with—

"Jason Koster could charm a porcupine out of its needles. Your panties never stood a chance."

"Stop teasing." I'd like to argue her point, but she's right on the money. I won't tell her that though. She'll hold it over me because Jason was everything—handsome, charismatic, talented, intelligent, and sexier than any man ever should be. But I thought I was his everything and I wasn't, so what do I know? "Did you book your flight?"

"Yep. You have one week to clean the house and get that farm back in order." She laughs. "Do you have a few minutes to go over invoices?"

The sound of tires grinding against the gravel of my dirt driveway alerts me to a visitor. "Actually, he's here. I need to go. We can go over them tomorrow."

"Don't sleep with him."

"What? There's no way in hell I'm sleeping with Jason. If that's what he thinks he's getting for dinner, he'll be sorely disappointed."

"How much do you want to wager?"

"I am not sleeping with that man, Shelby."

"All right," she replies, her tone sounding like she doesn't believe me. "So one of your homemade pies?"

"I'm not sleeping with him." She's ridiculous. "Fine. I'll wager a pie."

Giggling, she adds, "Good luck, little sis."

"Whatever. Talk tomorrow."

As soon as she says bye, I run to the bathroom, check my appearance, and smack my lips together to spread the gloss. While I make my way casually to the front door—like I don't have a care in the world, despite my whole body and mind caring too much—I dispute her claim. I will not sleep with him. I'm not attracted to Jason Koster anymore. I swing the door open, my thoughts still buzzing. We are two different people than we were four years ag—HOLY hell. Lord, help me. I'm in trouble.

The color brown was never fitting for Jason's eyes—vibrant, full of life, joy, love. Those words always seem to fit his shade better. All those things still light up that color I never could pinpoint with basic adjectives, but being this close to him now with the screen door open, there's a new emotion hidden inside near the darkness of his pupils. I'm thinking it's life. It gets to us all sometime or another, but his concerns me. What has stolen the light from his eyes?

"Hi," he says with a smirky grin that reminds me of my sister's warning that my panties never stood a chance. *Poof.* Yup, he's still got it.

I walk out. "Hi there yourself." Leaning against the railing, needing a few feet of distance between us, between me and those eyes and that smile, and from how amazing he smells. "So why did you want to have dinner together?"

The screen door flies from his hand, and he nods to his truck. "Because we have to eat. You hungry, Delilah?"

Honestly, I have nothing to prove, and my sister would never really make me pay up on any wager, fictional or real. But when I hear my name roll off his tongue like he just tasted the sweetest ice cream he ever had, my body and mind remember like it was yesterday when he used to say it prefaced by three little words I don't say anymore. His deep tone jumpstarts my heart, and I swear my fingers tighten around that old white wood railing.

He asks, "You okay?"

"Good. Yeah." I wave my hands in front of me, but when it looks like flailing, I pretend to swat. "Damn mosquitoes."

Looking around confused, his brow furrows. "Oh wow, I didn't notice. Do you want to go inside?"

"No," I shout. "I mean," I add, lowering my voice, "no. Outside is good." He's staring at me. I bite my lip, shake my head, and dash down the steps. "I'm starved. What'd you bring?"

I make it to the truck before turning back. Jason is still standing on the porch, his head tilted down, his eyes watching me while he scratches the back of his neck. "I'm sorry."

"For what?" I ask, leaning my hip against the bumper.

"I didn't intend to make you so uncomfortable."

"What are your intentions?"

He descends the steps with ease in his body and confidence in his stride. "To feed you." Walking right up next to me, he reaches into the bed of the truck and holds up a picnic basket. "I was thinking we could eat at the lake on the pier."

"Oh, that pier is long past safe these days, but I can grab a blanket or chairs for the grass."

Holding up a blanket, he adds, "I came prepared."

"Oh, I bet you did," I mumble under my breath.

"What was that?"

"Nothing."

He walks around to the passenger's door and opens it for me. "Hop in, honeysuckle."

Honeysuckle.

I wish I didn't like that so much, but the memories of how I got the name warm my insides, the taste of his kiss still lingering on my tongue as if it happened yesterday. He offers me a hand and I take it without thinking. If I had been thinking, I would have prepared for the current flowing between us like a live wire. I would have remembered how my body always came alive under his touch, and I would have remembered to breathe as my body brushed against his. Hell, if I were thinking at all, I wouldn't have accepted this date. But I wasn't, and here I am sitting in the cab of his truck with so many good times flashing back.

"I didn't realize your mom kept your truck."

"She didn't have to," he says, starting the engine. He

drives across the property as if he never left. "She even takes her out for monthly drives."

"I once saw it driving through town, but figured I must have been seeing things."

He smiles, but it slips away when his eyes find the lake ahead. Shifting the truck into park, he rests his arms on the top of the steering wheel. "Wow, it's exactly the same."

The lake doesn't get the same attention from me since he's stolen all of mine. He turns to me, catching my eyes on him. "Hi."

Jason's sweet enough to not embarrass me. "Hi."

"You were staring." Okay, maybe he's not so sweet.

"I'm sorry."

"Don't be. I like when you look at me." My cheeks heat because he not only likes me looking at him, but he's noticed me staring at him. I open the door, needing to get out of the close confines of the cab of his truck. "Hey," he calls. When I look over my shoulder, he adds, "You're making me look bad here. Stay there." He hops out and runs around. Offering me a hand to get out, he stands, not leaving much room between us.

"You don't have to worry about me. I can take care of myself."

When my feet land on the ground, he continues to hold my hand. I'm about to walk away when our hands part, and he shoves his in his pockets. "You were always very independent, so I know you can take care of yourself. But no matter how independent you are or how many years passed between us from then to now, I will always worry about you, Delilah."

My racing heart calms as if I was tucked into his arms like I used to be. It's wrong, and my head is swimming in confusion, but it feels good to feel cared for again.

8

Delilah

STARING.

I'm staring at him again. The way his muscles work fluidly together, the veins popping out with the least bit of effort he puts into a task.

His arms . . . they're better than any porn I can imagine.

Jason Koster was always gorgeous. Tall, dark, and handsome was envious of what that man possessed. His body is hard, the fittest I've ever seen him, and he was fit when he played football, but this is different. This peak physical fitness makes me even more curious how he stays in shape, and why to this degree. "Do you still play football?"

He stops and stomps a plank of the dock with his heel. When he glances up, he replies, "No. Billy and I have tossed the ball around a bit, but that's all really."

"You got a tattoo." I run my hand over his bicep and tilt my head. The tattoo is on the underside, kind of hidden. "On your arm," I add, as if he doesn't know it's there.

"Two years ago. It's a design I saw graffitied under a bridge in Seattle. I took a pic. I wish I knew the artist so I could show them."

"Why did you choose that design?"

"It spoke to me. If you look closely, the detailing of the clouds mixed with the darker sky. Blurring the night with the day." He shakes his head gently. "Can the light fight the dark? Can it survive?"

"Is that how you feel? Are you surviving the dark?"

"Right now? I'm living. For the first time in a long time I'm living."

Looking satisfied, he comes back to me . . . *back to me* . . . He's now staring deep into my eyes, and I can't seem to look away. When a smile crosses those full lips he asks, "Can I have the blanket, Delilah?"

Snapping me back to reality, my eyebrows shoot straight up. "Oh, yeah, here." I shove the blanket I was holding like a lifeline into his hard, brick-like abs. Peeking down, I can see the muscle beneath the button-up shirt, that six-pack calling my attention right to it.

From his close proximity, my heart begins to race. With the blanket bunched in his arms, his eyes lower to my lips before he leans forward. My lips part as I suck in air, needing help to breathe. Stopping, he looks at me and whispers, "Did you think I was going to kiss you?"

Mortified, my head jerks back. "No!" *Yes.* "Not at all." *Oh my God!* I'm so embarrassed. And I was going to let him. Not just let him but kiss him back. I know I was. Oh, good gracious. I walk around him and point at the dock like that is actually going to deflect the humiliation creeping up my skin in a fiery, blotchy haze. "Is the dock safe?"

Staring. He's staring again. "Yeah," he chuckles when he speaks. "It needs a little work, some planks replaced sooner than later, but for tonight, as long as we don't jump up and down on it, it's good to go."

He goes to the dock and spreads the blanket. I grab the picnic basket from the truck to keep my mind off the fact that I would have totally kissed Jason Koster if he'd kissed me. The man is magnetic, and I'm weak to his pull. *Will this never change? Even after he broke my heart?*

Reaching in after me, he grabs a small cooler, a few pillows, and follows me to the dock.

The scene is set, the sun going down. The cicadas get louder as early evening becomes twilight. He's thought of everything, including wine. He fills two glasses with Sauvignon blanc, while I pull the containers out of the basket. I expected beer, but he's pleasantly surprising me. "You went all out."

"I wanted to."

"Why?"

"Do you like chicken salad?"

He may have avoided the question, but I don't point it out. Sometimes we need time to work through things. I'm still curious why he was so insistent to see me though. "I love it."

"My mom taught me how to make her recipe. She makes the best with the grapes and celery."

"Hers is the best. She's a wonderful woman."

He takes a baguette out and starts cutting it into pieces. "She says the same about you."

The compliment makes me smile, but the baguette fascinates me. "Where did you get that? I know Smally's Grocers doesn't sell French bread."

Glancing up, his darker eyelashes highlight the golden centers of his eyes. "I ran over to Kerbyville. They have a bakery just this side of downtown."

"That's forty-five minutes away." I'm not so much asking a question as questioning why he drove so far.

Returning to the bread, he slices the pieces open, and takes the chicken salad container from me. "It was the closest bakery."

"But it's bread."

"You don't like it?"

I struggle to comprehend why he would drive two towns over for specialty bread. "I love it. I just . . . you really didn't have to go to this much trouble, Jason."

"I had some time to kill this afternoon." He hands me a sandwich and says, "Did you know Smally sold the store?"

Smiling, I reply, "Yes, I live here. It was big news when he announced it. Raina Smilth and her fourth husband bought it and promised to keep the name."

"I hope so. It's a legend around here."

"Well, Raina's fifth husband disagrees, but I heard she filed for divorce last week, so he won't have a say anyway."

He laughs. "Wow, isn't she only like fifty?"

"She brags she's had one for each decade of her life." I laugh now, feeling silly talking about this.

Silence seeps in as we eat our sandwiches. I notice how his eyes take in the area as if he's scanning more than casually looking around. He says, "It's not changed at all out here."

"The whole world seems to except this little plot of land, which forever remains unchanged."

"I like it. It's exactly how I remember." I look up when I feel his gaze lay heavy on me. He adds, "You haven't changed either."

My head lowers and I feel self-conscious. I hate that my cheeks heat under the most innocent of comments. Setting my sandwich down, I tug at my skirt with one hand and pick up my wine with the other. A single finger touches the base of my chin and lifts up. "I like seeing your eyes and your sweet face."

"I don't feel so sweet these days."

"Can I ask you something, Delilah?"

I know what it is. It's always the same. People are baffled with how I ended up with my boyfriend's best friend. Gullible. Naïve. So stupid. Something about Cole or the divorce.

Coming out on the other side of this nightmare I survived, I see how he twisted the truth and made me believe I wasn't good enough to hold on to Jason's love, to keep his attention when he would soon be surrounded by so many girls and then the NFL would call. I stood no chance at all. Sabrina taught me that jealousy makes women vicious. I'd be an embarrassment on his arm. My accent would be mocked. He'd eventually see what he could have would be better than what he had at home.

Cole did a number on my head, which destroyed my heart. I don't understand why Jason is back, but I can't deny I still have feelings for him. *Does one ever get over their first love?*

"God, I'm the most boring person ever, Jason. What could you possibly want to know about me?"

"Why are you still here?"

"I live here."

"No, why are you still in McKinney?"

Taking a sip of wine, the cool liquid is counteracting the heat of the evening. I like how I feel less pressure with a little wine in me, more relaxed, or maybe it's that Jason puts me at ease. He used to. I never had to be on guard with him. Not like Cole. He made sure I stayed on guard and the few unfortunate times I forgot that lesson, I paid the price. "It's complicated."

"I've got the time."

Leaning back, he relaxes as he settles in as if this story is worth the attention. "It's not exciting."

"I've had enough excitement. Now I want to hear about you."

I want to redirect conversation away from me, but I have a feeling he's much better at this game than I am. "When my dad died, he left the farm and all fifty acres to me and my sister. We also inherited a lot of debt that went with it."

"I'm sorry to hear that. Your father was a good man. I know he thought hard work was the answer to everything."

"Except to get him out of debt. He struggled to keep up with the crops."

"How do you keep up?"

Pointing across the property, I reply, "We only have two working plots. The others have gone to weeds."

"We?"

"Shelby and I. Oh, and Billy. He helps us more than he should."

"He's a good guy."

"Yeah, I've been trying to get my sister and him to go on a blind date." My giggle bubbles up.

"I don't think that's how blind dates work. They've known each other their whole lives."

"No," I start, my excitement to hook them up taking over my voice. "Not like this. They still see the gawky sides of each other. They need to see each other the way they are now. It's been a few years."

He finishes his sandwich and leans back on one elbow facing me. "Where is Shelby?"

"After college she went to Chicago. We thought she was

starting her career, but what she ended up doing was saving the farm."

"How so?"

"Although the debt was overdue, the bank gave us a three-year extension to pay it off. We have one year left. She works and pays money toward the loan." The *fun* of the dating conversation is over and the burden that weighs me down with worries returns. "I gave up leaving to stay here and work it."

"Is it what you want?"

"I used to. It's really lonely." I laugh humorlessly. "That's not a hint by the way."

"I didn't catch it if it was."

"I have a feeling you don't miss much." I finish my wine. "Tell me about what you've been doing since I last saw you."

"Hmm . . . the last time was when I saw you walk into Red River holding Cutler's hand. That was all I needed to see. I knew it was over. I realized there was nothing keeping me here anymore."

Ouch. If he only knew the truth. I missed him so much that I ached inside as I withered away. It was easier to pretend I'd never experienced pure love like I'd had with Jason. My sister was so worried about me, but I still couldn't bring myself to confess what was happening behind closed doors. The humiliation of them finding out the strong girl they once knew was weak. And then Jason was gone. Thin air, like the memories I held on to. "Your mom was here."

Lying all the way back, he rests his hands under his head and stares at the sky. "My mom can take care of herself."

I whisper, "*I* was here."

"You were being taken care of . . ." He pauses and looks out at the water and away from me for too long. When he turns back, I see some of the pain I feel inside residing in his irises. “You weren’t mine.”

You had already decided you were leaving whether I was with you or not. “And if I had been?”

“Then I would have had a reason to stay.”

What? He had been moving on. Without me. Even though Cole told me time and time again that Jason had moved on, should I have listened to my heart? Should I have known better, and not allowed my pride to stop me from finding out the truth? He needs to know maybe I’d been wrong. “It wasn’t over for me. That night you saw us. It wasn’t over for me until *he* told me how you’d met someone over at State. God, I felt so foolish and hurt.”

“It was lies, Delilah. I loved you so fucking much. What did he tell you?”

What didn’t he tell me?

“He said you didn’t want me. Cole told me everyone in town considered me used goods. He said he’d love me, and since I thought you were seeing other girls, I relented. Looking back now, I can see how he got me at my weakest and took advantage. He talked me into marrying him. Without my sister by my side. Alone. The county clerk was our witness. She took a call regarding an escaped bull on the highway in the middle of the ceremony. He thought I was crying from happiness. I was devastated.”

“Why didn’t you call me, return my texts, or come see me? Find out the truth.”

“I was humiliated. You left, I believed him. I saw the stares, believed others would only see me as sloppy seconds. People respected Cole back then. I felt like an embarrassment to my family. Cole was a second chance.”

“Fuck, Delilah. If I’d known—”

"See, that's just it. We can beat ourselves up, but it won't change anything."

My directness is unsettling. I'm used to sitting in my farmhouse alone at night and not having to answer to anybody anymore. Why confide true emotions to Jason? Why now? "I shouldn't have said anything."

"I'm glad you did, but I want to know why you're so upset. You broke up with me not the other way around."

"I broke up with you because you broke my heart."

"How did I do that?"

My mouth drops wide open. "Really?" *What the hell? How can he not remember something that's scarred me for life?*

"Yeah, really?"

I'm too wound up to sit still. I stand, walk off the dock into the grass, and start pacing under the same moon that hung high in the sky that first night I lost the love of my life.

When I turn to look at him, to possibly answer, I'm stunned into silence. His expression is one of pure curiosity as he watches me. "You don't get it, do you?"

"No, but I want to."

My emotional artillery falls like the walls I've built to protect myself. How can I stand here with weapons loaded when he sits there unarmed? He doesn't know. He doesn't understand how much he hurt me, which might mean he never intended to hurt me in the first place.

Whoa.

My head is spinning, my thoughts whirling with all the angles I thought I had covered regarding our breakup years earlier. Sitting down in the grass, I look at the man he's become. He's still so much the man my heart misses. Could I have had it wrong all along? The years we lost . . . they form a lump in my throat, but I manage to ask, "You weren't going to break up with me when you came over to tell me about the transfer, were you?"

He looks up at me with his head tilted, shaking it a little. He appears so . . . troubled. So sad, and I feel the same. He looks me straight in the eye. "No, Delilah, I wasn't. I was going to ask you to marry me."

9

Jason

I DON'T LIKE to lie.

I've spent the last three years living in an abundance of them—for my protection, for the protection of others, protecting secrets and lives.

In McKinney, I want to live in truth. I want to feel the warmth of sunshine instead of sneaking around in the cover of night. Here, I can breathe.

But there is something about this gorgeous woman that steals my breath and my heart just from looking at her.

Even when her mouth is gaping open by an admission I promised myself I would never confess. Pushing off the splintering wood of the dock, I stand and toe my shoes off. It's time for a diversion. Drastic measures need to be taken, and if I get to see what's under that dress, all the better.

Socks.

Belt.

Her interest is piqued, an eyebrow raised. Her mouth is open for other reasons it seems. My plan of distraction from telling her my deepest secrets is working.

I unbutton my shirt and drop it to the pile of clothes gathering at my feet. Reaching over my head, I tug the T-shirt off and tilt my head, looking down. I'm not shy, but she's looking at me like she's never seen a man half undressed before. "Do you go out much?"

"No. Why?"

"No reason." I slide the zipper down and step out of my jeans.

"Why are you undressing?"

"I'm going for a swim to cool off. Even with the sun down, it's a warm night. Join me."

"No. I haven't swum in that lake since . . . well, since we were a thing."

"A thing?"

"Dating, Jason. You know what I mean."

I also know how to rile her up. I'll have her in here before she has time to decide otherwise. "I liked being a thing with you. How about we try it, you know, while we swim?"

She crosses her arms. "I'm not taking a dip in that water with you."

"Why not? Are you scared?"

"Scared?" She scoffs. "Hardly. I'm just not a teenager anymore."

"Oh, sorry for mistaking you for someone who likes to have fun." I start on the waistband of my boxer briefs, but she says, "Wait. What are you doing?"

"Haven't we already covered this?" I take them down, and she's up and turning on a dime.

With her hands over her face, and her back to me, she says, "Oh my God. Jason Koster, if you are naked righ—"

I dive into the water. It's cold but not cold enough to make me want to get out. When I break the water's surface, I shake my head. My hair clears from my eyes only to find hers on me. She says, "I can't believe you just jumped in."

"I said I was going for a swim."

With a hand perched firmly on each hip, she's riled up. "What about our date?"

"Are we on a date? I thought we were just talking?"

"You're so infuriating, Jason Koster."

"I love when you say my whole name like I'm in trouble."

Her eyes squeeze closed, but a smile follows along with her stance softening. "Old habit."

"Come join me like old times."

This time I can see the debate—her eyes flashing between the water and me, then behind her like her father's going to catch us. "It's only us. No one has to know." I zip my lips and wait.

The debate is over, and she comes back onto the dock, looking down at me. "Feel any fish in there? I hate when they touch me."

"I'll keep them away."

A smile that starts small grows. "You were always good about that, but I'm not stripping down in front of you."

"There's not an inch of your skin that I haven't seen, or licked, or tasted, Delilah Rae. So that dress, although pretty, doesn't erase the memory of what's under it. But if you're scared—"

"Fine." Yup. She's riled up all right. "I'm coming in."

Mission Distraction is complete. She peels off that dress

like it offended her and without an embarrassed bone in her body, she stands on that rickety dock in mismatched bra and underwear as if I didn't think she was already the sexiest creature to walk this world.

"Like what you see here, Koster?"

Nodding, I reply, "I do," then laugh. "Now get in here, Noelle."

She jumps in and I swear she cannonballs on purpose to splash me as if that will cool down what's heating up between us. What she doesn't seem to understand is I love her moxie.

Her head pops up, and she wipes at the hair stuck to her face. A wide carefree grin caters to her expression and she laughs.

"Feels good, right?" I ask.

"It does." She swims away a little and asks, "So, now that you got me in here, what are you going to do to me?"

Tease. I lunge forward to swim after her. She squeals and takes off swimming into the moonlight-speckled waters. I reach her feet, grab her kicking ankles, and pull. This beauty lands right in my arms, and I hold on to her flailing body until she settles and her laughter softens. Her breathing deepens when our eyes meet, just like mine does. But I can't will myself to laugh, to enjoy the moment, or to say anything.

My bravado a minute earlier gets caught in my throat, and I look at her while exposing my inner thoughts—she can still bring me to my knees with that look in her eyes, and I'd happily kneel before her. I caress her slick skin, well aware that these curves *are* dangerous when wet.

"Jason?" she whispers.

"Mm?"

The playfulness returns to her eyes as her hands grace my shoulders. "Why are you holding me?"

"I don't have a good reason."

"Nothing at all?" she asks, appearing hopeful.

"No reason other than I want to hold you again."

A look of relief crosses her sweet face, and her legs drop from my arms to make their way around my middle. "It would be bad if we kissed."

"Would it?"

"So bad."

"I never claimed to be good." I pull her body against mine, and lean in, closing my eyes. Our lips touch and our breaths still. Our bodies float with minimal effort. Touch turns into a caress and I press harder, needing to feel her lips against mine again. Needing all of her against me again. God, I've missed this. Her. Her kisses. Her breath mingling with mine. Her soft body against the hardness of mine. No woman ever felt right, and now I know why. She was made for me.

But before we get in too deep, she pulls back and swims to the other side of the dock. "It's getting late. I think we should call it a night."

I swim a bit longer, watching as she climbs up the ladder. She grabs her dress and slips it over, leaving it unzipped. Looking down at me, she says, "Whatever that was, we can't do it again."

What the hell? "Why not?"

"I'm not in my right mind when I'm around you. Add wine and it's not wise."

"For who? You or me?"

Slipping on her shoes, she says, "I blame it on the moonlight."

"The moon was just an innocent bystander. It's the

sunlight we need to be wary of. The light of day often reveals more truth than we need to know."

"Maybe. Guess we'll find out soon enough." She takes a shaky breath. "You can see yourself home. I'm sure you know the way back."

"That's it?" I ask, waving my arms through the water.

"Yes."

She starts walking away, so I swim to the ladder and get out. "I can drive you back to the house.

"I know my way." She waves overhead and says, "Thanks for dinner."

"You barely ate."

She doesn't turn back this time or respond, and I'm standing there confused by what went wrong. The kiss? The conversation? The confession? Fuck that. This isn't the Delilah I once knew. She never ran from her problems. Is that what I am? A problem for her?

Screw that.

I grab the blanket and with everything inside, pick it up and set it in the back of the truck, except the wine, which I take with me. I stumble to the driver's side while putting my boxers on and hop in the truck to take off after her. She's not gotten far, but far enough for her to not hear me until I'm much closer. Flashbacks of our breakup and her stubborn side whip through my mind. I'm not going to let that get the best of us again. This time we're dealing with our issues head-on. I pull beside her and drive at the pace of her stride. "I have half a bottle of wine to kill. Care to join me?"

Taking the bottle from me, she stops to take a swig. "I know what you're doing, Jason Koster."

"What am I doing, Delilah Noelle?"

She points at me. "You're trying to get me drunk."

I put the truck in park, and lean my elbow on the door

through the open window. "Why would I want to do that? And since when do two glasses of wine get you drunk?"

"I don't drink much anymore, but you wouldn't know since you've been off doing only God knows whatever you've been doing."

"Hop in and I'll drive you back."

"I don't want you to drive me back. I'm perfectly fine with the stars and this wine."

"If you're so fine, why do you sound mad?"

She stills, her chest rising and falling with her feelings trapped inside. I know her. I remember all her moods and swings that maneuvered her through them. Delilah was never a girl to complain and always dealt with everything straight on, but she's not her usual self. She's holding back, and I hate it. Popping the door open, I step out—wet boxers and all. "Talk to me."

"I can't." Her shoulders fall in defeat. When the silence becomes uncomfortable, she brings the bottle to her lips, but I catch it, and lower it back down. Holding her by the wrist, her eyes have lost some of her fire that always burned inside, and she replies, "We broke up. That means you have no rights to make demands of me."

"I never wanted to break up, Delilah. I never wanted to make demands of you. I just wanted you."

"But you left me," she whispers.

Why does she feel I left her? *I left when she started dating Cutler.* I may have put distance between us with the transfer, but my heart stayed behind. "I'm back. I'm here now. Let's forget the past and enjoy this night."

"This night? Is that because you're only giving me one?"

"No, it's because I'd take all your time if you let me, but I don't think you're ready for that."

"What am I ready for?"

"This." I move in and close the space between us. This time our lips don't touch. They crash into each other's. Her arms move around my neck, and I slide my hands down the sides of her wet dress, feeling those dangerously sexy curves. Just when I feel her resolve slipping, I reach around my back and take the bottle from her hands.

Our lips part, and she whispers against my lips, "I missed you more than I should."

"There's nothing wrong with missing me. I missed you more than you'll ever believe."

A smile that endears me even more to her every time I see it appears. Leaning back, she looks into my eyes while keeping her arms securely around me. "Try me."

"Let me show you." I drop the bottle to the ground and kiss her.

And then I kiss her again, cupping her face in my hands and holding her to me. This time our kiss is gentle, a familiarity in the feel and flow of the movement. Our lips part and our tongues reunite with a soft caress and then more—deeper as if staking claims that can be staked without repercussions. We both know that can't happen, but in this kiss, we pretend it can. We pretend we can do this like we used to and the outside world doesn't exist.

Backing her up against the truck, this time I pull back and say, "Let me take you home."

She knows what I mean. My body gives me away as I press against her. "I bet my sister I wouldn't sleep with you."

I chuckle. "As much as I love a good cuddle after sex, I love to win a bet more. No sleeping together then."

"What? No." I hear the plea in her tone, and feel the way her body moves against mine.

"Oh, don't worry, honeysuckle. When I say sleeping, I

mean the slumbering kind of actual sleep. I plan on keeping you wide awake all night."

A smile slips into place and her head falls back with laughter. "You always knew the way to a woman's heart."

"I might want your heart, but tonight, I want everything else."

She laughs again. "I thought you were going to say you want my sex."

"When we hit the portion of the night that we start quoting songs from the nineties to get laid, it's time to go." Nodding toward the cab of the truck, I step back. "C'mon. The mosquitoes are brutal tonight."

Taking her hand, I lead her to the cab and open the door. When she's safely inside, I jog back around and steer the truck, getting us back to the farmhouse. When I cut the engine, the sounds of the cicadas surround us again. The light from the front porch barely reaches us. She looks over at me and, in that moment, I can see something so tragically beautiful in her eyes.

She asks, "Would you like to come in?"

"Do you want me to?"

"Yes." That's all the go-ahead I need to get out and help her down. The wet cotton of her dress clings to her body. What a fine pair of drowned rats we are. I don't lock my truck, but I do grab my clothes out of the back along with the blanket holding our food.

I follow behind her. Suddenly all the fun is gone, and we're left with the questions we should have asked and answered back on that dock. Her fight has slipped into the night and my stance on not having sex with my ex tonight returns. We have too much to work through to put ourselves at risk again. The quiet between us is unnerving, the doubts coming back, so I stop on the porch just as she enters the house. "Delilah?"

The screen door slams closed between us and she turns. Surprised to see me on the other side, she asks, "Are you coming in?"

I want to so badly. So badly that I doubt myself for not taking what I want. I can't though. Not with her. She means too much. She's the only one who can hurt me. Again. Instead, I sigh and look down. "I think I should go home."

Disappointment takes over in a return sigh, and she asks, "Why?"

"Because as much as I want be with you tonight, I can tell this is wrong. I don't want some weird thing between us. I want us kissing and laughing, making love because it feels good and because it's what we both want." I walk back down the steps. "I think it's best if we call it a night. Good night, Delilah. It was good spending time with you again."

"Jason?" Looking back over my shoulder, I wait to hear what she has to say, every word from her too important to miss. "It was a pleasure spending time with you too. Maybe we can do it again before you leave town."

"I'd like that." I start walking again, stepping on sticks and leaves as I cross that little lawn. I should probably get dressed. "And hey, let Shelby know you won the bet."

"I will. But if I won, why do I feel like I lost?"

Women are complicated. I try to do right by her. Read her body language and between the lines of what she says. Respect her and some bet she made with her sister. Now, she's disappointed I'm not ravaging her good and proper.

Dropping my clothes and the blanket back into the bed of the truck, I turn back. Analyzing that body now, I see all the signs I need. Fuck my stance. Fuck her bet. Fuck. She still owns me after all these years. I turn around and cross that lawn like my feet are on fire and get the distinct pleasure of her smile again.

I swing the screen door open and step inside until I hear her breath catch and her eyes go wild with anticipation. “You’re going to so lose that bet.” Capturing her chin between my fingers, I kiss her. This time I leave no doubt about my intentions for the night.

10

Jason

THE LAMP CRASHES to the floor, the light bulb flashing then going out. I bump my knee on a table and my big toe hits something metal. My lips leave hers as I bounce on one foot. "Fuck."

Delilah's arms are around my neck, but her lips leave my face, and she giggles. "Sorry about that. I've moved things around since you were last here."

Looking over her shoulder into the living room, there's enough light from the kitchen for me to take stock of the room. It's a bad habit I'd like to break, but living like I did it's one I needed. Even in the dark, I needed to know my escape route or I could be killed. There's a clear path to the back door if the chair is pushed in and the umbrella is righted.

She turns my chin with her finger. "Hey, remember me?"

Who needs lamps when her smile lights up the room. I tighten my hands around her waist, liking the feel of our bodies pressed together too much to let her go. "I remember."

"Where'd you go there? I lost you for a few seconds."

"I'm right here." Tucking some of her wet hair back from her face. "Right here with you." Her body is cold, the air in the house chilling both of us. I bring her to me, as close as I can hold her, and kiss her on the head. "You're going to get a cold. Maybe we should detour to the shower for a warm-up."

Tilting her head back, she rests her chin on my chest. "A warm-up like foreplay or to actually warm up?"

"Both."

I will never get enough of her smile. I'm warmer by being at the receiving end of it. I mentally add it to the list of things I missed about her. She replies, "I'll get the water going. It takes forever to heat up."

Just as she turns to leave, I catch her by the wrist. When she turns back expectantly, I ask, "What do you want me to do?"

Slipping her wrist from my grasp, her hand replaces it. "Come with me."

I follow her down the hall and up the stairs, stairs I remember climbing a million times when we were teenagers. We were only allowed in her bedroom with the door wide open and if we got too quiet, her dad would start asking questions.

When she reaches the top landing, she stops and turns around. Standing eye level with me, she holds my face in her hands, and as if someone might hear, she whispers, "I don't know what we're doing, but can we take it slow?"

Taking hold of her hips, I kiss her gently. "We can take it however you need to. I'm in no rush to reach the end of this night."

"I don't only mean tonight. I mean, I guess we kind of know what's about to happen and I want that with you. Again. I do. I'm just worried about tomorrow."

I kiss her again. Slower this time, letting our lips get reacquainted. "Let's leave our cares for tomorrow and enjoy tonight. Just a little time to feel good." I can't ask her for more. She deserves someone better, someone with a clear conscience and clean soul. But as I'm kissing her, I let the dark win because if I can have this chance, one last time to be with her, I'll greedily take it.

"You always did make it sound so easy."

"We don't have to make it hard either."

Embracing me, her mouth is to my ear, and she whispers, "Okay. We've got tonight. We'll leave our worries for another day." She turns and walks down the hall to the bathroom.

I'm left with my arms spread, my hands gripping the railings, and a whole hell of a lot of concerns about how we'll feel tomorrow. Because no matter how much I can convince her otherwise, I can't convince myself. She's the same woman I've been thinking about since the day we broke up. No one in the years since has come close. But here I am about to take a shower with her like I can walk away tomorrow not being utterly changed by merely being in her presence. *Fuck.*

It doesn't matter. I'm already walking down that creaky floorboard hallway and pushing open the bathroom door. She's standing there in the glow of candlelight with a towel wrapped around her and her hand hanging out under the water. Blue eyes that remind me of the pool in summertime look into mine with the trust she gives in that one exchange.

I can't screw this up.

I can't screw her over.

I can't take walking away from her the same way it played out last time.

If only for tonight, I have to be everything. All in. For her and for me.

Moving into the small space, I get all in hers. Taking the top of the towel, I lower my gaze as I unwrap her like a present just for me.

She says, "I'm nervous."

My eyes find hers again and I smile to reassure her. "Don't be."

Tending to the towel, I open it and look at her bare body. Every curve and shadow draws me in. Her body is perfection, a wonderland of discovery. The fullness of her breasts mixes with the familiar dip from her waist to her hips. The silkiness of her skin covers a toned but feminine softness to her body. "You're beautiful, Delilah."

A heavy breath is exhaled and relief filters through her. "Thank you."

Her reaction is unusual. She's always been a stunning girl. She turned the heads of all the guys at school. Before me now, she's a woman that needs reassurance. In the back of my mind, I know Cutler hit her, but did he beat her self-esteem down too? *Fucker.* How could he do it?

Why did he do it?

I doubt one night will undo the damage he did to her, but if I can give her a reprieve from her battered heart, I will. I hang the towel on the hook behind me and take down my boxers while she watches. I like how into me she seems. I love how her pretty blues meet my eyes and it's like we were never apart, like the love we once shared is within reach again.

Superficially, I like how she looks at me like she's about to drool. Makes me glad I went to the gym and got a few rounds inside the ring. I took a few blows to my stomach, but my opponent steered clear of my face. I told him I had to look good for tonight.

As much as I would wish to be taking a shower with Delilah, I didn't actually think it would be happening. Reaching out, I test the water, which has warmed. My gaze roams her body leisurely. That's when I spot it. "Is that a tattoo?"

I hear the fast intake of air and her eyes widen just enough for me to know she's embarrassed. Her hand covering the delicate skin just above her pubic bone and an inch to the right also tells me that. I'm intrigued. Really intrigued, I ask, "What's your tattoo?"

"Just pretend I don't have one. It was a mistake. A drunken night out with my sister during a visit to Chicago a few years back." She steps into the tub and under the shower spray, tilting her hips away from me so I can't see the artwork.

Following her into the tub, I ask, "Why are you hiding it from me?"

"Because I can't explain it without ruining the moment," she snaps.

I run my hands over her shoulders, leaving one hand on the side of her neck. "Hey, you can't ruin this. I want you. You want me. This right here is all good, honeysuckle."

After taking a deep breath and exhaling, she turns her hips toward me, giving me an open invitation to peruse her body, which I happily do. I squat down and her head goes up, hiding her face from me. It's only a number in black and gold—McKinney High School colors. It's meaningless to anyone else, but means everything to me. I run my finger over the eight and look up.

The heat from the shower isn't causing the red that

covers her face, but I pretend it is by standing up to reach around and turn up the cold water to cool us off. "It's getting hot."

Delilah's still refusing to look at me, so I lean down to find her gaze. "I think that might be the sexiest fucking thing I've ever seen."

There's the smile I adore. The apples of her cheeks are still pink, but at least the tension she was exuding has evaporated. "Do you think I'm crazy?"

"Yes, but it's a good kind of crazy." Moving my hand over the tattoo, I rub a few circles before going a little lower and a bit over.

"I didn't know there was a good kind."

"There is when it comes to you." I kiss her lightly on the lips.

Why am I *now nervous?*

I've been with women, though it'd be embarrassing to admit how long it's been. It's inhumane to go so long without doing something so natural, but it fit the job I was doing, a job that took an immense amount of attention. I was extremely focused when I worked. No break in concentration. Too many accidents happened otherwise. *Like innocent women being carjacked and shot.*

Her naked body is before me, reminding me how long it's been since I laid eyes on such beauty, such perfection, reminding me she was created to be my undoing.

We've had sex before. Many times. Although years have passed since I last touched her.

I never get nervous. I was good at my job because I was unshakeable, but Delilah Noelle has me anxious, wanting to please her.

Damn, I want to make her feel so good.

Moving her under the water, I watch as she closes her

eyes. I run the back of my hand over her cheek and then continue down her neck and lower. Her chest rises and falls with deepened breaths, her lips part so temptingly that I lean in and kiss her, my tongue connecting with hers. When I pull back, she opens her eyes, the tips of her fingers finally finding my skin. Her bottom lip finds the underside of her teeth while she runs her nails across my chest. "Why'd you stop?"

"Because I like looking at you." When a smile crosses those sexy lips, I have an epiphany. "But I think I like kissing you more." I step closer and take her face in my hands, our lips meeting in the middle. Her nails scrape down my ribs, and I run my hands over her shoulders. Holding her to the side, I reach up and turn the showerhead so the water warms us against the cold tile.

She giggles.

I grab a bottle of body wash and squeeze some into my palm. It smells delectable, just like her. Admiring the beauty before me, her eyes are bright with anticipation. I start rubbing it along those curves that become more dangerous when wet. "What are you laughing about?"

Shyness creeps in. Her hands leave my body to cover hers. "This. Us. We're standing here naked like we do this all the time."

"We used to. Maybe not in your room, but I remember all those nights in the bed of the truck, in the field that time we had no other choice, and in my house." I take her hands and bring them to my lips while keeping my eyes on hers. "I don't want you to hide. You're gorgeous. All over, and I can't wait to kiss you everywhere, Delilah."

Pink creeps up her chest and settles on her cheeks. She starts to raise her hands to cover herself, but I kneel in front of her instead while holding them at her sides. She never used to shy away from me. Never. "What are you doing, Jason?"

"Just enjoy."

"What?" Her voice pitches. "I'm, um . . . uh . . . I don't know."

"Shh." While kissing the apex of her thighs, I hold her hips still.

"Okay." She's breathy when she speaks, and I hear her head hit the tile. Determined fingers weave into my hair and tighten. When I peek up, she says, "Don't look at me like that."

"Like what?" I ask, smiling.

Her thighs clench together. "Like . . . like . . . like you want to eat me."

"I do want to eat you."

Sucking in a breath, another giggle exhales from her. Her tits look amazing. "What's so funny?"

"You. This. Us. I mean, you're staring at my girl parts."

"Girl parts?" Scrunching my brow together, I stand up. I rest my hand above her on the tile. Searching her eyes for any indication that this isn't the first time she's had sex since . . . I don't want to think about him, but the way she's giggling I'm thinking she needs this release as much as I do. "I'm not a guy who needs to know all the gory sexual details, but let me ask you something. When was the last time you were with somebody?"

"It's not like that for me."

"Like what?"

Her gaze falls to the tub, and the strength in her voice goes right with it. I hate that she feels weak at a time she should feel empowered. She's amazing. Has she forgotten? She whispers, "I've only been with two people and you're one of them." This time her hands find my cheek and the day's beard growth must feel rough under her soft touch. "You always saw me so differently from who I am."

"I saw who you really were. Not Douglas Noelle's daughter. Not Jason Koster's girlfriend. Not the most beautiful girl I'd ever seen even though you were. And are. No. I always saw Delilah Rae Noelle. She's the girl I would make the world spin backward to get another chance to spend time with her. You're magnificent."

Looking up under a wave of dark lashes, she's coy when she asks, "That was then. What am I now?"

"What did he do to you?"

"Jason?"

"Yeah?"

"We're standing naked in the shower and the water's turning cold. Maybe we can finish this talk another time. Tonight I want to be the girl you always remembered me to be."

"I don't need that girl when I have the woman before me." I follow up with a kiss on the tip of her nose.

She raises her arms into the air and says, "You missed a spot." Fuck yeah. The weight of our worries lifts, and the playfulness returns. I caress her breasts and kiss her neck. Her body vibrates as she laughs, then she adds, "We should really hurry this along before the water's freezing." I rub my body against hers, soaping myself up.

When she dips her soapy hands and takes hold of my erection, I waver. "God, that feels so good."

"Wait until I remind you what I can do with my tongue."

I hit the knob off and yank the towels from the shower rod, which comes down with them, bonking me on the head. "Ow!"

She screams and jumps out of the way.

"Shit. I'm sorry. I didn't mean to scare you."

Rubbing my head, she says, “Oh my. No. I’m so sorry. I’ve been meaning to secure it. It’s not the first time it’s fallen down.”

I pull her hands from my head and look into her worried eyes. “I’m okay, and I’ll fix it before I leave.”

The concern trapped in her brow eases and a smile appears. Leaning down and kissing my forehead, she says, “I’d like that. Hopefully that’s not until morning though.”

“I’m hoping for at least midday.” Now I’m smiling. Probably too big, but I don’t care. Taking her by the waist, I pull her close while pushing the curtain away from our legs.

“Come on. I want to show you something.” Her smile is mischievous and absolutely enticing.

“Please tell me you plan on showing me in the bedroom.” She wraps the towel around her, and I sigh in my discontent.

“Absolutely.” She winks, her brave and beautifully confident side returning. Patting myself down quickly, I am determined to speed this along. She asks, “Eager much?”

Nodding toward the bedroom, I reply, “Yes. Let’s get out of here so I can get dirty with you in there.”

11

Jason

When Delilah mentions she'll remind me what she can do with her tongue, I admit, my mind recalls the best blow jobs I've ever received, *all* courtesy of her.

Lying in the truck bed under a star-filled sky.

In the cab while driving across county lines after winning a Friday night game.

Once behind the DQ.

So many times in my room, and maybe more in hers.

Our parents never knew how bad we were back in those days. Although it was always so good for us.

What I didn't expect was her tongue sliding up my neck and taking my earlobe into her mouth. When her tongue grazes over it and she sucks—holy damn. She has me hard as a rock and ready to fuck. "I can't take much more of this torture, baby."

Straddling my lap, naked I might add, she smiles at me. "Is the foreplay too much?"

"No. It's done its job as you can tell." Taking her by the hips, I flip her next to me and maneuver over her. Her legs part enough for my body to slide into place. "As for you, are you wet for me, Delilah?"

Sweet pink lips form a little O as the shock of my question infiltrates the fine features of her face. I say, "Don't tell me you don't like a little dirty talk."

Her cheeks match those sweet lips, and she says, "I don't know."

While running two of my fingers on the inside of her thigh my gaze rises back to hers. "I want to relearn everything about you and this magnificent body." I drag my fingers along the side of her lower lips, teasing. When her eyes close, I run the tips of my fingers through her slickness. She's ready for me. "You are so incredibly sexy."

Our bodies begin a slow dance, coming together and moving apart. My emotions are too wrapped up to pretend this doesn't mean way more than I've let on. It does. Being with her does. From the pink bedroom to that look in her eyes, I believe this means more to her too. Pulling back, I touch the tips of my fingers to my tongue as she watches then say, "Tastes like honey, *honeysuckle.*"

"Kiss me, Jason. Kiss me."

I lower my body on the bed and place my hand on her stomach while her eyes go wide. "My pleasure." Licking through her wetness, I savor her, memories flooding my mind and my taste buds. She was always so fucking delectable. Her hips begin to wiggle, and I hear her moan. My hair is tugged, but when I stop to look up, her bottom lip is bitten and her eyes are closed.

Fucking stunning.

I make love to her with my mouth, the sounds of our pleasure the only sounds in the room. When she comes, she comes hard, pulling my hair and calling my name as if I'm the one she prays to. I can't take anymore. I'm about to explode. I've almost humped this mattress I'm so horny. I come up, sliding my body along hers as I lift myself. Holding myself in a pushup position above her, I realize I forgot a condom . . . in my jeans . . . which are in the truck. "Shit."

Her eyes go wide. "What?"

I'm embarrassed I'm so unprepared. Talk about killing a mood. "I left the condom in my jeans."

"In the truck?"

"Yeah."

I start to get up, but she stops me by reaching up and holding me by the shoulders. "I have something. Right there in the nightstand."

I don't care how stupid my smile looks at the moment. I reach over and open the drawer. With condoms in hand, I drop them on the bed. "Tell me these aren't the same ones from back in the day."

She laughs. "No. Newer condoms."

"How new?" I ask, waggling my eyebrows. I really like her being prepared.

She slinks down on the bed a bit and covers her face with her hands. Speaking between her fingers, she says, "This afternoon."

"Oh no. You don't get to hide your eyes." I take her wrists and move them to the side with little resistance. I see her vibrant blues, her carefree smile, and when she giggles I add, "You bought condoms because you were hoping to get lucky."

"Was not. I just figured—"

Pinning her wrists above her head, I say, "Admit it. Tell me how much you were hoping to have me naked and in your bed tonight." When she laughs and rolls her eyes, I push for more. "Come on. Admit it, Delilah. Tell me how much you wanted or hoped to have sex with me."

"I guess enough to drive to Cleverton for condoms."

"You didn't buy these at Smally's?"

"Nope. You win, Jason. I drove thirty minutes out of my way just to score some condoms without judgment or gossip getting around town."

"I may not blush like you do, but I'm flattered nonetheless."

"So much talking. How about we get to the main attraction?"

I kiss her cheek. "Wow, you get feisty when you get some action."

"I'm all warmed up, baby."

Baby. I sure like the sound of that. "Are you now?"

"I am. So ready for more."

More. I'll have her begging for more all right. I slide a condom over my erection and hold it proudly. Women aren't impressed with large dicks. They're impressed by how they're used, so I don't need to wave it around to brag. I just need to make her feel every hard inch, filling her not just for my pleasure, but hers. I position myself back between her legs and press the tip against her sweet abyss.

My nerves from earlier are buried under the desire I feel for her. "More," I mumble, her heat engulfing me as I slide inside. "Fuck." I want to say it's sex, the blissfulness of having it again, but that would be a lie. It's her—wet, tight, angling, moaning. Fuck. Delilah's heaving chest with perky tits on top, her tongue sliding over her lips, her back arching. Fuck. "You feel so fucking amazing."

Her nails drag over my shoulders and then her fingers lace behind my neck, pulling me to her. "Kiss me."

I do.

I kiss her and thrust—tongues and other parts of my body going deep, claiming her in ways I haven't in years. Our breaths are exchanged, one lifeline sustained by the other. When her hands find my ass, she squeezes. "Faster."

Harder.

All of her.

I want her next orgasm and the one after that.

I want to hear my name coming out like a curse word and to mess up that pretty hair.

I want to see her eyes wild with lust, insatiable desire for me.

I want to fuck her again—faster, harder—and make love after that—slower, feeling every damn slow movement together.

My forehead drops to the mattress next to hers, and I thrust and feel, savor, and devour the heat that has ignited a fire down deep. "I'm gonna c—"

"Come," she urges, her body writhing beneath mine in search of her own orgasm.

Like a wave rushing through me, I come, my body and soul dragged under with her when she calls my name like it's a sin she's just confessed.

My lips part and air enters my lungs, filling my chest. The blackness disperses and the small room with a little lamp shining next to the bed comes into focus. Swallowing is rough, my throat dry, but my body feels free from the confines that had shackled me for days, months, even years, and I find peace.

Soft touches and little kisses cover me, and I open my tired eyes to find hers as bright as before, and her face more beautiful in its sated state. "Hi," I say.

"Hi," she breathes, my weight causing her more trouble than she admits.

I smile and roll to the side. "Sorry about that."

"I liked it. I liked feeling your weight holding me down."

Peeking at her, I rest my arm across the top of my head. "Why do you need to be held down?"

"Feeling this good, this light, surely, I'd float away."

It's interesting how such a simple shared emotion makes me feel lighter. Or maybe it's her. The lightness, this peace, is something I've craved above all other things the last few years. "C'mere." I encourage her over on top of me. When she's settled, her body relaxed and her head resting on my chest, I add, "I feel the same."

I can't see her pretty face, but I can feel the smile that graces it, and I can hear it in her voice when she says, "That stunt you pulled this morning, stopping traffic and making demands you had no right to make . . . I'm glad you did."

Fuck yeah. My smile could probably rival hers. "I am too."

Her fingers run through the light hair on my chest. "I know I don't have a right to ask more of you, but I'd like you to stay the night. No pressure, but if you want."

I kiss the top of her strawberry-golden locks. "I have no intention of leaving tonight."

She rests her chin on my chest and looks at me with a smile that lights up the room brighter than the small lamp ever could. "What intentions do you have?"

Repeating her words from earlier, I say, "So much talking. How tired are you?"

"What do you have in mind?"

"To show you exactly what my intentions are." I move her to the side of me and kiss her until those little mewls begin again, signaling the start of the second round.

~

THE SMELL of bacon and eggs rouses me. I reach over to find the bed empty beside me, much to my dismay. I love a hardy breakfast after a night of hot sex, but I'd rather have Delilah waking me up. Maybe with her mouth on me or with my mouth on her.

Fuck.

I'm hard.

I rub over my hard cock, attempting to get him to go down, but I'm not sure that's possible with her scent all around me. Turning my head, I close my eyes, the faint scent of oranges covering her pillow. I could rub one out quickly in the bathroom, Delilah none the wiser, but I'm not ashamed I'm hard. I'm horny because I'm here with her.

Flipping the sheets off, I get up to find my clothes I'd left in the truck during the rain yesterday, clean, dry, and laid out at the end of the mattress. I pull on my underwear, still warm from the dryer. She's good, too good. Hopefully she washed them because she wanted to and not because she felt obligated. That bullshit about women being barefoot and pregnant and waiting on a man hand and foot doesn't fly with me. I can hire a maid. I don't need my wife to serve me.

My hand stills with my jeans halfway up.

Wife?

Where the fuck did that come from?

I pull them up and head to the bathroom. The word *wife* didn't kill my erection like I'd have thought, but my mind is spinning over the words, letting it rumble around, trying to find where it fits. I take a piss and wash my hands, but when I look into the mirror I see myself in a light I thought I had lost touch with a long time ago. Maybe I can be who I used to be. I wasn't so bad back then. A little heartbroken. A lot ego-shattered. Losing your girl to your best friend wasn't something I could control back then, but it's nothing I should be ashamed of now.

We may not have wanted to talk last night, but we'll need to soon. I splash my face with cool water and pat it dry. When I finish in the bathroom, I head downstairs. Passing through the living room, I follow the sounds from the kitchen and find Delilah scrambling eggs.

Her back is to me, which gives me a second to take her in. Her hair is up in a messy bun on top of her head, the delicate lines of her neck visible. She's in a black tank top that shows off the curve from her waist to hips, and leads my gaze lower to her ass—round enough to fill out that pair of cutoff shorts that her daddy would never approve of. Me? They've got my stamp of approval. Bare legs and feet anchor her to a mat with an ugly teapot design. With a hand planted on her side, she tilts her hips as if she's lost patience for how long it's taking to cook the eggs.

I ease up behind her. Sliding my hands around her waist, I kiss the back of her exposed neck. Her body tenses at first and then quickly relaxes. She leans her head back on my shoulder then kisses my neck. "Good morning," I say, sliding my hands over the top of the tank and taking two handfuls of her breasts.

The spatula is discarded and she spins in my arms, weaving hers around my neck. "Good morning."

Reaching around her, I turn off the stove and move the pan to a cold burner before pressing her ass against the counter next to it. "You smell amazing."

"That's the bacon."

"No. It's you."

"I haven't showered. I'm still dirty from last night."

With my lips against her neck, I hum. "Yeah, dirty. So dirty. I'm so hungry. For you. Want to come back to the bedroom with me?" Lifting her, my eyes meet hers. "Or we could test out that kitchen table like we used to joke about."

Laughter fills the kitchen and she languidly looks into my eyes, something more than lust filling the centers. Like . . . *love*? The word wife comes back to bounce around the space in my heart I've left vacant since Delilah left me.

"My parents used to have a cup of coffee every morning together at that table and eat a meal every night. They said it was the only time they were guaranteed together with the busyness of their lives."

"So that's a yes to the table?" I tease.

"That's a—"

"What the hell?" Her response is cut short when the screen door opens and a man's voice booms. "Jason Koster's truck is out front."

12

Jason

"MORNING, BILLY," Delilah says, as her hands press against me.

I take a step back and let her tend to the eggs in the pan like we weren't just caught. Looking over my shoulder, I see a goofy wide grin spreading across his face as the screen door slams shut behind him. I shake my head. "Your timing sucks."

"Good morning to you too, sunshine." He sits down at the table, making himself at home like he's staying awhile. "So what ya cookin' over there, other than some delicious-smelling bacon and freshly brewed coffee?"

Replying while crossing my arms, I glare at him. "Nothing now. What brings you out to the farm?"

He chuckles and takes off his hat just as Delilah sets a plate in front of him. "I could ask you the same thing." He smiles up at her. "Thank you."

She pats his back. "You're welcome." When she turns to me, she says, "Hungry for food?"

I catch the food emphasis. "Starved."

"Sit down and let me feed you."

"I can make a plate."

"I'm happy to make it for you, Jason."

"Thank you." I head upstairs into the bedroom, getting my exercise for the day, and grab my shirt. Pulling it on over my head, I return to the kitchen. Sitting across from Billy, who waggles his eyebrows, I give him a harder glare than before. He just laughs and shovels more eggs into his mouth. After drinking some coffee, he says, "Man, your eggs are the best."

My jaw tics. I don't like him talking about her eggs and how they're the best. I try to shake off my annoyance at how casually he walked into her house, moved around her kitchen, and sat at her table like he'd done it a million times before. She's mentioned that Billy had been helping out a lot, but they're so familiar with each other. *Am I setting myself up again for a huge lot of hurt?*

She sets a plate in front of me and sits in a chair between us with her own plate made. "Thanks, Billy. You're out here early."

"I'm heading to Kerbyville for supplies for the week. Wanted to check in with you to see if you needed anything other than the usual."

Delilah starts to get up, but I touch her knee. "You should eat breakfast while it's hot. I can help you guys after."

"Okay. Thanks." A soft smile plays at the tip of her lips. "Not much to get, but I'll make a list when we're done eating."

After cleaning the kitchen, Delilah and I go back

upstairs while Billy heads outside to the barn. "How much does Billy help you out here?"

"Don't get jealous," she says, poking me in the side as she passes. Sitting in a chair, she pulls on a pair of socks and then steps into her work boots. Heaven Almighty. My memory seriously had failed me when it came to this woman. She is no girl at all. With grownup curves and a sense about her that draws me to her like a moth to a flame, she's a fantasy come to life, easily outshining any centerfold I've ever seen.

Rolling in the hay and riding in the saddle take on a whole new filthy, oh-so-dirty meaning with the vision standing before me.

"What?" she asks, with her hands planted on her hips again.

"You sure do have a lot of sass with that hot ass."

Shaking those same sexy hips as she passes by me, she says, "You seem like the type who knows how to handle a woman."

I smack her hard on her back end, making her squeal, as she turns to me. I pull her by the belt loops until we're face-to-face, a breath away. "You know I do. No seeming about it. If you want to be bent over this bed or a hay bale in the barn, I suggest you keep doing exactly what you're doing now."

Watching her lick that bottom lip is about to do me in, but then she douses the fire burning inside me. "As tempting as you make hay sound, Billy's waiting out back." She takes my hands and lifts up to kiss me. "Spend the day with me."

"That's a hard offer to turn down."

"Then don't, and I'll make sure hard is all you are later on."

Cupping her jaw, I bring her in for another kiss. This time with purpose and passion, a *thank you, ma'am and I look forward to later* kiss. A deal struck and sealed with our lips. "I'm going to hold you to that."

She nips at my jaw and then kisses the spot. "I'm hoping you'll hold me to a lot of things later. But first," she says, walking away, "we've got work to do." I'm still standing there admiring the view when she stops and looks back. "C'mon now. Daylight's burning."

"So am I," I mumble and then laugh. She heads outside and I sit and put my socks and shoes on. When I'm done, I go into the bathroom and scrounge around until I find a toothbrush. I bust open the package and brush before I head out to help. I feel better just in case we need to kiss at the feed store.

In the cab of Billy's dad's truck, they talk upfront. It's a nice ride, so I get more comfortable in the backseat and stretch my legs out when I decide I should text my mom. She's not been my keeper for many years, but I know she worries about me.

Me: *Hi Ma. Helping Billy and Delilah out today at the Noelle farm. Just checking in.*

I lead with Billy, hoping that doesn't tip her off to ask too many questions.

She doesn't reply right away, but I get a return text before we reach Kerbyville town lines.

Mom: *Hope you got some breakfast out of the deal.*

Me: *I did.*

Mom: *I meant food, Jason.*

My mom's got jokes this morning. Although I'll always be her baby, as she constantly reminds me, it's nice that she treats me like I'm a man.

Me: *Ha! I'll be home later. Let me know if you need me to stop and get anything for you.*

Mom: *Have fun.*

Me: *You too. Love you.*

Mom: *Love you too, son.*

Delilah rests her arm on the seat and looks back at me. "What's so funny?"

I lift my eyes to her curious ones, and reply, "Just texting with my mom."

"That's sweet."

"I hate worrying her."

"She's such a sweet lady." She glances out the windshield and then back to me. "Have you spent any time with Fred Carver?"

"No. Just when I went to General Hardware a week or so ago." What an odd question. "Why?"

Her eyes go slightly wide and she turns to face away from me. "Oh, no reason."

"Why would I spend time with Fred Carver?" I see Billy glance over to her and she looks at him before she tries to keep avoiding the question. "Delilah?"

With a heavy sigh, she angles back in the seat again to face me. "I shouldn't have said anything."

"Yes, you should."

Worry creases her forehead, the look not good enough to grace her face. "Tell me. Please."

Looking at her side, her hands twist together. When she finally looks up, she says, "Your mom and Fred have been dating. From my understanding it's casual, but she told me she likes him."

"What?" I'm shaking my head in complete denial. "No, no way." She turns around, but I see her cringing face. "Is she really?"

Billy says, "Rumor has it that it's more than casual."

"Why do I get the distinct impression that you are enjoying this a little too much?"

He shrugs. "Because I am."

"Fuck you, man."

Delilah says, "Hey. Hey. Settle down. She's a grown woman with needs."

Grabbing Billy's cowboy hat from the hook across the cab from me, I put it on and sink in the seat. I lower the brim, and say, "No. I do not want to hear about my mom's needs, so let's end this now."

Her hand taps my leg. "You might have to get used to the idea of her dating, but I'm surprised she hasn't mentioned him to you or that you haven't seen him hanging around."

I grumble, "He's smart enough to stay away from my mom."

The sound of her laughter fills the truck, and then Billy joins in and says, "While you're in town."

"I'm not in a hurry."

Delilah looks at her lap, but from this angle, I see the smile on her face. Billy busts into our moment and adds, "It's been good to have you around again."

"It's been good to be around again." Leaning forward, I give her elbow a little squeeze. "How are you doing up there?"

Looking back, she flashes that sweet smile like she's been saving it all day for me. "Good." Her eyes tell me all I need to know and remind me of how they shined at two in the morning after we finished another round of fun under the covers.

"Can we just get it out in the open because all this sexual tension between you two isn't so subtle, if you know what I mean."

I chuckle. "No, what do you mean?"

"It's obvious I interrupted something this morning. I'm curious if what I walked in on started last night."

Leaning back again, I lower the hat to cover my eyes. "Sorry. I'm not one to kiss and tell."

Delilah is laughing, and then I hear her say, "Don't look at me like that, Billy Langston. A girl has a right to keep some secrets, even from her friends."

The truck parks and I sit up, hanging the hat back on the hook. He cuts the engine and says, "You two are ridiculous. It's obvious what's going on here. Let's just hope the whole town doesn't get wind. Boy willy, they'll have all sorts of stuff to occupy their time and talk about." He hops out of the truck and shuts the door.

My eyes meet Delilah's before she gets out. We both know we can't avoid what we so easily avoided last night for long. Her smile has faded. Reaching forward, I touch her arm. "Don't worry. It's going to be okay."

The high we were riding has lessened, a damper put on our fun. It felt good to feel careless for a night. Nothing good can last forever. And then I look around.

Three garage doors on the right side for large load trucks.

Two sets of double doors in the far back corners.

Four doors at the front entrance.

"Jason?"

I look behind me. Delilah is standing there with a curious look built into the tilt of her head. "What's on your mind?"

"Nothing."

"Billy wanted your help over there."

"Oh. Okay."

I start to go, but she asks, "Where do you go in that head of yours when you disappear like that?"

"Nowhere good." Like her, old habits are hard to break.

I help load some bags of chicken feed then slam the tailgate closed. Billy had already loaded the rest of the supplies. While he pays, Delilah leans on the side of the truck, her boots kicked out showing off those long, tan legs of hers.

Two cowboys walk by blatantly checking her out. Jealousy rushes through my veins, striking deep in my chest. I step over her boots, straddling her legs and lean forward caging her in. "I don't like all these eyes on you."

Her arms come around my neck and she looks at me, seeing right through me. "I only care about your eyes on me." Leveraging herself against me, she kisses me as if she has a point to prove. Maybe she does.

I do too. I don't need to prove it here, but I'm no fool. Wrapping an arm around her waist, I lift her up and kiss her deeper, getting lost in the sensual caress.

"I knew it," I hear Billy from behind me. "Break it up and save it for later, preferably when I'm not here."

We start laughing, the kiss broken but replaced with smiles. We get back into the truck. We don't make it out of the parking lot before he asks, "So you guys are a thing again?"

It's strange that labeling something grounds a feeling that was freeing just minutes earlier. I stare out the window. I'm not sure what to say, so I'll let her say what she needs and back her on it, but I have a feeling that conversation is going to happen now whether we want to have it or not.

She replies, "We're not going to complicate things just yet."

Lowering my head, I scrub my hands over my face. What am I doing? What was I thinking? It was supposed to be a few days, visit my mom, and then head off. To where? I don't know, but I know I have to be careful. My past could catch up to me if I'm not. And here I am, possibly dragging Delilah into my messy life like there couldn't be any repercussions to hers.

Her hand covers my knee, and I look up. She doesn't have to use words for me to know what she's thinking. The crinkle in her forehead, the lilt of her lips, and the sorrow that's returned to her eyes tell me everything I need to know. I take her hand and raise it to my lips and kiss. There's not much else I can do while trapped in this truck.

Most of the ride back is in silence, the three of us in our own thoughts. I don't mind the quiet. I've spent more time alone than with others in the last three years. Being a loner was sort of a job requirement, so I was a natural since I was looking for a way to escape. *To hide.*

I made a few friends, bonded with a woman on the last job, but that bond only went friendship deep. A deeper connection is what I've been missing. Looking at her through the space between the front seats, I'm feeling connected to Delilah already. I don't know if I should protect my heart, but it's feeling like it's already too late.

13

Jason

A SMALL BASKET of eggs is just inside the barn when we arrive back at the Noelle farm. Delilah grabs it while Billy and I unload the truck. It's good to do manual labor like this. It burns off the restless energy I feel inside, the same energy I used to burn off running away from my problems.

Billy comes up behind me and grabs the last bag as I haul some rolled up fencing. He says, "So between us, it's obvious you two are on again. Does that mean you're sticking around?"

"Are you asking out of curiosity or concern?"

"A little of both. She's a good woman."

I drop the fencing along the outside wall of the barn and give him a good hard look. "You interested?"

"Nah. We're friends. Nothing more. Doesn't mean I don't care about her or her well-being." Tilting the bill of his hat up, he wipes his arm across his forehead. "Heck, I wouldn't be out here so much if I didn't."

"How are you running your farm and this one?"

"My family is still running our farm. My brother secured some grocery chain deals. We've got new equipment and hired some guys."

"What about the Noelle farm? Be honest, how's it doing?"

He slides up on the tailgate and chugs from a thermos. Water drips from the cap when he pulls it away and pours some on his face. A bandanna is swiped across his face, and then he says, "Sometimes I think she wants this place to work and sometimes I wonder if it's a chain holding her back." Shaking his head, he looks at the house. I follow his gaze and we watch Delilah chopping wood. Chopping wood is not an easy job, but she seems to be managing quite well *and* looks sexy as fuck doing it.

"She's pretty independent and self-sufficient, but how long can she run this place on fumes?"

"Fumes?"

"Her sister's in Chicago working to save this place."

"Yeah, she said the bank gave them an extension on the loan."

When he looks back at me, he lowers his voice, and says, "Cutler made Delilah take a second mortgage out on the property to start his business."

"What? When?"

"Two years ago." Scratching the back of his neck, his face is scrunched and he seems unsure if he should be saying anything. "Look, Jason, don't tell her I told you this. She wears her heart on her sleeve, but when it comes to this farm, her pride gets in her way."

I look back at her. Her body's tight, great muscle definition in her arms and legs. The farm works her in all the right ways, but it still pisses me off that she has to work it at all. She's always been a stunning woman, but that's the outside. Her insides are warmth to my cold heart. She makes me want to stay in so many ways. I just wonder if I'm too far gone to be the man she deserves, the man she needs, the man she wants.

Do I want this life again? This life comes with rumor mills and farming, and an honest day's work, a positive side effect. "How much debt are we talking about?"

Billy shoves off the truck and grabs the fencing at my feet. "I don't have the final numbers or anything, but I know they're well into six figures."

Shit. That's a lot more than I thought. Glancing back at her, I realize how strong she is. Who knows what else she's had to hide for so long? I hate that her pretty smile possibly hides more troubles than anyone is aware.

He says, "C'mon. I need to fix the coop and get back to my farm by noon to get some stuff done over there."

Taking the fencing from him, I say, "You head out. I can handle the coop and anything else she needs done today."

Laughing, he lowers his cap but releases the fencing. "I bet you can."

"Fuck off."

His laughter turns hardier. "Beers later?"

"You're on. Text me."

"Do you ever take calls anymore?"

"No."

He slams the tailgate closed. "You're back in McKinney, man. Time to slow down and reconnect with the real world."

"Yeah. Yeah."

Tossing his keys in the air, he catches them and says, "See ya at beer o'clock." He gets in his truck and starts the engine. "Call me if you need anything, Delilah."

She looks up, smiles, and waves. "Thanks, Billy. You're the best."

Billy's truck kicks up some dust. I set the fencing down and walk over to her. "Hey."

One side of her mouth lifts when she looks at me. "Hey yourself."

"I thought I was the best."

"Aw, don't be jealous. You're the best at so much."

"Like?" I ask, teasing, but curious.

The weight of the ax falls to the ground and she rests her body on the handle. "I've never known you to have low self-esteem."

"I don't, but when it comes to you, I wonder."

The ax is dropped, and she comes to me, wrapping her arms around my neck. There's a sheen to her skin that makes her glow from the inside and ignites need within me. I want this woman. Damn, I want her. I take her by the waist and lick along the base of her neck.

"Jason?" she squeals in shock, but giggles. "Oh my God, you're an animal."

"I find you utterly impossible to resist. You taste divine, by the way." Despite her words, she settles into my hold, our bodies pressed together. Kissing her neck, I taste her skin again and find my way to her earlobe, where I nibble. "Do you know what you do to me? Do you know how incredibly sexy it is watching you wield that ax?"

She laughs again, squirming. She's ticklish, and I love that too much. I'll definitely have to indulge my enjoyment of that trait later, when we're naked. I lick the shell of her ear, making her moan. Her legs are straddling mine, her middle seeking pleasure. She says, "Sure is hot out here."

Swinging her by the hips over my shoulder, I dash for the door. "We should go inside then."

She's hanging upside down against my back. I have a firm hold of her tight ass while she's drumming on mine. "Animal."

"You love it."

Her laughter trails behind us. "I do."

"Admit it. You love it." I'm about to go to her room, but I detour to the bathroom to wash my hands. I want to feel my girl on the inside, so I need to get this filthy farm off me. The water faucet is on as I scrub the dirt from my hands.

"I do love it, but you do realize I'm still on your shoulder, right?"

"I do." I dry my hands and then turn around.

She reaches down like a good girl and washes her hands. "Then you must also realize this is the weirdest foreplay I've ever done."

"Cleanliness before . . ." I don't finish that thought. Considering what I'm about to do to this woman, I don't need to drag God into it. Unless, of course, it's being called at the top of her orgasm. Then she can go right ahead and scream his name all she wants, and I'll take it as a job well done.

Slapping my ass hard, she says, "All done."

I like this time with her. It's full of fun and her sunshine. She's just what I needed, a prescription to help heal my ailments.

I make it to her room and toss her on the bed. "Okay, there you go. See you later," I tease, pretending to leave.

She grabs the back hem of my shirt. "Oh no, you don't." When I turn back and waggle my eyebrows, her smile settles as she lies back, arms wide, legs spread. "C'mere."

Not waiting another second, I land on top of her, settled between those sexy tan legs, and shamelessly squeeze her tits. She's still smiling so I know she enjoys this too. Rubbing her hand along my cheek, the smile disappears, and she continues, "I like you being home."

"Is that where I am, honeysuckle? Am I home?" It's a loaded question I shouldn't have asked. I know better. I hate being put on the spot, but she makes me want to hear words I have no right to hear. Not this soon. It's not even been twenty-four hours in her presence and here I am clinging to her words as if they determine the rest of my life.

Do they?

I don't know, but then she says, "You could be," and I'm totally lost to her. Kissing her, I'm not gentle or easy, and she's not polite or reserved. She's the opposite—demanding and grabby hands—and I fucking love it.

Pushing my pelvis against hers, I'm so turned on I could fuck her through these jeans. But I want her naked, so I push up and start stripping down. I'm almost done when she lifts a leg. "Help me with my boots, cowboy."

"Yes, ma'am." Taking her by the heel and toe of the boot, I wiggle the boot until it comes off, then pull the sock off. I take the other boot and sock off and kick them to the side.

"My turn. Take off your clothes."

Our clothes go flying, and there's my goddess—bare innocence with a good helping of vixen mixed in. I'm rock-hard just looking at her. She reaches up and grabs a condom from the drawer while I climb back on the bed, taking hold of that fine ass of hers. "I want you like this."

She stills, the giddiness from seconds earlier dissipating under my heated request. Looking back over her shoulder, she asks, "From behind or . . ." leaving her question open-ended.

Reading people is something I've become very good at over the years. Tracking them down, reading between their lies, research, when they beg for their lives—it all comes in handy in the most interesting ways. Like now. She's intrigued, but a little fear resides in her tone. I don't want Delilah scared. I want her turned on. I want to be the one who turns her on. I lean to the side and say, "Hey. Look at me." She catches my eyes and waits. Rubbing my hand gingerly up her spine, I gently grasp her fine neck. "We only do what you want to do, what you're comfortable doing. If you want it slow, want to make love, then we go slow. You want me to fuck you hard, fast, and so deep until your orgasm bursts free, then I fuck you. You can trust me, Delilah. So tell me. How can I pleasure you?"

The tips of my fingers find stillness where her pulse was just beating rapidly. I add, "Breathe. For me. That's my only request."

She sucks in a jagged breath and swallows. "I want all of that with you."

A slow smirk slides into place before I kiss her shoulder. "Good. I want all of that with you, too. How about we start with slow and steady right here." I dip my hand between her legs and run my fingers through her slick silkiness. Her back bends and arches when her head drops down. "When you touch me, I lose myself. It's good to be out of my mind and in your world for a little while."

Moving to the side, I hear what she needs, her body speaking to me through every reaction. Lying on my back, I look at her and she looks at me, a small smile appearing. "Don't you want me like this?" she asks.

"Don't you know, baby? I want you any way I can have you. So tell me. You want on top?"

"Make love to me so I can see your face."

I lift up and kiss her while slowly moving so I'm above her. When she's lying on her back and tucked beneath me, I angle my middle. I could slide right in I'm so close. Fuck.

Her heat. Her sweet nectar. Fuck. I grab a condom and pull it on quickly before moving back into place. "Where were we?"

"I know we decided slow and steady, but seeing you here again, feeling your body . . ." The smallest of lines form on the outside of her eyes, her happiness shining through. "I hope you don't think I'm shallow, but I really like your muscles—your biceps, your abs, your . . ." Her breathing deepens and her eyes leave mine when she whispers, "Ass."

"What was that?" I tilt her chin in my direction and her gaze follows. "Did you say you like my ass?"

She seems to gather her courage, looking determined. "Yes, I did say I like your ass."

"That has to be one of the hottest things I've ever heard." I push in just enough to make her feel what's to come. "I want you to grab it."

Her eyebrows shoot up. "Huh?"

"You heard me. Grab my ass and squeeze to your heart's content."

Rolling her eyes, she smarts back, "I bet you say that to all the girls you sleep with."

"I don't sleep with any girls." I push in another inch or so.

A gasp escapes her, and she struggles to keep her eyes open, but she does it as if on a mission. "I know that's a lie."

"It's more like let me call you an Uber."

"Now that does not surp—Oh God, yes."

Filling her to the hilt, I pause not for some grand effect but because she feels so damn good I'm about to blow before I can make her come. Lowering my head, I whisper in her ear, "You are amazing."

She whispers right back, "I'm not doing anything but lying here."

I lift up to find her eyes. "You don't get it, do you? It's not about all the other stuff with us. It's about being together, our physical and emotional connection. I'm glad I came back."

Her eyes shine, a glassiness covering them as her expression softens. "I'm so glad you came back." Caressing my cheeks, she adds, "Please start moving."

I do, my body finding a rhythm with hers. Her eyelids close and I lean down and kiss her sumptuous lips, parting them as my tongue meets hers and everything deepens when I start thrusting. Just like her, it feels so good to lose myself in something bigger than my thoughts.

We hit that bliss together, our bodies wracked with pleasure and lust melding together. We lie on the bed, catching our breaths. My arm is curled around her as she curls around me. This feels normal, like we do this all the time. Nothing feels out of place. Nothing feels wrong or rushed.

Everything about this day feels good.

Everything about being with her in this house feels how it should.

Everything about *her* feels right.

With the only girl I ever loved in my arms, my restless heart finds rest. Comfort.

Solace . . .

14

Delilah

I STARE at the man beside me. There's not much light in the room, but there's enough afternoon sunshine sneaking through the bent blinds for me to see the differences between the boy I once thought I'd spend my life with and the man sleeping next to me.

Restless.

Like most of my nights.

Even behind closed lids, his eyes never seem to settle. With my hand on his chest, his heart beats fast even in slumber. There are small lines that remind me more of cat's whiskers than crow's feet. They're soft, but I see them digging in for the long haul. They look so much more distinguished on him than the ones setting in on my face from too much squinting in the sun.

Jason's nose has a small bump that wasn't there before. I like it. I'm tempted to run my finger over it and land on the lips that look like pillows where my lips could rest easy. The stubble is thick, but not so thick that it's a beard needing to be shaved. It's hard to decide if I like this look or a clean-shaven face on him best. Both highlight the jaw that's gotten sharper over the years.

I see the clouds of the design of his tattoo so much better now. The sun is barely peeking through. The artwork is both beautiful and sad. I hope that was him then and he can find happiness now because I love the comfort of being in his arms again.

Too soon?

I'm not sure.

I don't like to think about it. I want to enjoy this too much to overanalyze it to death. Why did I walk away from this man? He's never been anything but honest with me, so forthcoming with how he feels. I won't be that stupid again. I need to trust in the journey. I won't deviate from this path again if it feels this good to be with him.

"Hey," I whisper.

As if he's been awake the whole time, his eyes open, showing me those gorgeous brown eyes that always held too much emotion for him to hide from me. Despite his body's restlessness, his soulful eyes are at peace, staring into mine. His arm tightens around me, pulling me closer. "Hey," he whispers, brushing some strands of my hair behind my ear. "Everything okay?"

Resting my chin on his chest, I look at him. "Everything's good. Better than good."

A languid smile moves into place and holds steady. "Guess we should get up. I slept harder than I thought I would for an afternoon nap."

"I'm glad. You needed it."

He bends his neck to the side, stretching it. "Something about this place."

I don't beat around the bush. Neither of us has time for that. "I like having you here." Pushing up, I slide up and kiss him. Our bodies move the way that feels so good, and we fill the afternoon with moans, expending our desire, and satiating our lust.

Left with smiles that feel shy, although I don't know why, we take a shower and get redressed. Watching me as he puts his jeans on, he says, "I told Billy I'd fix your chicken coop."

"Do you know how, city slicker?"

Laughing, he dips his feet into his shoes and winks. "I think I can manage, but I need to start tomorrow if that's okay. I promised my mom I would change her oil today."

"You don't owe me anything, Jason. I can manage."

Coming over to me, he rubs my arms. "I know you can. I want to help. Is it okay for me to take that job off your hands? You have plenty to take care of yourself."

My arms go around his middle. I rest my head against his chest and close my eyes. His heart is strong like his muscles that make me weak in the knees. "Thank you."

I love being tucked inside his arms. It's safe here, like the world can't touch us, and all our problems belong to someone else. He kisses my head. When we part, he asks, "You busy tonight?"

"No," I reply, laughing lightly. "My schedule is pretty wide open most days."

"Let me ask you something."

Here it comes—the questions I've been happily avoiding. "Okay."

"Will you come to dinner tonight at my mom's house?"

"He, uh . . . wait. What?"

His forehead crinkles from my response. "Dinner. You. Me. My mom. Will you join us?"

That's not what I expected him to ask. I thought for sure

he'd bring up Cole, but I'm so glad he doesn't let him invade our time together. "Dinner?"

"You know," he says, his hands motioning like charades as he feeds himself. "Food. Eating. Talking. That kind of thing."

I smile. "I'd love to."

A wide smile appears but there's always a little mischievousness in his eyes. "How's seven?"

"Perfect. I'll bring dessert."

"I always loved your desserts."

"Are we still talking about food?"

"Nope."

I roll my eyes and head for the living room. "I'm not sure I can keep up with your appetite."

"I'm insatiable *because* of you."

Stopping in the hall, I turn around and press my hands against his chest. I rub lightly over the cotton of his shirt. I want to feel his hard muscles through it . . . yeah, I do, and I'm not making any apologies for it. "What are we doing, Jason?"

By the way his smile turns light and his eyes darken with the change in my tone, he says, "We're getting to know each other. Again. That's all."

"I like that." I nod, and then take a deep breath before exhaling. "I come with baggage I didn't have last time around."

"We all do." Kissing my cheek, his mouth lingers on my skin, sending goose bumps across my arms. "I lied earlier."

"What about?"

"When I said I rest better because there's something about this place. I lied. It's not this place."

"What is it then?"

Cupping my face, our lips meet, but he doesn't kiss me.

"It's you. You give me the peace I've needed, and the emptiness inside isn't so empty anymore."

He fills the emptiness inside me too. Our lips meet, and we kiss, exchanging the words that aren't needed.

"I'll see you tonight, Delilah."

He walks around and right out of my front door like it's his own to return through. I lean against the frame and watch him through the screen door. He starts his truck and looks back at me, leaving me with a nod of his head and smile on his face that feels genuine. Dirt fills the air behind his tires, and I watch that old beat-up pickup drive away, feeling anxious as the distance grows.

What are we really?

Are we playing a game or is this real?

I miss him already and it hasn't been a minute since he left.

That feels pretty darn real, to my heart at least.

With more than four hours until I need to be at dinner, it's time to wrap up some chores.

This goofy smile on my face might be the answer I'm looking for. I head out back and return to chopping the wood I'm going to need to store for winter. It's backbreaking work, but I can't afford the wood delivery service anymore. At least I don't have to work out anymore. The chores around here are enough to keep me in shape. And Jason seems to really like my body . . . perhaps more than before, which surprises me. I haven't felt attractive . . . well, since Jason used to appreciate me—emotionally and physically.

After the wood's chopped, I inspect the coop. I can fix this easily, but I like that Jason wants to help, and I like him hanging around more than taking the job away from him. I hop on the ATV and drive around the fields to the two active ones. Ricardo oversees the plots with Billy, but he also lives on the acreage that bumps against the fields in a two-bedroom cottage my dad built when I was little. I used to dream of living in the little white house with its gingerbread trim and door.

Paloma, his wife, takes care of the house, keeping it in shape despite time wanting to wear it down. She brings me food too often, but she knows how I love her cooking. She also says I'm too skinny. I'll happily take her pralines to help widen my hips to bear children, as she puts it. They're too delicious to pass up.

She's watering the flowers out front when I drive up. "Hi, Delilah."

"Hi, how are you today?"

"It's a beautiful day," she replies with a motherly smile on her face. "I saw a truck leaving the property earlier."

Her mothering instincts go beyond a smile. I've known her since I was eight, so we've been through a lot of changes together through the years. I don't have to say much. She's happy to fill the air with her wisdom and observations, which have often been comforting over the years since I lost my mom and dad. "Your old boyfriend, the one I liked, used to drive a truck like that."

I take the watering can from her and take over the task. As the water sprinkles across the flowerbed, I keep my tone level, careful not to give more than I have a right to away. "He still does."

I don't have to see her face to hear the smile in her voice. "It was a good visit?"

Looking at her, her hands are clasped together in front of her chest.

"You don't have to pretend. Tell me what you know."

"Ricardo said the truck stayed overnight."

I giggle, the usual burdens feeling lighter, almost effervescent today. "It did. Along with Jason."

"Jason," she says in such a dreamy way. "I always did like how he treated you."

"Even in the end?"

"The end? Hmm. You weren't one to reason with back then."

I've yet to process what Jason said last night. I felt like a fool. No, more than that, I felt heartsick at what I must have put *him* through. How could he come back here and want to reconnect with me? He must have hated me, especially when he saw me with Cole that time at Red River. *Why? Why hadn't I gone back to him and given him a chance to speak?* He wasn't a selfish man. He never had been. My assumptions were based in an insecurity that I placed on myself, not from his actions. Cole is to blame for his part; he was devious. But I fell for it. Naïve. My heart hurts thinking about what I did. God, how I hurt Jason, but here he is despite the pain he's felt, and potentially offering a second chance. He's so much stronger than I ever was.

I set the empty watering can down and move to sit on her steps. Resting my arms on my knees, I stare ahead at the field that meets the end of her yard. When I glance over at her, I say, "He wasn't going to break up with me. That's what he told me."

"I could have told you that too."

Softly laughing, I reply, "You probably did. I just wasn't able to hear you through the noise in my head."

"But you hear him now?"

"I'm not sure."

She sits next to me. Resting her head on my shoulder and wrapping me in a loving embrace, she says, "Sometimes it's not the loudest voice we hear, but the soft whisper our heart feels. Back then the sting of *perceived* betrayal clouded your judgment and clogged your ears. Someone took advantage of that pain and twisted it to his own needs."

Although I can't remember exactly when Cole first talked to me about Jason leaving, I can recall some of what he'd said.

"I'm sure you know what guys are like, Delilah. He's leaving this town—you, me, Billy—and moving on." He reaches over and rubs my shoulder, as if consoling me. I'm not even sure what he's talking about, which worries me more. Is Jason keeping secrets from me?

My hands tighten around the handles of my cheerleading bag, and I look toward the stadium tunnel that leads to the locker rooms. Jason is long gone, the coach calling him in to talk about something. Is it about leaving? Leaving school? Leaving me?

As I worry my lip, he continues, "He's kept you on a string, someone to come back to when he wants you." He runs his hands through his sweaty hair. When he looks back at me, it's a look of excitement . . . like? Lust? Surely not. I've seen this look before, but dismissed it as nothing since I'm with his best friend.

He says, "I'm sick of the rumors I've heard about him when he's visiting State's campus. Rumors about him and other girls. You deserve better. Why do you put up with that?"

. . . I remember doubting Cole, thinking that wasn't the Jason Koster I knew and loved. But each time Cole looked at me with sympathy and held me as if to comfort me, I believed him. *But was it true?*

No.

That wasn't Jason at all. But somehow I fell into more confusion when I didn't hear what Jason had to talk to the coach about, or why he suddenly had to stay after practice a few times for meetings.

Was Jason lying to me or waiting to tell me what he

considered good news? I know now, but I wish I had known then.

Cole had pursued me. Had turned up every day to spend time with me, to *help* a friend he'd said. And when I saw Jason at Red River just before he left again for college, I didn't know how to understand the look in his eyes. He'd looked angry. At me. Definitely at Cole. But I remember what I felt that night. I'd been just as angry. By then Cole had told me story after story of all the women Jason had been with on every visit to other campuses. He'd told me about the *many crude jokes* he'd heard Jason say about me when out drinking with the guys.

Were they all lies? And if so, why had I been so stupid and naïve to believe him?

Because I'd been devastated. I'd believed he was leaving me and heading off to his world, a world I had no place in.

"Cole was a force to be reckoned with. He played upon my insecurities until I couldn't see anything beyond the lies he was feeding me. I owe Jason an apology." My swallow is heavy like my heart thinking about how I hurt him.

Sitting up, Paloma pats my back. "If I still know Jason at all, I have a feeling he doesn't want or need an apology."

"What does he want?"

"The same thing he always needed. You."

"Can I be what he needs, what he deserves now? Am I stronger?" After last night, I think I am.

"Strength is found in the ashes of the fire. You've been burned, but you must rise because there's so much life ahead of you to live. Wouldn't it be nice to share that life with someone who cares for you so deeply?"

Pushing up off the little cement steps, she takes the watering can in one hand. With her other, she covers her chest. "Trust what's in here, Delilah." Then adds, "Ricardo is in the back quarter if you're looking for him," before she disappears behind the house.

Paloma has never needed to fill her days with a lot of chatter. I think the love she feels for life is fulfilling enough. Her thoughts aren't veiled. She always makes her views heard. I screwed up four years ago, and it cost me the future I once dreamed of. I won't make that mistake again. I stand and head for the field to find Ricardo and get an update on the farm.

~

FRESHLY SHOWERED, I'm baking with my robe on. I put the cobbler in the oven and return to the bedroom to get ready. I've timed things perfectly and am dressed when the timer goes off. Dashing into the kitchen, I hit the timer button to turn it off and set the cobbler on the stovetop while I gather my purse and slip on my shoes.

One final once-over in the mirror and a big smile in place, I'm ready to go. I stop under the arch in the kitchen.

What the hell?

As he scoops cobbler onto a plate, I watch in horror, frozen to the spot.

15

Delilah

"What are you doing here, Cole?" I ask, gripping the corner of the wall next to me. Officially, he's been out of my life for two months. He finally left—*coerced* not willingly—about fourteen months ago, but I had only really begun to feel safe again during the last few months since the divorce. For such a long time, I'd locked my doors at night. I had looked over my shoulder more times than I could count, and even now, hearing a man yell makes me shudder a little in fear. But now he is on my turf, somewhere he most definitely has no business being, and I am pissed.

The metal feet of the chair screech against the floor, and he makes himself at home. I watch as he shovels a big bite of the cobbler in his mouth before he looks up. His eyes are the color of faded blue jeans that have seen better days. "I'm eating. You always did make the best cobbler."

"You would know," I smart back, my better sense forgotten.

"What does that mean?"

I debate on holding my tongue, but I never did abide by his rules. Most of the problems in our relationship can be summed up in that confession. "Means you were eating cobbler all over town and not caring that I knew."

The vein in his forehead becomes prominent in his anger.

Stage one.

His spoon hits the dish, clanging to the table. "You and that mouth of yours—"

"Are none of your concern anymore. I want you to leave right now." We stare at each other for what feels like minutes. It's seconds, but time with him always did drag. I repeat, "Leave."

He stands, the veins in his neck prominent in his anger.

Stage two.

I remember the stages well. They were ticking time bombs leading to the finale.

The pop of cracking knuckles.

Stage three.

I have to stand my ground or he'll come back. The rubber soles of his shoes stick to the linoleum as he walks, the sound ominous in his approach.

My breath shallows, but I won't cower.

"Delilah Rae Cutler. That's my fucking name on the end of yours, meaning you are mine. Always mine."

Stage four.

I flinch when his hands come at me. When I'm not hurt or hit, I open my eyes and realize I'm caged by his body. His expression is laden with disgust as he snarls at me. "What do you know about Jason Koster being back in town?"

My silence must be telling. My body trembles, my breathing staggered. My throat closes in on me. He grabs my jaw as soon as I turn away and forces me to look at him. I press my hands against him and push, but his hold on me tightens, the taste of blood coating my mouth. When my eyes begin to water, he steps back, and sits down to eat more cobbler.

Don't cower.

"Leave, Cole."

"Stay away from him, Delilah."

My heartbeat picks up, the fear I felt when I first found him in here returning and shrouding my bravery. "Don't tell me what to do." My voice sounds meek, and I hate it. *I hate him.* "We aren't married. This is not your home. Leave."

Grabbing his heart, he fakes offense. "Oh, that hurt, but you know what will hurt more?"

His questions are all leading, and I don't have to respond. He never expects an answer. He's way too impressed with himself to let me actually guess. "You," he replies. "*You* will hurt. Stay away from him. That's your only warning."

"Get out."

Laughing, he stands and grabs his plate. Tossing it into the sink, the sound of shattering ceramic fills the space. "Oops. Tastes like shit anyway." He grabs his hat off the table and kicks the screen door open to leave. I see the dent in the metal before it slams closed after him.

I grab my keys from the hook, the only weapon I have within reach. His truck roars down the drive away from the house.

I'm safe.

Leaning against the wall, I try to calm down.

I'm safe.

Looking at the dessert from here, tears spring to my eyes. I no longer have a dessert to take tonight. As much as that should worry me more, it's not my biggest concern. We can live without dessert.

But my dish. He knows this was my mother's. I only have a few pieces left of the original set—thanks to my ex-husband—and now I'm down another dessert plate.

I refuse to cry despite the lump formed in my throat. He's not worth shedding another tear over. The plate yes, but there's no point. I pick up the pieces and the tip of my finger is sliced. "Oh." I lift it up as blood pools. It's a deep enough cut for me to worry. Fuck. *Fuck him.* Once again he hurt me, but I refuse to cry. I rinse it under cold water and then wrap it in a paper towel while going to the bathroom to bandage it up.

And then that's when anger takes over.

Anger dominates every other emotion as I grab my keys again to leave.

Anger that he thinks he can come into my home.

Anger that he thinks he can tell me what to do.

Anger that he broke something precious to me.

Anger that at one time he broke me, and I'm still putting the pieces back together.

Anger that I believed his lies.

Anger that I have nothing to offer Jason and his mother tonight.

Anger that I'm not stronger.

My head throbs with the memories of being bent, my body curled over itself as my blood pooled on the bathroom floor.

My naked body shakes uncontrollably as my mind returns to reality. This is my life, the life Cole allows me to live—bruised with fear owning my thoughts and now my body. Not again. I will never let him do this to me again. I push up off the floor and avoid the mirror as I crawl through the house.

Cole left. "Going drinkin'," he'd said.

I pull my purse from the kitchen counter, the contents falling onto the floor, including my phone. I take it and dial the only number I know will keep this a secret.

"Are you calling me about the hash brown casserole?" He laughs. "You know I'm weak to your home cooking."

"Billy?"

The laughter is gone from his voice in response to mine. "Delilah? What's wrong?"

"I need help."

. . . Billy bought me a gun, but can I use it? Will I?

Wanting to check on the gun, I go to the side table in the living room and open the drawer. This time I load the bullets. One by one until all five chambers are full. I don't touch the safety. I don't like guns and had hidden my dad's shotgun in the back bedroom closet after he died. I know how to shoot, but I hope I don't have to.

My body shakes involuntarily every time I see Cole, but now minutes later, I'm much calmer. I run my hand over my hair, making sure it's still in place. It's a silly concern after what just happened, but I need to focus on one breath after the other, pulling myself slowly back together.

With a clearer head, I think about grabbing something pre-made at the market, but I'd rather be on time than take something that feels last minute.

I KNOCK on the door and Meredith answers quickly. "Delilah, come in. Come in."

We hug and she takes my hand. I'm quick to retreat when the motion hurts my finger. She asks, "What happened?"

"Kitchen accident. Nothing to worry to about."

"Of course I worry, but I'll leave it be. Looks like you did a good job of wrapping it. Jason's grilling out back. We're having fish. Hope you're hungry. He bought a ton of food today."

I smile. "Starved. I'm sorry I don't have a dessert like I promised. I burned it."

We go into the kitchen and she pulls out a bottle of white wine. "I don't need the calories anyway. But that's not like you to burn food. You're such a good cook. Everything okay?"

"Just busy." I hate lying. I really hate lying to her. She's been so good to me, but Jason will lose it if he finds out that Cole came by. "I was sidetracked doing something else and didn't hear the timer go off."

"No worries, dear." She hands me a glass of wine. "It's been awhile since I've seen you. I'm glad you're here."

"Can I help with anything?"

"Yes. Head on out and enjoy the evening. The lightning bugs are out tonight. There's something about them that's so magical, don't you think?"

"Something so small but is powerful enough to shine light in through the dark is magical indeed." I open the back door and add, "Call me if you need anything."

"Go entertain my son. I'm almost done in here."

Giggling, I reply, "I'm not sure how entertaining I am, but I'll try."

I shut the door behind me and whistle at him. He looks up and says, "Are you catcalling my meat?"

"You've got the best-looking meat around."

He takes me by the waist and swings me into his arms, and I don't spill a drop of my wine. We make a good team. With my back to his chest, I look over my shoulder and he kisses me. "You don't mind a little PDA in front of my mom, do you?"

I see her looking through the window. When I catch her, she busies herself, turning away. "I adore your mom."

Coming around in front of me, he says, "I told her about us. That I stayed the night with you. I didn't want to lie."

"What did she say?"

"She smiled and said I told you so."

"What had she told you, Jason?"

Leaning in, his cheek rests against mine, and he whispers, "That my feelings weren't one-sided."

"What are you feeling?"

"Everything. All at once. As if the world had dulled before you were back in my arms."

Swooning's a thing, right, because I totally do it. "You say the most amazing things to me."

"You are amazing to me." Sliding our hands into the air, his other holds my waist, and we start slow dancing even though there's no music. "What's with the bandage?"

"Just a little cut. Nothing to worry about."

"It's bleeding through. Let me clean it up for you." He turns and closes the grill lid and leads me inside by the hand. "Ma, check on the fish, will you?"

"Got it handled. You're not going to be too long?"

He laughs, but I don't. "She thinks we're going to have sex."

"And you noticed she didn't stop us?"

I elbow him. "I don't want her to think I would be disrespectful like that."

"This will take five minutes. No respectful man can make love to his woman in that amount of time."

"You sure do give me a lot of credit," I tease.

"I'm going to clean up Delilah's cut. We'll be right out."

She doesn't reply, but I'm laughing too hard to know for sure. I sit on the toilet lid, and he digs out a first aid kit from under the sink. "Hold up your finger." He carefully unwraps the white bandage. "How'd you do this? It's a deep cut. You don't need stitches but it will leave a scar."

"I have plenty of them already. Most you just can't see."

His eyes flash to mine momentarily, but he lets the comment slide. *Shit. Shit. Shit.* I shouldn't have said that, but Cole's earlier visit has knocked me off balance a bit. When it's rewrapped with clean cotton and tape, he kisses it. "All better?"

Not able to take my eyes off him and the care he's giving me, I whisper, "Yes."

Touching my chin, he lifts it. "It's okay. It's just a bandage. I didn't perform surgery." I stand and lean my head against him. The fear I felt earlier had unnerved me, but here I'm reminded that I'm safe now, safe in Jason's arms. He whispers, "Hey, everything okay?"

"Yes. Now."

He leans back and looks into my eyes. "Now?"

"It's nothing. I'm just feeling sentimental is all."

A reassuring smile creases his lips. "Me too." Kissing my forehead, he whispers against it, "I also told my mom we were dating. I know we said we didn't need to complicate things, but they're complicated already, aren't they?"

We hold hands between us, and I nod. "Very."

"How about some wine and dinner?"

"I think that sounds like a good idea."

~

SITTING AROUND THE FIRE PIT, I have my feet kicked up on

the stones surrounding the flame. Jason's not usually very talkative, but he is tonight.

We've covered the fixes he's made around the house.

His trip to the hardware store, which I promptly steered him clear of since his mother doesn't owe him an explanation.

We even covered a little about the motorcycle parked to the side of the garage hidden from the street. That one he guided us away from fairly fast after the topic was broached. I did get him to promise me a ride on it soon though. It's a side of him I'm completely fascinated by. And find sexy as hell.

But then his mother, on her third glass of wine, asks him, "Are you staying?"

He looks at me. Jason takes my hand, not shy about it at all in front of his mom, and replies, "I'm thinking I might."

My tongue curls around the front of my teeth as I hold back revealing my feelings. Too soon, I remind myself. I grasp his hand in one of mine and the wine glass in the other. I can hide my feelings, but I can't hide my smile. His mother giggles in drunken delight and I finish off my wine, feeling tipsy myself.

Jason changes the subject, something I'm learning he's very skilled at doing, and asks, "Are we ready for dessert?" Rubbing his belly, he adds, "I know I am."

His mom says, "We're skipping dessert tonight." She looks at me conspiratorially as if we've just pulled off a big caper.

"What?" He looks to me.

I fess up, and by fessing up, I mean, I lie while pouring more wine to forget the real reason I didn't bring my cobbler. "I burned it. It's tragic, actually."

"Damn. I'd say so. I was looking forward to it."

"I'll make you one tomorrow and not burn it. Promise."

His knee knocks into mine. "Well, since you promised and all."

Two bottles are emptied before we decide to call it a night. After clearing the table out back, we bring the rest of the food inside and wrap it up. I'm trying to pretend I'm not feeling every bit of that wine, but it's hard.

Jason hugs his mom. "I'll finish up in here, Ma. You can go to bed."

"You're the best." She kisses his cheek.

She comes to me and with my face between her hands, she says, "I'm so glad you're back in his life."

"Me too."

"You're a wonderful person, Delilah. It's good to see you smiling again." She embraces me before she retires for the night.

Meredith has always been a loving woman, but tonight I feel closer than ever. "Thank you for having me over."

"My pleasure, dear." She glances to her son. "Jason, you're seeing her home, right?"

"Yes, Ma. I'll drive her home."

"Good. Good night then."

"Good night," we say in unison as she slips out of the kitchen.

After cleaning the dishes, Jason comes over and takes my hand. "You ready?"

"Born ready for you."

His chuckle is deep, but he keeps it under wraps by his hand so it doesn't travel through the house. "You're drunk, Delilah."

"Not drunk . . ." I waver. "Okay, maybe a little tipsy, but you make me feel the same way."

"You get drunk on me?"

"Being near you, I lose my better judgment and inhibitions. You're a very dangerous man to my self-control."

A thumb runs over his bottom lip while he looks at me. "What am I going to do with you?"

Throwing myself at him, I wrap my arms around his neck. "Take me home and have your way with me?" I hear the hope in my voice when I was going for sultry.

"Who needs dessert when I have other ways of satisfying my sweet tooth? C'mon. I'm taking you home."

"You're staying though, right?"

He holds the door open for me. "You couldn't keep me away, honeysuckle."

There's something in the way he says it that makes me think he might be right. Luckily for me, I don't want to keep him away. I sure do like having him around again.

He grabs a backpack by the door and adds, "Change of clothes."

"I like that you're prepared."

"Always, baby."

We walk to my car and I toss him the keys. In the country, when it gets dark, it's pitch black. I'm glad he's driving to handle the curvy road we have to drive to get to the farm. It's not a long drive, but it's long enough for the wine to settle my mind and lull me.

When we arrive, he parks the car out front, comes around, and picks me up. "You don't have to carry me," I lamely protest by relaxing in his arms.

"I like to."

Just that simple.

Jason Koster never put on a show for anyone or hid his feelings. I'd once believed I knew exactly where I stood with him. If I hadn't been blinded by feelings of betrayal and hurt, I would have realized he hadn't changed. He just opens up and tells it like it is. He says what he likes and what he wants, and I like that.

Making our way to the couch, he sets me down, but I quickly crawl onto his lap as he turns on the TV—some manhunt show that is way too boring to keep my eyes open. "Stay with me."

"I never left you. Not really," are the last words I hear before I fall asleep in his arms.

16

Jason

DELILAH SNORES.

I think it's just from being drunk and sleeping so deeply. I never noticed it before. It's cute when she does it, like a little snuffle-snort. My body shakes with laughter. I've tried to hold it back so I don't wake her, but I can't. It's cracking me up more than it should.

It's bedtime. I lift her into my arms and carry her up the stairs to her room. As soon as I lay her down, she rolls to the side away from me. I take her shoes off and work the covers over her. I'm not that tired so I go back downstairs. I turn off the TV and the living room lamp, wanting to head out on the front porch to enjoy the quiet night.

Grabbing a beer from the fridge, I twist the cap off and flick it into the sink, landing it exactly where I wanted. Amused with my minor achievement, I go to retrieve it but stop when I look down. A full cobbler dish is angled in the sink with a big scoop taken out. The remains of that scoop are splattered across a broken dish.

When I pick a piece of the shattered plate up, I notice the blood that has seeped into it through the jagged edges. I recognize the pattern of the plate as one Delilah always cherished. We were never allowed to use these floral-trimmed plates because they were her mother's. They're on display above the cabinets. Looking up, it's easy to find the vacant spot. She had to make quite the effort to eat off it. Wonder what spurred her to use that plate, and why did it end up broken in the sink with what looks to be not burned, perfectly delicious cobbler?

But what I find odd is why Delilah lied about dessert. I can guess all night, but I'm not getting any answers until morning from the snoring beauty upstairs. I find myself smiling, thinking about her. I pull the pieces of the plate out of the sink and put them in a brown lunch sack I find in the pantry.

On the porch, I sit down on the steps and set the bag next to me so I remember it on the way out tomorrow. I hear the bugs and see the fireflies in the field. The light above Paloma and Ricardo's front door shines in the distance. I should probably go by tomorrow and say hello. I'm sure they know I'm in town so it's rude not to stop by.

A car drives down the main road, coming toward the curve just past the farm. If they keep driving that speed they could end up in the ditch. I watch, keeping my eyes on the car just in case. But the car slows down so much so that it comes to a stop at the end of the long drive that leads to the house. When the lights are cut, I stand up. What the fuck are they up to?

I maneuver off the porch from the other side and duck behind a tree in the yard. Making my way to the edge of the fence, I stare. The driver remains in the car, but the inside's too dark to tell who it is from here. I'm about to sneak through the field and approach from behind, but the lights flick back on and the car drives off. But not before I get the make and model—white BMW 3 Series.

I've not seen many BMWs around the county. It's a rich man's car when most here live mortgage payment to payment. Trucks are much more practical. Was that a wrong turn, ending on this road, or more?

With no sign of the car returning, I go back inside the house. All doors and windows are double-checked on the first floor before I go upstairs to Delilah's bedroom.

She's still sleeping soundly, which relieves me. Knowing she's comfortable gives me peace of mind. I hope she feels the same from me, that I can bring back the same confidence she once had, the confidence the motherfucker ex of hers took.

Cole Cutler is lucky I let him go with a minor takedown outside Red River. I'm not sure how or when, but he better hope we don't meet in a dark alley anytime soon. I go through my nighttime routine like I live here, which makes me wonder if I eventually will.

I'd never considered it since Delilah never thought she'd be living here after college, but plans change, life happens, and sometimes we end up exactly where we were always meant to be. Standing over the bed, staring at this stunning woman—snuffle-snorts and tattoos from drunken nights—I'm starting to feel this might be where I was meant to be all along.

Shifting the covers on the free side of the bed, I slide her over. Her skirt scrunches up around her thighs and I let my eyes follow the long lines of her legs. Reaching down, I toss the blanket to the end of the bed and slide down the zipper on her hip and shimmy the skirt off. I work her sweater from her shoulders and down one arm and then the other, leaving her hopefully a little more comfortable in a tank top and underwear. Pulling the covers over her, I lean down and kiss her head before slipping in next to her.

I don't worry about macho pride. I get right in, bumping up against her, and then spoon the hell out this woman. *My woman.*

Sleep evades me.

Headlights. A BMW. Stopping on the road in front of her property isn't normal in the country. Not that spot. Not this time of night. It feels off. My instincts are on high alert. The problem is I'm not sure if I'm dealing with a threat from my past or a present danger.

I kiss the back of her head and tighten my hold on this angel of mine. Have I put her at risk by being here? What about my mom? Was it a mistake to come home?

It's hard to think I made a mistake when I'm currently holding the one reason I survived through the last few years. I can continue the lie that she wasn't on my mind, but I'm tired of lying to myself.

"Jason . . ."

My name breaks through the stormy clouds of my thoughts. "Yeah?" I reply softly.

"Please . . ."

That's when I realize she's still asleep. Sitting up, I hover over her, and watch her face as it contorts in pain. Shit. I don't want to hurt her. I hurt her once, which I'll regret forever. If I had only told her, but that damn surprise backfired before I could fix the damage my secret caused. Her dreams should be filled with the good memories, not the bad.

I run my hand over her arm, trying to comfort her.

"No. Please. Please, Cole. Don't hit—" She balls up, her words choking in her throat as she starts to cry. "Jason. Help . . ."

What the fuck? "Delilah?" My voice is louder than I intend, firmer. I want to wake her up. *Need to.*

Air whooshes from between her lips and her chest lowers just as her eyes open. Her throat must be dry by how she takes a moment to swallow and coat it, hopefully drowning the bad dreams along with it. "You awake?"

A hand covers her head, and her gaze finds me in the dark. "What's wrong?"

"You were having a bad dream."

"Oh." Her reply is flat, and she looks at the ceiling. "Sorry if I woke you."

"You didn't."

Glancing back to me, sadness comes over her expression, sinking into the corners of her eyes. "Can't sleep?"

"No." I lie back.

"What is it?"

"I hate that you have bad dreams."

"They're just nightmares. They're not real."

"But they were."

She sighs. "Yeah. Not anymore though."

"Can I ask you something that's rattled me for years?"

"Sure," she replies, unsure of where this is going by the way she extends the word, dragging it out.

"I remember this one time after I transferred, after we broke up. I made a touchdown, winning the game my junior year after transferring. The team piled onto the field, tackling me with cheers and congrats. I knew you weren't there."

Her body tenses, but I keep going. "I knew you weren't there, but I looked up into those stands anyway like a bad habit I couldn't break. You know what happened?"

Hesitating at first, she finally replies, "What?"

"You *know* what happened. Tell me."

Her body molds to mine, but she keeps her head down. "I watched you score that touchdown. I watched your team lift you onto their shoulders. I watched the crowd cheer for you. I watched you."

"I saw you. I ran as fast as I could, jumping a wall to get into those stands, and work my way to the section where you were, but you were gone."

"I shouldn't have been there."

"But you were." I sit abruptly and she lies down. "You were there like you were supposed to be. And then you weren't. Why?"

"Because Cole was playing, and I left his game to come to yours. I only needed to see you to breathe again, to feel whole, to feel what I'd missed. It was always so much better with you."

I keep my back to her and move to the end of the bed. I have no energy, the emotional toll wiping away all my strength. "Then why'd you stay in this town?"

When she doesn't answer, I turn back. She's leaning her head on the mattress, the pillow pushed behind her. The covers expose her shoulders, but she seems exposed in other ways—vulnerable—even in the dark. I want to help her, to fill in the space where her words can heal, but something tells me they won't heal but hurt us both if spoken. I'm about to end the pain she's reliving in her mind by the distance that's taken over her gaze, but she finally says, "He didn't just hurt me after we got married."

Fuck.

"At first I stayed to help my dad, but he said I was meant to fly. I was going to move to Chicago with my sister. Cole didn't like that idea, and always knew just the right thing to terrorize me with. He threatened to set fire to the fields, and then he threatened to set fire to me, to ruin me for all others."

I drop my head into my hands. The pads of my palms dig into my eyes before standing and walking to the window. I hate these damn blinds. They're useless, making me want to rip them from the frame. I don't, but I want to. Instead, I yank the cord, the metal slats slamming together.

"Jason! What are you doing?"

I open the glass and climb out, my muscle memory strong from all the times I came and went through this window. Pacing the roof above the porch, I don't know how to make this right. I don't know how she can even allow me back into her life. I didn't protect her. I've proven I can't protect her. I didn't when she needed me most.

How can she look at me?

How can she act like she forgives me?

My feet stop, and I look back at the window as she climbs out. Standing there, she says, "Why are you upset?"

Sitting down near the corner where the trellis hangs, I look over the property, too ashamed to look at her. "I'll never fucking forgive myself for letting him put his hands on you."

"Is that what you think?" I glance at her while she comes closer and sits, keeping a foot or so between us. "You think you *let* any of that happen?"

"I didn't stop it—"

"You couldn't stop it." She reaches over, stretching across the distance that seems wider than the visible space. "Don't go blaming yourself for something you had nothing to do with and no control over."

"I loved you."

"And I loved you," she replies easily. "But it wasn't love keeping us apart. It wasn't you transferring schools either. It wasn't a lack of want on my part. I wanted you. Mostly, I needed you. You meant so much to me that I struggled to live life without you in it."

"But you stayed with him. Why?"

"Like you, I didn't feel I had much choice in the matter. I tried to leave once. He dragged me from the truck before I could stick the key in the ignition. It didn't matter how hard I fought, his hands tightened around my neck, forcing me to the lake." She stops talking. I'm so tempted to fill in the space. I want to take away her pain, tell her it's okay, but I can't. I wasn't here for her when she needed me most. I have to let her work through this now. "We stood on the dock. While I gasped for air, he looked into my eyes and told me he would drown me before he let me leave him. He would kill me before I embarrassed him in front of the whole town like that."

I don't think she realizes her hands are on her neck, rubbing lightly as if she's soothing her throat.

I say, "He knew."

"Knew what?"

"He knew I was going to ask you to marry me."

A scoff-sob escapes her as she looks at her lap, her chest denting in momentarily. When she turns her eyes toward the sky, I can see how they shine, a layer of tears ready to fall. "Of course he did. Cole had his eyes set on the prize long before that argument between us."

"Why didn't you come to me? Why didn't you trust me enough to tell me?"

"I believed him." She turns to me, her arms wrapped around her knees. "I believed him when he said you transferred because you didn't have the nerve to break up with me. I believed him when he told me you had been bragging about how many girls you'd been with. I believed everything because he was my friend and your best friend and surely everything he was telling me was true."

"Delilah, you have to believe me. None of that was true. I never, *never* slept with any other girls. You were my everything. I knew what I had, how special you were. *Are.* I've been so fucking angry with you. Through miles of travel and years apart, I never understood why you left me without another word, without giving me something I could hold on to enough to let you go. Or how you could be with him."

And that's the most honest we've been for some time. Now I know the truth. Now I know why. Years late, but knowing allows so much of my anger to evaporate.

He had lied to her.

"I'm so sorry, Jason. So, so sorry. I—"

"No. Don't apologize. I'm sorry you believed him then, and I'm angry because of that you were hurt. But you need to believe me now. I love you."

Her eyes flash to mine. "Loved. You loved me like I loved you."

I never stopped loving her, even when I wanted to hate her. My pretty girl has simply owned my heart forever.

"What about me?" I didn't mean to step up the second after the pretty girl turned Cole down. But my thoughts were voiced before I knew what I was doing.

I may have been used to throwing a ball in the spotlight, but I wasn't used to being the spotlight. The guys looked at me. Cole stood up, offense defining his face.

The girls turned around and stared at me. Delilah smiled when she looked my way. "We barely know each other, Jason." That's not a no.

She had cheered for me for years, but for some reason, hearing her say my name that day was different. It was personal and made my throat thick, causing me to clear it before speaking again. "I'd like to get to know you."

With the tilt of her head, her ponytail swung to the side. "I'd like to get to know you, too."

That was the last day I walked home with the guys. Starting the very next day, I carried Delilah's backpack home for her—two miles out of the way. I got my truck three months later and started driving her and her sister. I think I loved her from the minute we saw each other, but I knew I was a goner not long after the day she said she wanted to get to know me. By the end of that school year, I wanted her for my forever.

. . . "No, Delilah. I love you. Present tense. Hearts and flowers. Kisses over morning coffee and poetry down by the lake in the afternoon love."

Tears spill over her bottom lids, but her joy isn't contained. She giggles and says, "That's intense."

I scoot over until our hips are bumped together. Wrapping my arm around her, I hug her close. Her arm sneaks around my back. I say, "That is intense and so honest that I don't even think I can look at you right now."

"What?" She squeezes me. "Why can't you look at me?"

"Because then I'm going to see that look in your eyes that tells me I told you too much."

"It wasn't too much."

"I meant that you're going to have hearts in your eyes and a goofy grin on your face, because I've given you ammo to hang over me like a carrot teasing a rabbit."

Her head leans on the top of my bicep. I tighten because now I want to impress her even more than I did before, and I didn't think I was holding back before. "You know me so well, Jason Koster. I love a good blackmail, and you've given me a doozy."

It's all fun and games, good-natured teasing, but she's

still over there laughing while my stomach gets tied up in knots. Apparently she notices because she adds, "If it makes a difference, you can hang something over me too."

"What?"

"I love you." *Fuck yeah.*

Free and easy.

Without stipulations.

She just lays it out there without fear.

"Are you saying it because I did?"

"No. I'm saying it because I know it's true. I never stopped."

"Me too." I point to the sky. "Look. A shooting star."

"You sure that wasn't a spaceship?"

"Oh, ye of little faith. That was a star receiving our message and sending it into the cosmos."

"What does our star say?"

"Nothing heals a broken soul like the love of a true heart."

Looking back up at the sky, she says, "You should write poetry."

"Most people think poetry has to be lines of words strung together. That's not poetry to me."

"What's poetry to you?"

"One word. Delilah."

17

Jason

"Why do you sleep in your old room?"

Floating on her back with her eyes closed and her body still, Delilah replies, "I feel safe in that corner of the house."

I wade through the water, mentally running through the floor plan of the farmhouse. Her room is the farthest from the front door, the back door, and the common areas. "You never wanted to take over the master bedroom downstairs?"

As if an unforeseen force pushes her down into the water, she loses her balance when she loses her concentration. She pops up.

Glorious in the mid-morning sun shining on her wet lashes and water droplets covering her skin, she swims away from me. After being here practically every day and night for over a week, I've discovered when she turns away from me she's either avoiding a question or hiding her eyes from me. She can't lie when looking into my eyes. Either way it's avoidance. Simple as that.

Swimming after her, I catch her twenty yards from the dock, but keep swimming to give her the space I know she needs. "I can dog-paddle all day long."

"Why do you want to know all the stuff that doesn't matter now?"

"Because it matters to me."

"Fine." She splashes me. "If you get to ask questions and I have to answer, same goes for you. I'll make you a deal. We take turns and when one doesn't answer, the game is over. How's that?"

She may be good at avoiding those grenades of questions I drop around her sometimes, but I'm the king of keeping secrets. So this proposition gives me pause.

For us to be together, she needs to know about the life I've been leading. As much as I hate admitting the bad stuff, there were good things to come out of it. What if this is my chance to redeem myself? What if she thinks I'm a monster? What if she loves me more because I survived when I didn't know if I would at times? What if she can't forgive my past? What if she hates me? What if . . . letting her in will free my soul from these sins I've carried with me?

I swallow my pride. "Okay," I whisper. "Deal."

She swims closer but stops ten or so feet away. "When my dad died, Cole moved us straight into my parents' bedroom. I didn't want to sleep in there. I was still grieving, and it felt disrespectful. It hurt to be in that room at all, much less take over it."

"Why he'd do that?"

Smiling gently, she reminds me, "My turn, remember?" I swim a foot or two closer to her. "Where have you been the last three years?"

Easy. "Alaska for a brief stint on a fishing boat. The money was great, but the work was hard."

"You never minded hard work from what I remember."

She's tricky. It's not a question, but a statement I feel the need to answer. "It wasn't the work I wanted to do. Also, it sucked being on that boat for weeks at a time. Limited booze. Horrible sleeping conditions. Fish every meal." The left side of my mouth quirks up. *No women.* "After that I was up and down the West Coast and then cross-country to New England. I've traveled all over between jobs and sometimes for the job."

Rolling her eyes, she retreats a few feet, which makes me laugh. She says, "To answer your earlier question, I'm not sure. I have theories that Cole wanted to control me and when he didn't feel he had enough power over me, he'd hurt me. At first it was emotional, then it escalated." Wading closer, she asks, "What did you do, or do now, for work and for money?"

Diving forward, I swim until I reach her legs. Her scream can be heard underwater it's so loud. Pulling her under, I kiss her before we pop back up for air together. "Ah." She sounds so satisfied, my cock awakens despite the cool water.

"C'mere." Her limbs wrap around me, and I swim back to the dock.

"You still have to answer, Jason."

"I will, but it may take a while."

While she climbs up the ladder, I watch that fine ass move with ease and chase after her. One of our towels is on the splintering wood, and we sit on the edge with our legs dangling over. I'm not going to make her ask again, but it's hard to start this conversation from a place of truth when I'm so used to hiding the details. I exhale and say, "I wasn't a hitman."

"What? Good God," she exclaims. "I didn't expect that.

What the hell do you mean you weren't a hitman? And if that's what you weren't, what were you?"

I don't think I've ever seen her eyes both wide with curiosity and narrowed in shock, but that's what I'm seeing, and I feel an explanation rushing to ease the lines digging into her forehead. "I was a hired gun, a soldier, maybe a mercenary is more accurate, but not for the military. Private citizens who needed help righting wrongs." Daring to peek over at her, her mouth hangs open. "Are we still playing the game?"

"Jason . . ."

That's all she says and turns away from me to stare ahead at the lake.

It's a lot to process, and I'm willing to give her time to do so, but damn am I squirming in my skin. My heart's racing and I'm sweating, even though I'm still wet from swimming.

Sitting here is torture of a different kind than any form I've endured. She finally speaks, but it's not what I want to hear. "When you say hitman, did you kill people?"

"I said I wasn't a hitman."

The playfulness of the game is gone like I knew it would be. One way or the other our pasts were going to dampen our time together. I just hope it's temporary.

"I need you to be serious with me, Jason. Have you killed someone?"

"Yes."

On her feet, she's pacing the dock. "You've killed someone? Oh my God. You've killed someone."

"It's my turn," I say as she mumbles and rants. I need to bring back some of the lightness from before.

She stops, too far for me to grab her ankles and beg for mercy. "Jason."

"Delilah."

"This isn't funny. You've murdered somebody or you killed them?"

"Is there a difference?"

Her hands go to her head and she starts pacing again. "Oh my God. Oh my God. Oh my God." When she stops again, she says, "There's a difference. Killing someone accidently is very different than murdering somebody."

"What if they murdered your friend, or someone you loved? Hurt them. Tried to kill them. Is it okay then?"

"It's never okay."

I put my back to her. This will be the end of what I hoped was a beginning. The sun is high in the sky, morning turning to midday. I can feel the heat on my skin, the burning, but I don't move. Sunburn I can handle. Her disappointment in me, her *disgust* isn't something I can live with.

Closing my eyes, I remember how Connor Johnson slept beside his wife. I remember the weight of the metal and the wood grain of the gun handle. It's slower in my memories, like a lot of things. Except Delilah. All my time with her has always been too short, gone by too fast.

King can't do it. I'm glad. He has a chance to recover from the dirty deeds he's done. I need to help him keep his hands clean from the crimes he's so determined to commit. That was one of the promises I made my boss.

Johnson is worse than his partner who already took two bullets. He's the mastermind, and he won't stop until he reaps his vengeful reward.

The bullet flies from my gun straight into his head. Not much sound but enough to wake his sleeping wife. We're out the window and running before she's aware of what's really happening.

. . . I'm not sure when she sat down, but her body presses to my back, her words softly spoken, "When I said I love you, I meant it. I love you, Jason. I won't stop because you're honest with me. I'll only stop if you're bad for me."

"I'm bad for you, babe. So bad you don't even know." *And I hate how true those words are.*

The wind blows and the song of the birds is carried with it. I'm not sure what to say. "I hate that I've done it, but I can't take it back, and I wouldn't if I could."

"Why? How can you not regret taking a life?"

"Because he took many lives, and he tried to take the life of someone I cared about, someone who deserved better than to be shot on the side of the road and left for dead."

She rests her head against me and sighs. I try to end the debate she's having inside. "I'm charred inside, burned from the hell I've been living. It's probably best you know now. Save yourself, Delilah. No good can come from being with me."

"But—"

"No." I stand up, moving out of her heat, her love, her misunderstanding of what needed to be done versus what we would all wish we could have done if the world was a better place. Staring at the farmland surrounding me, it's easy to believe only good exists. Even when we struggle to pay bills or crops don't produce, this place, this land, it's magical—like time stands still here—and I'm not judged as harshly as I am out there. "I can't turn back time, and I can't take back the sins I've committed."

"You can be redeemed. You just have to believe—"

"I don't regret what I've done. It was either take him out or allow him to kill a dozen innocent people. I'll burn in hell like I've been burning here on earth, but I'll face that fire with a clear conscience."

"Jason?" She stands, her little pink bikini so damn distracting to the conversation we're having.

Grabbing my alma mater snapback, I pull it on and lower the bill. "What?"

"I meant what I said. I love you."

"I know you do, but love isn't going to be enough this time." And it's those words I now hate the most. The truth. She doesn't need the shit that is my life in her world.

She doesn't need me.

She's brave and bold, stepping right up to me with no fear of consequences. She knows I could never hurt her even if I've hurt others. "It wasn't last time, but here we are."

"We didn't survive last time, honeysuckle. What makes you think this time will be different?"

"Because *we* are. We've seen what life is like without each other. It's not pretty. We only get blue skies when we're together."

"I don't understand what you want from me."

"That's just it, Jason. It sounds like everyone has wanted something from you. They've trained you to believe that no one can be trusted. Whoever *they* are did quite the job on you, and for what? Their benefit or yours?"

"It's not like that."

"Then tell me what it's like because it's our memories that bind us, but it's who we are now that will carry us forward. And I want that, Jason. I want to move forward. With you." She slips a little dress over her head. It's ill-fitting, but she still looks so gorgeous. The gravity of this conversation strikes my heart. I see the depth of concern for my soul residing in her eyes. No one has ever loved me the way she has. I can't lose her. Not again.

Stepping closer, I take her hand. She doesn't pull back, which gives me the strength I need. "I will tell you anything you want to know. I just don't want to lose you in the process. So tell me, what can I say that will keep you here, and by here, I mean in my arms at night and waking up to you in the morning. I want to talk about our day in the evenings and swim in the lake in the middle of the day. I want you. I want this life with you. I want whatever life you want, Delilah. I just want you. Any part of you that you're willing to give me I'll take like a greedy thief in the night."

"I'm trying to understand what would turn the man I used to know into somebody who could harm someone, instead of saving him."

"Save him?" I walk to the end of the dock and spin the hat around. When I turn around, she's on the other end, and once again I feel the distance between us. "You're not understanding. This is not a man you can save by taking him to church or introducing him to the Bible. This was a monster that would hurt you if it hurt me. He killed an innocent kid just for being in the wrong place at the wrong time. A kid who came to help out his friend. He was shot without a chance to plead for his life. Killed only to hurt other people."

This is the most I've talked in forever and it's taking a toll. My patience is gone. I shouldn't have to justify what I've done to her, but I will because it's her. "I needed money. I came off the ships in Alaska and was robbed, gun to my head, robbed by one of the other crewmembers. I thought I was going to die. We didn't get along on the boat. He called me too good-looking to be working a real man's job. Taunted me the whole time. First night off the boat, we walked to the closest brothel. We got drunk. So fucking drunk. I left when the guys started going to the back with the girls. I made it outside to the alley before I was hit from behind and knocked to my knees. Ten thousand stolen right from my jacket pocket with the barrel of a gun to my head."

"Oh, Jason," she says.

I see the sympathy in her expression, but I don't want her sympathy. I want her. "They said, 'Say a prayer, pretty boy.' But what I thought were the last words I'd ever hear didn't bother me. Neither did the money. I didn't care about the money right then. All I could think of was how I would never get to see you again and tell you how much I loved you."

She runs into my arms. Her body is wrapped around mine. Her tears run down my bare chest and I embrace her fully, never wanting to let her go. "I love you. I love you so much." When she looks up at me, she asks, "Why didn't you come back for me?"

"Because the next day, I called my mom and found out you were getting married before I could catch a flight. I was too fucking hurt. Too angry. Too disappointed. I'd lost you, Delilah. You were no longer mine. And my heart broke that day."

"You should have called me." *I certainly hadn't seen the point. She was marrying another man, for fuck's sake.*

"I didn't want to bring you anymore pain, especially on your wedding day."

"So much has changed and yet so much is still the same, but I see you. I see how you hide inside your thoughts. I see how you watch, how you tick the boxes everywhere we go. I see how you put on an act that you're the same guy we used to know. I see you, Jason Koster. The real you. That's the man I love. Your secrets don't scare me, but the reality of what they are, do. I can't turn my love on and off for you. There's always a steady stream when it comes to us, but I need time to understand, to learn more about the life you left behind. It doesn't have to be today, but promise you'll never lie to me, and you won't keep your secrets barreled up inside."

"I'll make that promise if it means I get you."

"I'm not a prize. I never was. But I like who I am these days, and I like you too much to not give you the benefit of the doubt."

My body relaxes, knowing this isn't it. Maybe we can get past this.

Maybe.

"I want to hear more, but maybe we can finish this over lunch. I'm starved, and I never expected to hear what you were doing."

"If it makes you feel better, it wasn't all bad. I was a stuntman in Hollywood on two films. I was a bodyguard for a visiting dignitary in San Francisco for a couple weeks, which is how I met the woman who became my boss for almost two years."

Her mouth is hanging open again. I lift her chin to close her mouth, but she asks, "Is that all?"

Despite the sarcasm of her question, I go on, "Oh, and I worked at a mini-mart for a few months in a small town in the mountains."

Rubbing her temples, she asks, "Anything else I need to know right now?"

"I was shot once."

"What? Good Lord. Are you okay?"

I wrap my arm around her shoulders, and we start walking. "I'm better now."

18

Delilah

SITTING in the kitchen while eating lunch, we've not suffered from a lack of conversation. "Is that scar on your leg from when you were shot?"

"Yes." He bends down and rubs over the spot. "It's just a graze, now a new story to tell."

"It's still pink. You were shot recently?"

I can see how uncomfortable he is answering questions about what he's been doing from how he is shifting in the chair, but I'm compelled to know everything about him. He is not the driven and carefree boy from my youth. He's now a man who seems to have struggled and fought with many demons. And most probably alone. As much as I hate the thought that he is capable of killing someone, I've learned that sometimes things in life are not as black and white as we've grown up to believe. How many times had I wished Cole dead after he took out his *justified* anger on me?

After exhaling and sitting back, he says, "A couple months."

My throat tightens and I grip the sides of my chair. "You came back because you were almost killed." I'm not asking, but I can see I've stumbled onto the truth.

He nods. "Even though this is only a graze, there were times I didn't think I would live to see daylight. Near-death experiences make you grateful for another opportunity to make things right in your life."

I relate too well to this. "Your turn."

"Tell me about the tattoo. You didn't have that when we were together. What made you get it when we weren't?"

It's a fair question. I was just hoping for more time before addressing it. After the heaviness outside this morning, I'm just going to be straightforward and rip the Band-Aid off this sore subject. "Cole had been pressuring me to get his name tattooed on me."

Jason growls under his breath. "He was pressuring you?"

"It all makes sense to me now, but back then I didn't understand how he was twisting things to make me his."

"You used the word prize earlier. You were a prize to him. He used to tell me how lucky I was to have you, but he didn't mean having a girlfriend. He meant *you* specifically."

"He wasted no time, Jason. One moment I only saw him when out with all of you, and the next he was over every night offering a shoulder to cry on. That's when the stories started about you and other girls, although he'd already whispered such things before we broke up. He told me story after story about how much he had loved me for so many years, and how he was so disgusted that you, his best friend and my boyfriend, would cheat on me. That no woman of his would ever know such betrayal. That he would look after me, because there weren't any other men around here who would look at me twice after being with you. Once we married, it ended up being true, but it was because I was with him, not you. He was an enemy in disguise." I've never spoken these words out loud. I feel like such a fool.

Pushing my plate away, I add, "One night he came home drunk, although that wasn't unusual. But the guys had been teasing him that he got your sloppy seconds." Just saying that phrase makes me feel cheap. "We had a huge argument. That was the first time he ever slapped me. He had been rough before, but it had never gone that far."

"Hitting a woman doesn't make him a man or more powerful. It makes him a coward." Reaching over, I take the plate from his hands, his knuckles white from his hard grip. Our eyes meet, and I move back over to cover his hands with mine. "I'm here. I'm okay."

His silence is eerie. When I see his eyes, he's about to burn a hole through the table. He's still. So still I almost back away, but I'm not afraid of him. I want to soothe that anger away. Just as I reach for him, he says, "Do you know how much it kills me that you were ever touched by him? How could he hurt you like that?" It hurts to see him in so much pain . . . especially because of me.

I squeeze his hands a little more. "You're not to blame. I know you want to take the blame because you weren't here, but I don't blame you. The blame sits squarely on my shoulders. I'm still so angry with myself that I got mixed up with him in the first place."

"Because he twisted shit around to look like a hero. He took one fight between you and me, a fight I realize now that never should have happened, and worked it to his advantage. But if I would have fought harder for us—"

I'm standing and hugging him, his head against my chest. The anguish he wrestles with, the guilt that seems to fill him, comes in waves of rage, and I feel it too. I understand. I've been there. I'm still there, if I'm honest. "We can't go back and change those things."

The feet of the chair grind against the linoleum, and I'm pulled into his lap. My arms are around his neck and his hands find my lower back. "I never stopped thinking about you. I never thought I had chance of getting you back. If I'd known you weren't living the life you wanted, I would have been here. If I'd known he hurt you, I would have killed him."

"Don't say that."

"Too soon?"

"Maybe." I rest my head on his. "What am I going to do with you?" When his arms tighten around me, I have the same thoughts I'm sure he does. "We can't solve our problems between the sheets."

Pulling back, he says, "You sure about that?"

The smile that stirs long-buried sensations makes me smile. "I've not been this happy in years. We have some stuff to deal with, but I feel good around you."

He runs the back of his fingers along my cheekbone, and kisses the corner of my mouth. I love how much he loves touching me, looking at me like I might disappear if he's not watching. I never felt this with Cole. I doubt I ever loved him, or him me. When I look at the adoration on Jason's face when he looks at me, how he cherishes me as if there is no other choice but to do so, I see the difference.

I love him.

"What happened with the tattoo?"

Replying, I look down, playing with the hem of his shirt. Damn shirt hiding the good stuff underneath. "After he hit me, he told me I would get it done or he'd hold me down and do it himself." Jason's hands aren't tight, but I feel his fingers flex around my waist. "I had already planned to visit Shelby in Chicago the following weekend. Shelby and I were blowing off steam. I never felt better than when I was away from him. We got drunk, and that night we passed a tattoo parlor. I took his threat seriously, and I wanted to control any art that would become a permanent part of me."

The figure eights he was drawing on my back stops, and he says, "Eight is a long way away from twenty-two."

Exhaling loudly, I know how bad this sounds, but I tell it how it was. "I told them to tattoo my husband's jersey number, but like I said I was drunk."

Understanding passes through him and all the tension that was straining his muscles moments before eases. "You keep saying you were drunk. Did you tell them my number on purpose or the alcohol's to blame?"

"I blame the alcohol?" Closing my eyes, I shake my head.

"Are you asking me?"

"No. I blame the booze."

He smiles. "You know what I think?" I don't reply, instead wanting him to figure it out on his own. "I think the number eight may have accidentally slipped out, but you didn't correct them. I've gotten tattoos. They don't just ink you without your final go-ahead."

The gold centers of his brown eyes are bright with happiness. I want to kiss him, but I don't want to hide behind a distraction, even if he's hard to resist. Tapping the tip of his nose, I say, "You're enjoying this too much."

"You're right, but as much satisfaction I find in this, I imagine it didn't go over so well once you got home."

"April fifteenth. The day most people dread because their taxes are due, but for me, I thought it was the last day I would ever see."

With me still on his lap, Jason stands abruptly while

setting me carefully on my feet. He walks to the back door, but instead of looking out, he lowers his hands. The rise and fall of his torso matches the pace of his heavy breaths. As if something draws him outside, he walks out. But when I look out he's pacing the yard, popping his fisted knuckles. I push the screen door open. "Jason?"

He stops and looks back at me. "Billy said he took you to the ER once . . ."

"Billy shouldn't have told you about that."

"Why?"

"Because you can't fix it. This anger coursing through you"—I take his hands to try to settle his anxious energy—"is fruitless. It happened. There's nothing to be done about it now. I'm divorced. He's out of my life." I think back to recently finding him in my kitchen. "Hopefully for good."

Taking my face between his hands, he looks into my eyes. "You don't believe the lies you tell yourself. Why would I?"

"I'm not lying."

"Okay, then you're fooling yourself into believing you're safe when you're not."

He sighs, appearing to calm down. Backing up, he goes to the back steps and sits down. "What kind of vehicle does he drive?"

His question is so far out of left field that I struggle to remember now that I'm on the spot. "Um, uh. A Ram. A black Ram truck."

"Shit," he says, looking disappointed.

"What?"

Now a debate colors his body language and he shifts. "I don't think it's a big deal, but I saw a car parked in front of the farm one night. I thought it might be Cutler."

"Was it a BMW?"

His stare hits me hard, and he stands. "Yes."

"I forgot. He has a BMW, but he rarely drives it except for work meetings. He bought it when we were together, but we couldn't afford it so it became another source of contention."

"Does he drive by often?"

"I don't know. I've not seen him drive by, but I'm not really looking."

"The divorce has only been finalized a few months, but have you seen him since then?"

When I hem and haw too long, he says, "Tell me, Delilah."

Forward. No secrets. Trust. Honesty. Security. That's what love is. "He came by the other day. It was the first time in months."

Steepling his fingers together, he runs them up the bridge of his nose, struggling to contain his rage. This I can relate to. "He's a fucking dead man already, so be honest with me. You didn't burn the cobbler. You didn't break your mom's plate. That's when he was here, wasn't it?"

I feel ashamed that I didn't handle myself better. "I told him to leave. I don't think he'll be back."

"He'll be back. He's obsessed with you, but I also think he'll be back because I am. He hates losing, but to me, it's as if his whole world revolves around securing that victory."

"Me and holding that over you."

He's nodding. "Why didn't you tell me that night at my mom's?"

"I knew you'd be upset."

"Not with you."

I cross the yard and lower my voice. "I knew you'd go after him, and I don't want you getting hurt because of me."

The laughter comes from deep within, too big to hold inside. "Trust me, baby, he can't hurt me."

"He's volatile. Angry and possessive. He's an alcoholic who makes everyone else pay the price for his failures. He'll start a fight with you."

"Let him. I can handle Cole Cutler."

"Things are finally starting to settle down with him." I pause and look away momentarily. He knows me too well and can spot when I'm lying, so I try to hide my eyes. I can't hide forever. When I turn back, I plead, "Don't start a fight with him. Promise me."

"I promise you I won't start one, but I will finish it. This has been going on too long. It's time to put an end to it." Pulling me into an embrace, he hugs me and then dips me. With my head resting in his hands, and my heart on the line, he says, "And I promise you right here, Delilah Noelle, I'll give you the ending you deserve, the one we're owed."

He kisses me slowly as if we have all the time in the world. Maybe it's possible for us to find the peace we're both searching for. It sure feels it when we kiss like that.

When I'm lifted upright, he adds, "There are so many things I want to make right, that I want to make you proud of me for, that I want for us in this life. Thank you for giving me the chance."

"Oh, sweet man. You don't have to thank me." It's time I steal the title back. "I'm lucky to have you back. I feel more me with you around. Thank *you*."

His lips take mine, crashing our hearts, our love, our bodies together in a frenzy of passion. He gives all of himself in this kiss and just like the first time I kissed him, I fall madly, head over heels in love with this man. It's easy to promise my life to his with words, but we're deeper than that. It's not about the words or confessions, sins or pasts.

It's about the kiss.

This one right here. It's felt deep through my body and reaches my toes. This man. *This. Man.* He kisses me with such desire I realize all others don't matter. *This* kiss is the first kiss of our forever.

19

Jason

I'M FIRED UP, but I keep the hurricane of anger twisting inside hidden from her. I have to. Delilah deserves peace after all she's been through. I sit back in the chair in her room, my leg bouncing from the unsettled emotions inside. I need to move, to fuck, to drink, to beat something up . . . but I'm home. I have to temper how I've been trained to react. I don't want people here to see the cold mercenary I became.

I say, "I like that one."

Her hands fly to her hips. "You've said that about the last two dresses."

"I like them all. You look good in all of them."

Coming over to me, she presses my knee down with her hand. "It's going to be okay. I'm okay. You don't have to worry about me."

"I worry. That's not something I can change. It's not something I want to change."

She stands up. "I'll wear this one. Let's go. We both need a night out."

It doesn't take long to reach Red River. The ride is mostly quiet. We know we're making a statement when we walk in there together. People will talk to our faces and behind our backs. Word will get out, but it needs to. I want this night out with my girl, but I also want to tempt the snake out of his hole. Cole Cutler needs to know I'm not going anywhere, and he better not come anywhere near Delilah.

I help her out of the truck and hold her hand firmly in mine as we walk down the sidewalk to the busy bar. Just before we reach the doors, she pulls me to a stop. "Hey?"

Turning back, her eyes are gloriously bright blue with the setting sun shining on them. Wisps of her strawberry-blond hair blow in the light breeze. The pink of her lips draws my gaze and I bend to kiss her. She never says anything, but between her grip on my arm and the way she snuggles into me, I hear her unspoken words. Stroking her hair down her back, I whisper the words she reassured me with earlier, "It will be okay. I'll take care of you."

I kiss her temple before she pulls away and tugs me toward the door. "Let's just get this over with."

Cocking an eyebrow, I say, "You're such a romantic."

She laughs. "I'm sorry. I'm nervous. I wouldn't want to be here with anyone else. Now come on, hot stuff, and let me show you off."

I take hold of the door and let her pass in front of me. "I'm more than a pretty face," I tease, not so dumb to the fact that women find me attractive. There's only one woman I'm drawn to, and I'm feeling fucking fantastic that I get to show her off tonight.

"You're right. You have a great ass too, and arms. Oh, and

thank you for letting me pay homage to all eight of those ab muscles last night."

I slip my hand under her hair and rub the back of her neck. "I let you pay homage to more than my ab muscles. Any chance for a repeat performance?"

"A very good chance."

Guess getting caught in our own world is something we do more than just out on the farm. Willie Nelson is crooning through the jukebox in the back, but other than that, the place has gone quiet. Even the pinball machine has stopped dinging. I scan the area, always aware.

Front door. Top half glass.

Back door through the small kitchen in the left corner. One large window.

One window in the men's and two smaller windows in the women's restroom.

Five booths.

Twenty-one people.

Ten barstools.

Eight taken.

I need to stop doing this. It's a bad habit that needs to be broken. I'm safe. No one's going to get me here.

It's easy to get caught up in the stares and dropped jaws, to walk out of here like we don't belong or that we can stop the gossip before it begins. But I don't want to.

"Let them talk." I lead her to a table in the center of the bar and pull out her chair. "They're going to anyway."

She sits down with a big grin on her face. "They sure are."

The bar returns to life like we never walked in, conversations continuing with only a few sideways stares. McGilley calls, "Good to see, Ms. Cut—Ms. Noelle. It's been a while."

"Sure has, Mr. McGilley."

"First drink's on me. What are you having?"

Looking at Delilah, she nods. "Beer?"

"You'll be okay?"

"I'm fine, Jason. The bar is like five steps away."

She may think I'm ridiculous, but a lot can go wrong in a short span of time. I'm not willing to risk it with her. "I'll be back." I walk to the bar and tap it twice. McGilley knows our order before I even tell him. He sets the bottles down, and says, "She never comes in anymore."

"Maybe things are changing."

"For the better, I'd say."

When I turn back, Billy's pulled a chair up and is talking to Delilah. I deliver the beers and sit. "What's up?"

"Night out is all." He smiles, tapping the top of his bottle to ours. "Cheers."

We toast and all drink. "Good week?" I ask.

"Got caught up in an auction for a calf midweek and everything went to shit after that. Been meaning to mention the county fair is coming up in a few weeks."

Delilah says, "Wow, I haven't been in years. I want to go." Reaching across the table, she rubs my hand. "Maybe you can win me a giant bear or something I can cuddle with."

"I thought I was your cuddle bear?" What the fuck did I just ask? Cuddle bear? Billy looks disgusted, and I say, "God, forget I ever said that. That is seriously *chop your balls off* talk."

"I thought it was cute," she says, giggling. "Cuddle bear."

"No. No. We're not doing that. That name is not happening." I down my beer. I can be settled without becoming a pussy. "McGilley, another round."

Billy finishes his beer and then says, "It's good to know that even the great Jason Koster has a soft side."

Delilah says, "He doesn't. He's hard all over. Trust me."

Billy stands up. "This conversation has gone south fast, and I don't need to hear it," he says, laughing. "I think there's a lonely girl over there looking for company."

He walks off just as Sabrina Smith shows up with a straight face and an ax to grind. "Well, if it isn't Miss Freeland County herself. What brings you out, Delilah?"

"Sabrina," she replies.

Delilah's lack of real response is amusing. We both know Sabrina came over on a mission. We just have to wait until she's bored with us. Sabrina has always been fairly harmless, but she's bold enough to get on your nerves fast. It's almost impressive how quick on the draw she is tonight. Looking around the bar, her scrutinizing glare lands back on me. "No hello, Jason?"

"Hello."

"After all we shared too."

She loves to tell lies about us hooking up. It never happened, but years after high school she still holds on to them like they'll turn into reality if she continues dragging it out. Delilah shifts, causing me to look at her. I don't want her uncomfortable, so I reply, "Nothing ever happened between us, Sabrina. Your memory seems as foggy as ever."

"We did too. You're just choosing to hide the truth—"

"Sharing a microscope in biology our sophomore year doesn't count as intimacy. It was an assigned partner project."

She taps Delilah's shoulder with a satisfied smile on her face. "See? He remembers me. Anywho, where's that handsome husband of yours, Delilah?"

I'm about to stand up and shoo her away, but I know I can accomplish what I want sitting right here. Whispering, I warn her, "This town may let you pull this bullshit with them, but you won't with us. I will let you walk away without embarrassing you in front of everyone, but this is your only warning. I want you to stay away from Delilah and me. Do you understand, Sabrina?"

Her mouth was gawking open by "bullshit," so I know I got her attention. "Well," she starts, raising her chin in stubborn defiance, "a microscope is the only thing I ever intend to share with you, Jason Koster. Your meanness is noted." She scoffs as she walks back to her booth with the poor sucker stuck with her for the night.

I'm still shaking my head in annoyance when Delilah says, "I've noted a few things about you myself."

"And what might those be?"

Leaning over the table, she looks to her left and then to her right before returning to me and whispering, "The impressive size of your—"

"Delilah." She tenses immediately, her shoulders caving in.

I stand, coming face-to-face with my ex-friend. My voice is steady and firm, "Turn around and walk away, Cutler."

"Me? That's my fucking wife."

When I glance at Delilah, it's clear Sabrina rattled her, but now she looks more angry than fearful. *That's my girl.*

I lean closer, my shoulder bumping against Cole's and say, "Don't you ever fucking call her that again. And if I ever see you within ten miles of that farm, or my girl, I will fucking end you."

With our eyes hard on each other, we stand there, both of us unwavering in our silent standoff. McGilley finally yells, "Break it up, boys, or hit the streets."

Cutler ignores the bartender. "You need to check yourself, Koster. That woman—"

"She's not *that* woman. She's *my* woman."

My words seem to cause him to choke. "Your woman?"

I'm shoved but don't budge. "Yes. Mine. I suggest you go back to wherever you came from and don't come back over here."

"Back off, Cole." Delilah stands, her hand wrapping around my forearm. "Jason, let's leave."

That's when I see it. Not her, but the look he gives her, the one that comes loaded with threats he intends to carry out. "Leave?" he grits. "Together? What did I tell you about him?"

I give my last warning. "Don't look at her."

Her hold on my arm tightens. "Jason." My name comes as a warning in and of itself. Facing Cole, the fear has disappeared, and she says, "You and I are done. Leave us alone."

He reaches to touch her, but I knock his hand away. Cutler shifts, and then faces me. "You got a death wish, Koster? Cuz I'm happy to fulfill it."

"You're drunk. Go home."

"Fu—"

Billy rushes between us, his body separating us. "Hey. Hey. C'mon, guys." Looking at Cole, he says, "Stop causing trouble where there is none."

"He needs to stay away from us."

Cutler says, "You do realize I own half that farmhouse you're fucking my wife in?" He laughs, but there's no humor in it. *Speaking of death wishes, he's close to making that wish come true.*

"*Ex.* You seem to be forgetting that important detail."

Cole swings, but Billy pushes him back on his ass. "Time for us to go. Put it on my tab, McGilley."

"Sure thing, Billy," McGilley replies.

Cole pushes off the floor and yells at Delilah while Billy pushes him out the door. Before the door closes, Cole yells, "You're my wife. A piece of paper doesn't define us."

I look at Delilah who says, “I want to go home.”

Holding out my hand, I say, “Come on.”

When her shaking hand takes mine, I wrap my warmth around her, hoping to ease her fear. I toss a fifty on the bar as we pass. “Thanks, McGilley.”

“You betcha. Hope to see you again, Delilah.”

“Thank you,” she replies with the smallest of polite smiles.

Pressing the door open, I look both ways on the sidewalk before I help her out. She’s shaken. I don’t blame her. I thought I was about to come to blows with Cutler, and I was willing to because it’s clear he’s gotten into her head again. *And she put up with that asshole for how long?*

While walking down the street, I scan the area. The only thing out of place is the car parked next to my truck.

Which I recognize from the life I left behind.

Shit.

20

Jason

UP AHEAD, leaning against the passenger door is someone I never thought I'd see again. When I stop walking, Delilah presses against my side and asks, "What's wrong?"

"Nothing." I lower my voice so only she can hear me. "Will you wait in the truck for me?"

"You're scaring me, Jason."

My gaze slides to her. "I don't mean to. Everything's fine. I need a few minutes, okay?"

"Okay."

She walks ahead, staring at the man as she passes. When she looks back over her shoulder, I catch her eyes and give a smile I hope reassures her. As soon as Delilah's in the truck, I take a few more steps. I always expected my crimes to come back to haunt me. I just didn't see them coming back tonight. Crossing my arms, I ask, "What brings you to town?"

Cruise, an old ally, isn't uptight, but seems particularly at ease tonight. He comes over and offers his hand. "You left in a hurry."

Happily, I shake it. "You been missing me?"

"Ha." He smiles and steps back, always a respectful friend. "Kind of."

Chuckling, I drop my guard. "Yeah, I'm a very likeable guy. I think I was underappreciated in the Kingwood world."

That makes him laugh. "Probably so, but it was easier to not trust than be stabbed in the back."

"Understandable." I glance at Delilah, who's watching us through the truck window. I give her a nod to make her feel safe, but after my confessions, I don't think she's feeling as comfortable as we are about this encounter. "This a social visit?"

"Not really. Got some time?"

I can trust him, so I tell him to follow me to the farm. When I hop into the cab of the truck, Delilah asks, "Who is that?"

"An old friend." I reverse the truck and put it into drive.

"Who is he, though? Why is he showing up here at almost nine o'clock at night looking for you? Please don't lie to me."

"I don't lie to you, Delilah. I told you more than I should already." Cruise is behind me as we head out of town. "We used to work together."

"Killing people?" She gasps an octave too high for the small space of this cab.

Resting my hand on the bare skin of her thigh, I give her a gentle squeeze. "I don't think he's killed anyone. You can ask him when we get to the farmhouse."

"Wait, what? He's coming home with us?"

"He's one of the good guys, Delilah. You don't need to worry about him."

"Are you one of the good guys?"

"Depends who you ask."

"I'm asking you, Jason."

"Yes, I am."

"How are good and bad defined in your world?"

"The same as in your world, but with bloodshed."

She turns away and looks out into the inky night over fields dotted with the occasional farmhouse. "That's dark."

Pulling my hand back, I grip the steering wheel, tempted to turn on some music and not have this conversation. No more avoidance. "That's why I came home."

"Why are you home? You didn't come back for me. You thought I was still married."

"I wasn't living the life I wanted. I missed my mom." Checking my rearview mirror, I mumble, "I missed you."

Her hand warms my arm. "I shouldn't have, but I missed you too. I have a confession."

I glance over. Her fine features are barely visible in the dark, but I see her eyes on mine. "Tell me all your secrets. I want to know everything about you again."

She laughs. "You make me sound so interesting when I'm just the same as I always was, stuck in the same town where you left me."

"I hate that you think I left you on purpose. I left dejected, but guess what?"

"What?"

"Together, two broken hearts can be whole again."

She unbuckles her seatbelt and slides across the seat. When she leans her head on my shoulder, I kiss her head. She puts on the middle seatbelt and I ask, "What's your confession?"

"I feel silly telling you this, especially knowing I'm to blame for the mistakes I've made."

"We all have things we'd like to change. Some we can. Some we can't. Doesn't matter as long as we grow from the experience. Tell me and please let it be about me." I smirk, though she can't see me.

After a soft laugh, she says, "I used to fantasize about being married to you and how glorious each day would be. We would have a family and run the farm but go on great adventures around the world. I never made it to Paris."

"I've not been to Paris either. How about we go together?" I turn onto the property and drive up the dirt road to the house. Her smile is clear as the lights from the front porch scan across the cab as we pass. "And there's nothing wrong with fantasizing about a future together. We were dating, and it was serious; it's only natural. I had the same thoughts too."

"It was when I was married."

Oh. Wow. I shift the truck into park and cut the engine. With my arm wrapped around her shoulders, I say, "Your fantasies are how it should have been." And how it will be if I have my way.

"Thank you for never making me feel ridiculous or dumb."

Cutler is a fucker.

Cruise parks behind us. We should go in. Both of us move to get out, but before we do, I say, "I think you're incredible and so smart. I've never seen you as anything less than magnificent."

"Jason," she says, barely above a whisper, "you're so good to me, good for me. I'm never prepared for your words."

"They're not words, Delilah. They're the truth."

"How did I ever get so lucky?"

"It's not luck, it's love." I get out and turn back to help her out. "Come on. I want to introduce you to my friend."

CRUISE HAS CHANGED in the short time I've been gone. What he's gone through has darkened his already reserved demeanor. Guess he has more demons than he started with as well. He's a quiet guy, but Delilah has a way about her—everyone opens up to her. Laughing, Cruise is on the tail end of a story about getting his ass kicked in an alley by a drug lord and his gang. "King just looks at me and laughs."

"He laughs?"

Staring down at the bottle of beer in front of him, he picks it up, finishes off the lager and replies, "That was before we knew what we had gotten ourselves into."

Delilah asks, "What had you gotten yourselves into?"

His eyes shift from her to me. "We were lucky to have Jason on our side."

She knows she's not going to get the details she's wanting. Cruise, like me, is a pro at leaving secrets good and buried. Delilah stands and walks behind me. Rubbing my shoulders, she says, "I'm going to head to bed. I hope you consider staying the night, Cruise. We have a spare bedroom down the hall with clean sheets and a view of the lake for in the morning."

"You drive a hard bargain. Thank you for the hospitality."

I add, "He's too drunk to drive anywhere anyway."

"Not drunk enough to let the night slip by without talking."

Delilah says, "Well, on that note, I'll leave you to it." Bending down, she kisses my neck then whispers in my ear, "You okay with me going to bed?"

Tilting up, she waits for me to answer. "You don't have to ask me for permission." I wrap my hands around her neck and bring her closer until our lips meet in the middle. "I'll be in shortly."

"I'll keep the bed warm for you." Just as she leaves, she says, "Last one to bed, turn out the lights please."

As soon as I hear those creaky floors upstairs, I lean forward. "As fun as it is to reminisce, why are you really here?"

"We miss you."

"King doesn't miss me."

"No, he doesn't, but the rest of us do. I'm here with a job offer."

Never saw that coming.

I'm surprised he found me in all honesty, and now he's thrown a job offer on the table. "I'm surprised they need my help."

"It's always good to have backup."

"Backup for you?" I can't help the chuckle. "Saving your ass more like it."

"Right. That's the job offer." His sarcasm game is strong. "Saving our asses when our asses need saving."

I can match him. "Here's some advice: stay away from criminals and psychopaths with a vendetta, and you'll be fine."

He turns the bottle around on the table—a nervous tic. The social part of the visit put to rest and the business finally at hand. "I'm told to offer you double your old salary."

The money is tempting, but I've earned more than I can spend in this lifetime. Anyway, Delilah is more than enough reason to say no. "I'm out of that line of work now. I'm settling into this life with that beautiful creature upstairs. It's a slower pace here, but it's good for clearing my head. And when it's really quiet, I can hear the cicadas buzzing, frogs croaking, water rolling over the lake, and Delilah's snores. They're not loud. It's actually kind of cute. I like the sound of her next to me."

"I'm not sure what to say to that. I do think she might kill you if she knew you told someone she snores." He chuckles.

"Yeah, she might, but it'd be a damn good death coming from her."

"I don't know what's happened to the guy I knew a few months back, but you're not him. Whatever this place has done to you is good." He laughs. "You're almost tolerable now." He stands and cracks his neck to the side. "I'm going to bed. I'll be out of your hair by morning."

"You can stay a few days. I've got plenty of manure for you to shovel."

His laughter gains strength. "I know you don't know much about me, but manure is not something I'm familiar with or looking to learn about. Thanks for the offer though."

"Anytime."

He heads for the archway but turns back before he leaves. "You're always welcome back. Delilah's welcome, too."

"Thanks. Wanting a solid future with her, man. Not sure working for King can offer that."

Nodding, he says, "Understandable. Night."

"Night."

~

CRUISE STUCK TO HIS WORD. He was long gone by morning. Delilah was disappointed. She probably hoped she could gain more insight into me if he stuck around a little longer. Probably could have. I slide my hands around her waist from behind and look over her shoulder into the mirror. “Now you’re stuck with me telling you all the stories.”

“But you hold back.”

“I don’t hold back. I just don’t share the ugly details you don’t need haunting that pretty head.”

“I’ve told you. I can handle the truth.”

“Okay. I once stood guard outside a dressing room while an A-list actor fucked two women. It took him ten minutes to get off during a fifteen-minute break. He rehearsed his lines while doing it. When he returned to the set, he nailed the scene. He nailed them too, but—”

“Eww, Jason”—she spins in my arms—“it’s not even nine in the morning.”

Laughing, I ask, “Is there a better time of day to tell a story like that?”

“Yes, like when I’ve had wine or at least lunch. Or not at all. That’s not a good story.”

“I didn’t say they were all good. I said they were ugly. I learned a lot about people and how they operate. How power is used and abused and the way money twists the human psyche to make them greedy. It’s not like that here. It’s still good. You’re still pure.”

“I’m not so innocent.”

“None of us are, but we don’t have to live like it’s the apocalypse either.”

She finally agrees with me and nods. Sweet girl. “What time did Cruise leave?”

“I heard him leave around five.” It was good seeing him, but nothing felt quite right with him around. It was as if he carried the cloud of darkness I thought I’d left behind.

When we go downstairs, I laugh when I see what he left me on the kitchen table. A sealed envelope propped against a bag of Oreos. Delilah passes me and grabs the cookies. "I love Oreos. Can I have one?"

"You can have as many as you want." My gaze goes to the envelope. Taking it in hand, I recognize the name on the front—Eric—and smile. I open it, pull the note out, and read:

Glad you found a reason to stay.

THE NOTE IS NOT SIGNED, but I know who it's from. Seems Cruise had been given an alternate mission as well. I take a cookie from the bag and eat it in one bite. A friend once told me that everything is sweeter when you've found your reason to stay. *She was right.*

21

Delilah

JASON and I have been playing house for weeks. We don't go out much, just to do the regular errands. Billy hangs out with us, sometimes to help and other times to drink a few beers. It's a peaceful existence.

Too peaceful.

As soon as I hear the screen door slam close, I run into the barn to find Billy. "Billy?"

He comes out from the area where we keep old equipment. "Yeah?"

"Have you heard from Cole lately?"

"Saw him yesterday. What's up?"

"He doesn't usually take his ego getting bruised so lightly."

Sitting on a stump of wood my dad used for a chair, he takes off his cowboy hat and runs a hand through his hair. "Are you talking about what happened at Red River between him and Jason?"

"Yeah. I've been worried, living every day like he's about to strike. Is he?"

"You have Jason around. You don't have to worry, Delilah."

"I don't want Jason fighting this battle. I don't want Jason near Cole at all. It won't end well. You know that."

"Jason can handle himself. I saw him pin Cole to the ground by a neck hold. The guy's got a lethal side to him."

You're telling me. "Wait, when did that happen?"

"When Jason first arrived back in town. Same place. Red River."

Jason didn't tell me that. We both look back toward the farmhouse when we hear the screen door slam again. My heart picks up speed. "I'm serious. I don't want Jason and Cole near each other. You'll let me know if you hear about Cole coming out here, right?"

"You know I will."

Finding some relief, I smile. "Thanks. I appreciate it."

From behind, Jason walks into the barn. "You sticking around, Billy?" He's far enough away to not have heard us talking. "I was thinking about it. I was also thinking about getting laid."

"Billy." I shake my head and pretend I was tending to the rusted tools hanging on the wall. "Gross."

"Really? Are we fifteen? A man has needs, Delilah. I'm assuming a woman does too, so I'm going to go help one out with those needs tonight."

Jason's laughing too hard or is smart enough to not get involved in this conversation in the first place. I start walking away, but I stop and go back. "You can't say stuff like that in front of my sister when she comes to visit."

"Why not?"

I cross my arms and roll my eyes. “Because she’s used to men with class.”

“Annnnnd?”

“And,” I say, then huff, frustrated he doesn’t get my drift without me spelling it out for him. “And, do you have a tie?”

“Delilah.” Now Jason joins in.

“What? I’m just asking if he has a tie.”

Billy responds instead, “Yes, I do. Why are you trying to set me up with your sister?”

“Because I like you and I love her, and I think you guys might work well together.”

“Your sister has hated me since I was eight. I don’t think she’s going to like you trying to set us up.”

He’s not saying no. Actually, he’s not saying he wouldn’t be interested in being set up either. Maybe he likes Shelby more than he’s letting on. “Nobody even remembers you pushing her into the mud.”

“Except you.”

And my sister. “Doesn’t matter,” I reply. “We’re not kids anymore. Right, Jason?”

His hands are up and he’s backing away. “I’m not getting involved in this one.”

Rolling my eyes, I turn back to Billy, and say, “Wear the tie over for dinner on Friday night. Okay?”

“Am I going to church?”

“No, but if you play your cards right—oh God, what am I saying?” I laugh at myself. “Just wear something nice—not too dressy but not straight off the farm.”

“Some women like straight off the farm, but I have a feeling your sister is not going to like this setup one bit.”

“What’s not to like? Four friends getting together to hang out and catch up is all good stuff.”

“Guess we’ll find out. As for these tools, I think I can

clean 'em up and sell them. You don't use them, and Ricardo has his own."

"If we can make money off them, let's sell them. Every penny counts."

Jason says, "Speaking of money, I wanted to talk when you have a few minutes."

Although I'm curious to know what he wants to talk about specifically, I don't push for more with Billy standing here. "Okay."

Billy gets to work, pulling the tools out from the corner and I join Jason as he walks to his truck. I ask, "Is everything all right?"

"Yeah, it's good. I'm good. You?"

"I'm good. Since we're all good, I've been meaning to ask you about the fair again. With Red River not working out how we planned, how are you feeling about the fair?"

He pulls the tailgate down and sits atop it. "I'm fine with it. The reality is we can't stay holed up here forever."

Moving between his legs, I run my hands over his denim-clad thighs. "I don't want to be controlled by my ex."

"I fucking hate that you even have an ex." Taking me by surprise, he brings me in for a kiss.

It's possessive and greedy, abrupt and lustful. My body's temperature rises as does my need for him. "How do you turn me on from one kiss?"

"Because you know what follows." He hops off. "You want to go upstairs?"

Looking back at Billy, I debate briefly, but decide against it. "He works for free to help me out. I think we should wait."

"I'll wait, but I can't promise I'll be good."

"I love when you're bad."

"Hold on to your britches, Ms. Noelle, because I put the *bad* in bad boy."

"Bad boys are my weakness."

"Then I'm one lucky bastard."

I'm the lucky one, but I'll let him own the title for a bit. "We should finish the chores so we can have some fun sooner rather than later."

"I like the way you think."

"I like everything about you."

The tips of his fingers slide inside the waistband of my cut-offs. My body responds instantly to his touch. In the heat of the day, he manages to make my body shiver from desire while goose bumps pebble my skin.

Billy comes out of the barn, "I'm taking off."

I back up a few steps from Jason, who says, "Your timing really fucking sucks."

"*Thank you* would be nice. I'm leaving. You guys can roll in the hay or whatever it is you're wanting to do. Just don't tell me about it and don't make me watch."

I close the tailgate for him. "Thanks for helping out."

"You're welcome. So the fair tomorrow—"

"We'll be there. Want to ride together?" Jason asks.

He shakes his head. "Nah. I'm hoping to bring whoever I meet tonight to the fair tomorrow."

Laughing, I say, "You've really thought this through."

"My needs come with plans. I'm not a love 'em and leave 'em kind of guy, despite what you hear around town."

"Noted," I reply. "Then we'll see you there around six?"

"I'll be there. I'm judging the Mutton Bustin' race."

Elbowing him, I tease, "You old softie."

"It builds character in kids to participate in competitions like that. Guess they figure the all-time winning champion in Freeland County will make a good judge."

I'm just about to aww from his sweet support of kids, but then he says, "And, cowboys tend to screw up their marriages. I bet there will be a lot of hot single moms there."

"Ugh. I thought you were bringing a date."

"Date, not wife."

"Again. Ugh. Why'd you have to go and ruin it? I'm going inside. See you tomorrow."

I leave the guys laughing in my wake. I grab the iced tea container from the windowsill after noticing the deep, bright coloring from steeping in the sun all morning. Jason comes in the back door just as I finish pouring the tea over two large glasses filled with ice.

"It's not sweet," I say.

"That's okay," he says, coming to me. He licks up the side of my neck. "You're sweet enough."

"Ahh," I sigh. "I'm sweaty though."

"I know. It's fucking sexy as hell." His hands wander as my eyes dip closed.

"We shouldn't," I whisper in all the ways that counteract my feelings.

"We should."

"I have so much to do."

"I want to do you." His voice is muffled as he sucks on my neck.

Squeezing my hands between us, I push back. "Jason, stop."

Shock and hurt run across his face. "What?"

"No. No. I don't mean this. Us." Whispering, I say, "If you leave a mark, he might see."

"He?" It dawns on him before I can answer. "I don't fucking care about Cutler. It's none of his fucking business what we do. He's your ex, Delilah. He doesn't have a place in our lives."

"I know. I just don't want to incite him. If he sees a

hickey on my neck, he'll flip out, and who knows what he'll do."

"The fuck?" By the hands clenching at his sides, the tic in his jaw, and wild eyes staring at me, he is angry. It's not like Cole's where I felt frightened for my life, but it's not the Jason I recognize.

He doesn't understand. He wasn't here when tiny things would set Cole off. *I was. Alone.*

Jason walks out, and I see him rounding the corner of the house. It's not like him to walk away from me. He's never been afraid to take a conversation head-on. I run out the front door just as he approaches his truck. Stopping on the porch, I ask, "Where are you going?"

"I need my bike."

"Don't leave."

My words or maybe the plea in my tone stop him. With his back to me, he says, "I need to take a ride and clear my head."

"Jason, look at me."

When he looks at me, his soulful eyes reveal such pain, and I hate that I've caused that again. "I'm sorry I upset you. I don't want any more trouble with him."

His shoulders lose tension as he comes to me. He stops on the bottom step so much like he did the first day he showed up. His respectful nature, his respect for me has been shown in many ways. Even now, he remains a few steps lower. He doesn't try to intimidate me like Cole. Jason humbles himself before me, and it's a genuine sign of respect I'm still getting used to.

He communicates *with* me, not *over* me. "I'm not mad at you, Delilah. We're not fighting. I've been here every day like I live here and reality just hit me. I don't. This *isn't* my farm. And as long as you're worried about him and how he'll react to my presence, it's as if you're not really my girl. This isn't an ultimatum. I'm here for you however I can be, however you want me to be. I don't care if I lose to him in football or in a fight or whatever. That's all shit that's built on ego and pride. But when it comes to you, I can't be second to him."

"You're not. You never will be. I don't want him near you. I don't want you hurt."

"How many times do I have to tell you I can handle him?"

"He's not the same person you used to know. You were never stuck in the glory days of your football years. He is. Two things matter to him—his ego and me. You've effectively taken both from him since you came back."

"You're divorced. He can't hold on to you anymore."

"He's an alcoholic with a gambling problem. He didn't want the divorce. I petitioned for it after I got a temporary restraining order. The judge granted me a quick divorce, but that restraining order was lifted the same day because the good ole boy judge admired Cole's football record." I lean against the post, four steps dividing me from the man I love. *I hate that Jason has come home to this. To me, with this dreadful baggage.* "It's not a matter of *if* he'll try to get me back or hurt me. It's *when*. And I don't want you caught in the crossfire."

He covers the steps, staying one down, which puts him eye level with me. "I'm not afraid. He can come after me as long as he doesn't come after you. I won't let him come after you, Delilah. You're my everything."

Taking this stunning man by the jaw, I hold him in my hands. "Were you always this foolish?"

"Only for you, honeysuckle." We kiss and I sigh, melting against him. "Look, if it will help ease tension, I'll talk to him."

"He's not a reasonable man."

He winks. "I have ways of helping him see the light."

"Do I want to know what that means?"

"No, better not. It's safer that way. In the meantime . . ." He kisses my neck. "Want to go for a ride on my Harley?"

Now that is an offer I can't refuse. "Absolutely."

22

Jason

THE WIND WHIPS around us as we chase the sun. The road's wide open. I could keep riding. I could steal her away from this life that's holding her back. Would she stop me?

Would Delilah want to keep going or turn back?

We're both caught in a whirlwind we can't control, and it sucks. I know she loves me. She doesn't have to tell me, though she does often. She shows me. I see it in her pretty blue eyes. I feel it in the way she touches me and in the way she cares for me.

I love her.

I cover one of her hands with mine before returning it to the handlebar. Having her on my bike, wrapped around me, was yet another fantasy I never thought would happen. Here we are though. Trust in me to care for her—to keep her safe—has been handed over without question.

Delilah took the helmet and put it on before I had a chance to insist on it. It was as easy as her saying, "Share this piece of you with me." An hour later, we haven't made it far, but we've crossed county lines. I veered off onto a small, hidden-from-the-highway dirt road about ten minutes ago. I don't think she'll remember when I brought her here back in college, but it felt like a good time for a visit.

The river comes into view, and I love the sight of the mountains with the gray and purple of twilight. We dismount and she sets the helmet on the bike before wandering toward the river. "You brought me here a few times. I always remembered it, but could never find it."

"Why were you looking for it?"

Standing at the water's edge with her back to me, she says, "I thought if I could find it again, it would lead me back to you."

When her head tilts down, her shoulders shake with a sob. I go to her as she covers her face with her hands. Holding her from behind, I whisper, "My heart was always with you. The beat was just silent until I returned." I turn her around and hold her as she cries on my shoulder. "I'm not mad at you, honeysuckle." Stroking her hair, I whisper, "And I'm not leaving."

She looks up, her puddled tears running down her face. "For now?"

"I'm thinking about forever. What do you think?"

A smile cuts through the sadness that had overtaken her face. "I'd like that."

"Remember how I said I wanted to talk about money?"

"Yes, but I don't."

Chuckling, I ask, "Why is money such a taboo topic?"

"Because it brings out the worst in people."

That's not the Delilah I know. She's never been one to focus on the negatives, but after what I've learned regarding the human condition, she's right. "Does it have to be that way?"

"I don't know anymore."

"I've saved some money, Delilah. I was thinking about our future and the farm."

"What? Why would you be thinking about the farm?"

"I want to be where you are."

She steps out of my reach and crosses her arms. Staring out over the lake, she's nodding her head before she speaks. "I'm not letting you spend your money on the farm if that's what you're suggesting."

"What if I want to?"

"You were shot. You've done unimaginable things for that money."

"Is it too dirty for you to want to use it for a good cause?"

She laughs. "I'm not that high and mighty, Jason. I meant, you've had to sacrifice so much to earn every dollar."

"Everyone who works makes sacrifices."

"Usually not with your life."

"I didn't think I would, but shit happens. Things go wrong. Bad people sometimes get ahead, but they didn't win."

"What happened to them?"

"They died." I walk to the edge of the water and squat down. Picking a weed, I rub it between my fingers before tossing it to the ground. "You have more questions, so can we just get them over and done with?"

"Why did that note from your friend Cruise say Eric on it?"

"Because it wasn't from Cruise. It was from my old . . . boss, a friend. Acquaintances. I don't know what to call them. I consider them friends and allies more than anything else."

"So it's like an inside joke?"

"It was an alias I went by at one time."

"Eric? Eric," she repeats, trying out the name. "It doesn't fit you."

Chuckling, I ask, "And Jason does?"

"Yes. To me, it's just a part of who you are. Like Cuddle Bear." This time she laughs.

I go to her. Taking her hand in mine, I say, "You can call me that if you like."

She bumps up against me playfully. "Okay, Cuddle Bear."

"Anything else you're wondering about?"

"The Oreos."

"Now that is an inside joke. It's not even funny. I like Oreos, and I ate someone else's."

Digging the toe of her shoe into the ground, she says, "Yeah, guess you had to be there."

"What's wrong?"

"When you tell these stories about being shot or working on movie sets, I feel like you've lived a whole *exciting* lifetime without me. You went on adventures and saw the country. You lived a life I thought I'd be sharing with you. I worry I won't be enough for you."

"You feel left out because I was shot?"

That earns me a half smile. "Not that. You know what I mean."

"I do, but no matter where I traveled or who I met, nothing compares to being on that farm with you. If I could change things I would. I would come back after college for you." We start walking along the bank. "I've been meaning to ask you something."

"All right."

"I know you're recently divorce—"

"Oh my God. Are you going to ask me to marry you?"

"What? No." A hand flies to my hair, and I run it through. "Wait. I mean—" The heartbreak on her face does me in. I rush to cup her head in my hands. "Don't cry."

"I'm so sorry. I thought you meant you were going to ask me." She looks away, as if she's too embarrassed to look at me. "Forget it. Forget I said anything."

An ache grows in my chest seeing the pain on this woman's face. "If you'd say yes, I'd marry you right now." Beautiful eyes the color of bluebirds peer up at me. She wears her heart on her sleeve for everyone to see. It's battered like mine but filled with so much love to give. "I would."

"I'm a recently divorced, almost bankrupt farmer in the middle of nowhere. My spirit has been bruised along with my body. I have a lot more scars than I had when I was wearing that Freeland County tiara. I feel older than my years because of them. And here you come, riding back into town, and screwing up my plans of being a spinster the rest of my life."

"You know why? Because when I heard you were single again, all the plans I made suddenly seemed secondary to you. Scars don't scare me. I have a lot of my own. As for your divorce, I say this is my lucky day. It's as if Cupid himself had a say in the matter. I also think you're more stunning than the day we fell in love."

"Which time?"

"Both. Age doesn't hold a candle to your beauty. But who cares if we get lines and both age if we're living a good life and growing old together?" Taking her by the hips and wiggling them back and forth a bit, I say, "I'm not sorry about ruining your plan to grow old alone."

With a pretty smile on her face, she asks, "Why are you so good to me?"

"Because you deserve good. Lots of it, and I intend to give it to you for the rest of your life."

"I love when you give it to me."

Leading her back to the bike, I say, "Speaking of giving it to you . . ."

WITH MY ASS pressed to the leather, Delilah slides down my hard cock. Seated to the hilt, her head falls back and her hair sways across my thighs. When she tilts forward, she says, "I will never get tired of how good you feel inside me."

Fuck. "Show me how good I feel to you."

"So good," she rasps.

My stomach muscles tighten from the sound. "Fuck. I'm not gonna last long, babe."

She moves faster, her eyes closed, her nails digging into my shoulders. "Don't come yet. I'm so close, Jason."

She's an angel under a halo of strawberry-blond hair. A vixen who knows how to command her pleasure. "Fuck, you're gorgeous."

"Oh, yes. Jason," she releases on a sharp-edged breath, her body tremors and her hands squeeze like that perfect pussy of hers.

"Fuck." I grab her by the hips and hold her down while I thrust until I'm emptied of everything held deep inside—my emotions, my secrets, my come, my sins. *Everything* is given to this goddess who rules my world and is healing my soul.

My lids are heavy, and I drop my forehead against her chest, trying to catch my breath. I look at her, her gaze on me. She runs her fingers through my hair, and says, "I'd marry you if you asked. I want you to ask not for me, but for you. We're not in a hurry. I'm not going anywhere."

"I love you." We kiss and things feel settled between us in the good kind of way. "We should get back."

"It's a shame to leave somewhere so beautiful. Thank you for bringing me here again."

"I'm glad we came." I wink, amused by the double entendre.

"So, do you always carry condoms in your pocket?"

"Only when I'm with you."

"Good answer, Mr. Koster. Good answer."

Once we're redressed and back on the bike ready to go, I lean back and ask, "You ready?"

"Ready for anything."

~

I'VE BEEN NEGLIGENT. I've been back long enough to have stopped by to say hi, so here I am, walking along the far side of the field. The little house looks to be in good shape. Ricardo and Paloma always did take care of it.

I find Ricardo on top of a tractor. He cuts the engine when he sees me. Leaning on the steering wheel, a smile that time recorded in the deep lines surrounding his mouth appears. "I was starting to wonder if you were ever going to come by."

Kicking the large tire, I gaze up using my hand to protect my eyes from the sun. "I should have come sooner."

He climbs down and we shake hands. "It's good to see you, son. How are ya?"

"I'm good. Staying out at the farm and helping Delilah with chores. You?"

He sits on the step, shadowed by the tractor, and takes

off his hat to wipe his forehead. "Keepin' on with the keepin' on. Heard you were hanging around these parts."

"Yeah," I say, looking toward the farmhouse in the distance. "Never thought I'd be out here again—"

"But here you are." He smiles. "She's always been a good girl."

"She has." I shove my hands in my pockets. The conversation is awkward when I don't want it to be. "I wanted to come by and say hi because things are getting serious with Delilah."

"Gettin'?"

"Maybe already are."

"That's what I thought, considering that truck of yours seems to be permanently parked over there." He stands, but puts his foot on the step, the lightness already making room for the talk I knew was coming. "It's not been easy for her. If you're planning on leaving anytime soon then best be doing it now. She doesn't need another broken heart."

"I'm not leaving anytime soon." I glance over when a car drives by. When I turn back, I look him in the eye. "I'm going to marry her this time."

"You do right by her if you do. She deserves better than she's gotten."

"I carry that regret heavy on my shoulders every day. If I would have known—"

"Don't let it weigh you down too much. I was right here and . . ." His gaze goes to the ground between us, and for the first time in my life, Ricardo looks . . . *regretful*. His body slumps. "We can't change what's happened." The dark brown eyes hold more than memories, but are still optimistic. "I know you well enough, Jason, to know you'll do right by her. But if you don't, we own two shotguns, and Paloma and I aren't afraid to use them."

"I'd forgotten how you never messed around."

"My days are long but there never seems to be enough time. I don't have time to beat around the bush." He reaches forward, and we shake hands again. "Good to see you, son. Since you're hanging around, feel free to come give me an afternoon off here and there," he jokes.

"I will."

Sitting atop the old tractor, he says, "Make sure to say hello to my wife or she'll give me a hard time. She's not home right now, but she's been dying to see you."

Delilah is fortunate to have them nearby. They care about her. They were there for her when I wasn't, and I'm thankful she has them in her life. "She could have come over anytime. Both of you. You're always welcome. You know that."

"Eh, I told her to give you and Delilah some time to grow together. I see it worked."

Chuckling, I reply, "It sure did. Thanks for that."

23

Jason

"WELCOME to the Freeland County Fair and Rodeo."

The greeting screeches through the parking lot as I park the truck and get out. I scan the area, but it's massive.

One main ticketed entrance.

Four gates to the left to exit.

Too many ins and outs.

I hate large events. Danger lurks everywhere. The lack of safety here is disconcerting, and I'm supposed to walk my girl right in there. So much can go wrong quickly. Reminding myself that I grew up coming here, I try to believe it's safe. But I can think that all I want. Deep down I know crazy shit can happen without warning.

Pushing these thoughts down isn't going to be easy, but maybe that's yet another penance I'll pay for living the life of a mercenary.

Delilah's a reminder of the good in people.

When I come around, Delilah slips out. The skirt of her

dress slides up while her boots land on the gravel with ease. Her long, tan legs cause my dick to stir. *As always.* Looking around, I'm tempted to take her here. There aren't many people here yet, but enough that we might be noticed since it's only six o'clock and the sun is still high in the sky.

I settle on a compliment. "Have I told you how pretty you look in that dress?"

She's blushing when she looks at me under the brim of her cowboy hat. "We're not having sex here."

My hands go up in surrender. "I wasn't going to suggest it."

"I know you, Jason Koster. I can see it on your face and the way you're looking at me."

Grabbing her around the waist, I pull her against my hard-on. "I can't help that you do things to me."

Her hands slide under my shirt, her nails scraping lightly against my stomach and arousing me even more. "I'll tell you what. You win me a prize, a big prize, and we'll try out what you suggested on the hay bale the other night."

Fuck yeah, I'll win that prize. "Beautiful ass up, stomach flat on the hay bale, pounding into you from behind."

Her pupils dilate. With a mischievous smile on her face, she bends and runs her tongue over my abs. "Wherever you want."

Fuck. My cock hurts from being restrained in these jeans.

A sexy confidence she used to have when we dated has begun to return. She's so damn tempting and maddening when she teases, but it makes it so much better when I'm deep inside her. She makes it to the end of the truck bed and turns back. "Well, c'mon now."

I grab hold of my dick and shift the best I can within the confines of the denim.

"Let's get a move on." She saunters off. Looking back, she winks. "Good times await, stud."

I WASN'T KIDDING on winning her that prize. The offer she made is worth the money spent on dumb carnival games. But the biggest prize doesn't come from hitting rigged milk bottles or tossing darts at balloons. Nope. The big prize of $500 cash is in sharpshooting.

Seems this is my lucky day. I sign up for the tournament against hunters and gun owners who shoot for fun. Everyone in the state pretty much has a gun on his or her property, but they've never had to use it like I've had to. I'm feeling confident I can win this contest. Billy was taken out in the second round of the previous bracket, and he warned me about the competition.

It's not just about hitting the targets. When I see Cole Cutler hanging out at the judge's table, laughing, working them over, I realize this isn't just about the cash prize for me. It is about dominance and instilling fear in him. Delilah isn't his, and I won't be intimidated. I'm hoping for the chance to go against him.

After signing up, I return to Delilah who's eating pink cotton candy. Can't avoid getting hard watching her tongue dip and swirl the sugar around it. "You're going to tease me all night, aren't you?"

"Sure am." She giggles as her hand finds mine. "When I said I wanted a big prize, it doesn't have to be this one."

"Yes. It does."

Her laughter stops. She's spotted Cole. Everyone has. The way he parades around here like he's Grand Marshall makes it hard for anyone to miss him. He's so fucking cocky. I can't wait to knock that chip right off his fucking shoulder.

That chance would come as if my wish was a command.

"You don't have anything to prove."

"I don't back down from a good fight, babe. Anyway, I have everything to prove, and I intend to."

"Bracket Four report to the stage." The announcer comes over the speakers, and says, "Up next, we've got our very own hometown hero, Jason Koster. Former quarterback for Freeland County High School . . . and Homecoming King."

I hear the laughter. A lame title is better than none, so what the fuck ever. A gentle squeeze to my bicep causes me to tighten it, and she gets the full strength of what lies under this T-shirt. Delilah's lips are close to my ear as she stands behind me. "I should call you king," she whispers seductively.

The life I left behind comes racing back, and I duck my head. Squeezing my eyes, they aren't bad memories on the whole, but some I'd like to forget forever . . .

The nights are the worst. This penthouse is too high. Too secure. Too removed from reality. I've been a bodyguard. I know how to protect someone, how to risk my life for theirs for money.

It's different here.

King and Cruise don't know what to make of me, but they need me and know it. What started out as a job has become more. I care about these people, and Ali—I don't let my mind go there.

A job.

That's all this is, I tell myself, and attempt sleep again.

When it doesn't work, I get up and head down the hall. I click on the coffeemaker and start snacking on some Oreos left on the counter. Staring out through the large windows my head begins to clear as the sun rises. It's always easier in the daytime to handle the dark crime I committed against another man, even if he did deserve it.

My mom would be devastated by the choices I've made. I wonder what Delilah would think of me now?

. . . Turning to my side, I say, "Nah, I don't need the trouble that comes along with a name like that."

"Okay, Cuddle Bear."

Chuckling, I roll my eyes. "Shh. We'll keep that one between us." She slaps my ass as I walk to the podium.

"Cole Cutler, owner of Cutler Cabling and former running back for Freeland County High School."

Cole shouts, "You forgot to add the one who got the girl."

I glance over my shoulder as he approaches. *He's such an asshole.* I want to add, the one *who lost the girl*, but it's best if I keep quiet. My shoulder is shoved and I turn, his throat in my hands within seconds. "Don't fuck with me, Cutler, or you'll get a repeat of what happened outside Red River."

"A bit touchy for a wife-stealing wife-fucker."

The announcer crouches down. "Gentlemen, save it for the shootin' contest. You've got five targets ready to take these bullets of anger off your hands."

He's right. *Delilah deserves better from me.* I find Delilah in the crowd, worry creasing her brow.

When I turn back, I see that giant check for five hundred dollars hanging high above the announcer's head. Cutler needs money, and he's got the skills to win this. That is of course if I weren't here to make sure he doesn't. This should be fun.

A case is presented to each of us. The rules state we don't get to choose our weapon, much to my dismay. I hate revolvers, but that seems to be the choice for this contest. Even worse, Cutler gets an Uberti handgun. I get a Smith & Wesson .357 and shake my head. His is made for competition. My gun is made for collectors, not precise shooting. *Fuck.* I refuse to lose, but it may be harder to win with this weapon.

I take the gun out of the case and check the chambers. Five bullets. Five targets. The fastest and most accurate moves to the final bracket. Four winners of their brackets will shoot to win. I have to take Cutler out first. We're led to the line. Cutler wins a coin toss to see who goes first. I cross my arms and take a few steps back.

He walks to the line and kicks up some dust. When he's given the go ahead, he shoots. It's an impressive showing for such an asshole. He used to kill every can with a BB gun when we took turns shooting. If he'd win one round, I'd win the next. We were always good at pushing each other.

The paper targets are changed out and Cutler's are brought to the judges on the podium.

I'm told to step to the line. As soon as the signal is given, time stands still. The colors that once surrounded my target turn a gray gradient, allowing me to focus on the bullseye. My arm flies out steady, my elbow locked to absorb any recoil. My eyes narrow while lining up the sight with the dead center of my target.

The first bullet flies from the chamber and I turn just enough to send the second toward its intended destination.

Third.

Fourth.

Fifth.

My arm lowers as the gray fades away and the sound of the crowd behind me returns. But the sound is muted, not like the talkative noise and chatter from before. I look behind me and am greeted with silence. The rowdy rodeo goers are staring—some with their mouths open, some closed but with wide eyes, and some sport both. I see the rise and fall of Delilah's chest, her eyes meeting mine. Barging through the gawkers, she comes toward me. "Jason?"

"What?" I ask, not sure if she's okay or if I'm in trouble.

"That was the sexiest thing I think I've ever witnessed," she whispers.

"My shooting?"

"Yes, your shooting." The exposed top of her chest is flushed. "Holy damn. I see now."

"What? What do you see?"

A sexy grin slips onto her lips. "I see why you were so good at your job."

"Former job."

"Whatever. Do you want to leave early?"

Now I smirk, amused. "You turned on, baby?"

"So much."

"I was just messing around out there." I try to see my targets, pretending I don't know that I hit the center of the bullseye. Every. Time. "We used to shoot BB guns for fun. You remember."

"That wasn't messing around, Jason. What you did was pure skill." We walk to the podium to return the gun, but she continues, "Your face. I've never seen you look like that."

"I wake up every day with the same ugly mug. Nothing to see here." I try to distract her by making a big deal about putting the gun back in the case.

It doesn't work because she's still staring at me. As soon as the case closes, her hand covers my forearm, and I look at her. She says, "I want you so badly right now."

"I would have shown you what I can do with a gun sooner if I would have known how turned on you are by it."

The announcer interrupts our foreplay, "Woooweeee. Holy cow! Would you look at them targets! Our hometown hero just might maintain that status. You've been cut, Cutler." A snicker echoes across the range, causing the crowd to join in at Cutler's expense.

"You fucking rigged it, Koster," he shouts. I turn around, and he charges, sending me landing hard on the ground. *Shit.* He swings, but I flip him to the side with a good shove to his chest and knee to his groin. I'm on my knees and get a solid punch in before I'm grabbed and yanked backward by two dudes the size of the Hulk. He has one guy who's been drinking too much to hold him back. Fucker hits me with an uppercut before I can free my arms and fight back.

I land heavily on top of him. Two punches and the sad sap is groaning in pain and hiding his face like he's a kid getting picked on at the playground. Security is there, and I'm pulled away again. "I already stopped."

Jeffrey Whaley, our town deputy, cuts through the crowd. "Why am I not surprised it's the two of you fightin' again?"

"Because Cutler can't seem to keep his insecurities under wraps."

Whaley grabs me by the elbow and the twin Hulks back away. "Come with me, Koster."

"What the hell? He fucking started it."

Deputy Whaley never saw things for how they were. He preferred to pick and choose who his criminals were. Today, I guess I'm the bad guy. "Shut it, or I'll take you to jail."

Delilah pushes through the crowd. "Jason was defending himself, Deputy Whaley. All these witnesses can back him up."

"Step back, Ms. Cutler."

"Noelle," she corrects.

He stops and looks at her. Releasing my arm, he says, "You jump from one bad decision to the next. Cut your losses on this one before I see you in jail along with him."

"No." She jumps in front of him, proving his point. "This is wrong. I'm not going to let you get away with this."

"Well, there's nothing you can do, Ms. Noelle, so step aside."

"It's okay, baby. He's not going to take me in. I'll be back."

Seeing her all fired up like this, fires me up in ways we can't act on. She's feisty and fierce. Her hands are on her hips, and she's passionate when she speaks, "It's not okay—"

Cole grabs her arm. I'm already in action to take that fucker down once and for all, but she's already swinging and lands a perfect right cross, his jowls shaking under the impact.

Deputy Whaley sighs. He yells, "Take her into custody."

24

Delilah

I'M NOT SCARED.

I probably should be, but I'm not.

I'm never scared when I'm with Jason, and you would think having been so close to Cole when he flew at Jason I'd be rattled. *I'm not.* And even though I'm leaning over a cop car handcuffed, I'm not worried.

His cheek is pressed to the same trunk as mine, both of us staring at each with smiles on our faces. "Maybe you shouldn't have told him his wife's famous blue ribbon recipe was a rip-off of your mom's."

Laughing, I reply, "Maybe, but it's true. Shows what cheaters the Whaley family have always been."

"Commit a crime and you walk away with a warning in this small fucked-up county. Expose the truth about an apple crisp and you get a night in jail. Sounds about right."

"They won't take us," I say. "They've got nothing on us."

His eyes narrow at me, confusion furrowing his brow. "Since when did you grow a pair of balls the size of Kentucky?"

"I'm just tired of it all. Tired of being called Cole's wife. Tired of being called a whore to my face from rumors spread all over McKinney. Tired of hiding who I want to be. Tired of hiding us. I'm so fucking tired of all the bullshit. Do you ever just get tired of it all, Jason?"

He smiles. "Yeah, that's when I decided to come home."

"But this is my home. I have nowhere to escape to."

We're both lifted by our shoulders and brought around opposite sides of the car. Our heads are pushed down as we're loaded into the back of the cop car. The doors slam closed and we look at each other. Blue and red flashes, lighting up the night around us. Jason leans his head forward and turns to me. "Marry me, Delilah."

Not a question.

It's a plea followed by a smile and nudge. "Fuck this town and marry me. We'll live like the shunned in our private paradise by the lake. We'll fish and fuck, raise a family, and pour so much love into that farm and each other that no one will have cause to say anything bad."

"I don't want to marry you to stop gossip."

"Then marry me to start it. I'll walk down Main with you on my arm, proud as the day is long. You're my girl. You always were. And you always will be. Let me be your man long past forever. Will you marry me, Delilah Rae Noelle?"

Jason, Billy, Ricardo, and my daddy are the only men who've never used my married name, which surprisingly the town refuses to drop. There's a lot to be said for men with manners. Besides manners, Jason's the man I was always meant to be with. I may be newly divorced, but I was never truly married. Not in my heart anyway. The answer is easy, coming forthright just like Jason is now. "Yes."

Leaning closer, with our hands trapped behind our backs, our lips meet in the middle. Words aren't necessary. Our kiss confirms the promises we're not afraid to voice, but don't need to say.

The deep and steadfast love we have for each other is felt in this kiss. A million yeses exchanged. An eternity of I love yous whispered through caresses.

The driver's door opens and Deputy Whaley folds inside. "Geesh, stop that or I'm gonna have to hold you in separate cars."

Jason's laughing, and then he licks his bottom lip making me wish I was the one licking it. He then bites that bottom lip as if the secret he's keeping from Whaley might escape.

Whaley says, "I don't know what's gotten into you, Delilah. Dragging my wife and her blue ribbons into your mess can land you in a cell for the night. You can't blow that low and not expect to pay the price. What if my wife finds out?"

"What if the Women's Auxiliary Club finds out she's been stealing blue ribbon recipes long before last year? Isn't she up for re-election of the Fourth of July Extravaganza this year?"

"Is that a threat, Ms. Noelle?"

Jason stares at me wide-eyed and mouths, "You're so fucking hot."

But Whaley ruins the moment by adding, "Your father is probably rollin' in his grave right now. What would he say if he saw you cuffed in the back of my car?"

Angling my chin up in defiance, I reply, "He'd be proud I stood up for what was right."

His dissatisfaction comes in a huff before he turns attention to my partner in crime. "I blame you, Koster. If you weren't on that football field, you were always causin' trouble. If my vote mattered, I'd have that billboard down by the highway demo'd and burned for the homecoming bonfire."

"Well, Deputy," Jason starts, "I actually wasn't in trouble much, but you did go to Kerbyville High, so maybe it's the rivalry that makes you hate me so much."

"I do not hate you." Whaley's voice rises. Looking at us in the rearview mirror, he says, "I'm gonna let you go with a warnin', but you best be leaving Mr. Cutler alone and mindin' your own damn business. Do you both hear me?"

Jason replies, "Loud and clear."

"Did ya hear me, Ms. Noelle?"

"I heard you."

"Good," Whaley says. "Just head on home and stop causin' trouble where there is none."

When I look at Jason, he's already looking at me. A small smile is seen as the flashing lights drift across his face. He whispers, "Even though I didn't win the money, I totally won the grand prize."

I'm about to tell him the money doesn't matter, but the doors open, and we're helped out of the vehicle. Facing each other over the roof of the car, he smiles at me and I smile back. This is not the way I expected him to ask me to marry him, but now we're on the other side of it, it was perfect for us.

We don't talk until we're out of eavesdropping distance. Rubbing my wrists, his hand lands on my lower back and he guides me away from the cops. His lips are near my ear when he says, "I had that shooting contest in the bag. How about a consolation prize on the way home?"

Sneaking a peek of him, I see the confidence embedded in that smile, and ask, "What'd you have in mind?"

THE WINDOWS ARE DOWN and Blake Shelton's "Every Time I Hear That Song" is playing through the speakers, floating into the night. With a palm on each thigh, he spreads my legs wide open. We've had a lot of sex since he's been back, but it's hard to get used to how he looks at me—my whole body under deep inspection as he studies every inch in the moonlight. *In awe.*

Lifting up, my eyes meet his briefly before his gaze lowers again and he kisses that spot where my most private parts meet the top of my thigh. My head drops back slowly on the blanketed truck bed, and I happily sigh while closing my eyes.

"You're amazing, Delilah. Your trust is a beautiful thing. I promise never to abuse it." He kisses me again—deeply with intention as his tongue sinks inside me.

I sigh to relax, my muscles and my mind getting lost in this moment, getting lost in him forever. Blame it on the moonlight or his magical tongue, or maybe a combination of both, but my orgasm comes fast and hits hard. My back arches as he holds me still. "You're so bad." My body relaxes into a puddle of blissful goodness. "You're going to send me to an early grave of ecstasy."

"Hey, honeysuckle?" When my eyes connect with his, he says, "I may be bad, but I'll always make you feel good." He maneuvers onto the truck and lies next to me. Looking over, he takes my hand, rolls to the side, and kisses me.

It's naughty and rough, raw, and God, so crazy. "I feel so

carefree with you, like we could disappear into that star-filled universe and never look back."

"Is that what you want? Do you want to leave here, leave the farm?"

Turning my eyes to the night sky, I lean my head to his shoulder. "I don't know what I want other than a redo."

"How about we start with an *I do*?"

I smile, my happiness bubbling to the surface through giggles like I'm a teenager. "Sounds good to me."

We lie there a little longer before grabbing the blanket and shutting the tailgate. We leave the windows down the rest of the way and listen to the music loudly as we sing at the top of our lungs.

Rolling down the window, I maneuver out and sit on the door, letting the wind whip through my hair. My arms are raised as I lean back and let the music take me away. My calf is warmed by Jason's hand. His touch feels good but I know he's really taking precautions.

My protector—of heart and body.

When we enter the city limits of McKinney, I slide into my seat and buckle up. I leave my window down and rest my head on my arm. I've seen these same buildings my whole life, passed under this stoplight a million times, and every time I do, I wonder what it's like to be somewhere else. To get . . . away.

My sister knows. She followed a job offer to Chicago and then stayed for the money. Almost every time we talk, she tells me she wishes she were back on the farm feeding the chickens and swinging on that rickety porch swing.

I'd trade the quiet of the country for six months in the city. Big dreams die in little towns.

Jason runs his hand over my thigh and under my skirt

before the heat sears my skin. I look up. He says, "You seem sad."

"Not sad. Confined to a life I didn't choose."

"What about us?"

"You're the best part of my reality." *My salvation.* I angle my back against the door and prop my boots on his lap. "Tell me a story about one of your adventures."

Goose bumps are left in the wake of his hand as it runs over my knee. "I once drove from Seattle to San Diego. That's some beautiful country out there."

"What's the ocean like? I saw the water in Chicago. They treat it like the ocean but it's a lake technically. Is there a difference to the beaches in California?"

We pull up the drive to the farmhouse. "They're different. There's nothing like a sunset over the Pacific Ocean. I'm going to show you one day."

I have no doubt he will. He's a man of his word. "I'm so grateful to have you in my life. As much as I want to travel and see the world, I feel like you've brought all that back with you."

"My stories pale in comparison."

"I'll take those over nothing at all."

Taking my hand, he kisses the top. "I'm going to give you the best life, Delilah, the one you always wanted. You'll never want for anything. What do you dream about?"

"I'm too broke to dream outside my means."

"Dreams are free. What does your heart long to do?"

"I love the farm. I've always seen myself living out my life here, but I've always dreamed of seeing the Eiffel Tower, and I wonder what it feels like to dig my toes in the sandy beaches of Southern California. Although I don't need to be rich to be happy, I do wish to see what's beyond these county lines."

"I have money."

I slide across the truck bench. "We've already talked about this. I don't want to take your money."

"I've saved it for my future. You're my future, Delilah."

Future Mrs. Jason Koster. I lift up and kiss his neck. "You're my everything."

25

Delilah

A BOTTLE OF WINE, two beers, and three grilled cheese sandwiches later, Jason is dancing with me in the kitchen.

We're happy.

We're stuffed.

We're drunk.

We're high on life.

We're turned on.

That's nothing new. I've never felt so alive, or is it more that I never knew how empty I felt? Like a summer storm, he wrecked all my plans. But in his destruction of that planned life, he gave me a sunrise of hope. I gasp in pleasure. "I suspect you wear these dresses to tempt me into sinning."

"Is it working?" I ask through broken breaths.

"It's working." He moves, going deeper. "The fair was fun, but if I could spend every night buried deep inside you like I am now, I'd never leave this farm."

"We were arrested. That wasn't fun."

Laughing against the back of my head, he says, "We weren't arrested, but fuck, you sure do know how to use that smart mouth of yours sometimes."

"Too much?"

"No, it's fucking sexy."

Currently pinned to the counter in front of the sink, my skirt is bunched above my ass. My panties are in shreds on the floor. His shoes push against my boots while he pushes into me.

Again.

And again.

Closing my eyes, I chase the darkness that alights with fireworks of desire. Fuck, I want it. Like him, I want it so badly I can taste it—salty sweet—from an hour earlier when I made Jason fall apart, dropping his guard and getting off as he watched me take him deep in my mouth.

He's close.

His thrusts are becoming erratic.

I'm close.

The thought of him being turned on turns me on. So much. My fingers sting from the pressure of holding the edge of the counter so hard. Leaning onto my elbows, his fingers dig into my hips as he comes. Mine follows fast. My mouth falls open, releasing a rough moan. "Jason." His name is dragged through my body's vibrations.

Reaching behind me, my breath returns as I fist his T-shirt. Opening my eyes, I scream. I push away from the window in front of me.

Those eyes.

The eyes that have haunted me.

"Shit! What? What is it?"

Pointing toward the window, I say, "Cole. Cole. Co—"

"Cole? What?" Jason spins me around to face him. "Cutler?"

"He's out there. He's out there, Jason. I saw him. I saw him."

His pants are up, and he's running out the back door. Is he real? Is he here? Surely I'm hallucinating. I run to the front door to look for his car, and as I swing it open I'm charged—one hand covers my mouth and the other holds the back of my head. I scream, my eyes wide while Cole pushes me into the house.

"Shut up," he demands.

I'm grappling for anything I can grab while being shoved too fast to comprehend what's happening. I'm pushed backward into the hallway. My back hits the corner before we clear it, but there's no slowing him. He pushes harder as I wince in pain. With his hand over my mouth, my attempts to scream are squashed. My eyes water in pain and fear, and I try to grab his wrists to pull them away.

Cole's body is hard, harder than natural. Staring into his bloodshot eyes, the pupils are pinpricks. His strength is extraordinary.

He's not drunk.

He'd be sloppy.

He's high on something.

I continue to try and scream as I claw at his arm. Nothing deters him. With the strength of an army, he pushes me into my parents' room. The door is locked, and I'm shoved to the ground. "You think you can make me look like a fool and get away with it? Is that what you thought?"

Scrambling away from him, I hit the bed with my back. "Listen to me, Cole—"

"No." I'm whacked with the back of his hand, and my ears ring. "I told you to stay away from him and what do I find out? You're fucking him, and he's living here." He stands over me, his anger surging. "I saw you in the kitchen. You let him treat you like a whore. Is that what you want? You want to be treated like that?"

"He's here, Cole. He'll find us."

"Do you let him fuck you in *our* bed?" His eyes dart to the mattress and back. "Like I used to fuck you?" Reaching for his belt, he starts to undo it.

White-hot fear runs up my spine. The sound of his belt through the loops. His rapid breathing. The crazed look in his eyes. Too many memories flash before me, and I become paralyzed with fear. But then somewhere in the white noise I hear Jason's voice. *"I won't let him come after you, Delilah. You're my everything."* He's here. He knows my house like the back of his hand.

I look back up at Cole. He's not in his right mind.

I won't be able to reason with him, but I won't die on his timeline either. Grabbing one of his legs, I yank it forward sending him to fall on his backside. He's too quick to recover for me to get far. My boot is grabbed as I lunge away from him. With my body free as he holds the boot, I move to get to my feet. We both are upright at the same time, and he charges me again. I get one good hit and start to run, but he grabs my hair and pulls me back to the ground, my head hitting the wood floor.

My vision is spotty. I struggle to stay alert as my body is dragged into the bathroom. I hold his wrists to take pressure off the hair that's being ripped from my scalp. Kicking my feet, my socked foot slips on the floor, and I have no grip.

The water is turned on in the tub, and I'm dragged closer. "Cole," I scream, tears streaking down my face, my heart racing. "Please."

"Please what? You've ruined everything. Everything was for you."

"Please stop. You're hurting me." He steps into the tub, pulling my body with him. As he slides down the tile, he cradles me against him, my back to his chest, his hand squeezing my neck. My head is pushed under the water. Even as my air is cut off, I find comfort in the warmth of the water.

I kick while struggling to loosen his hand from my throat. The black spots spread, the bright light of the bathroom dimming under the pressure of death.

I always thought death would follow a filtering of flashing memories, the ones that made you happy, feel alive and loved. I was lied to. Every regret I've had in life is given a front-row seat to my breaking heart, the memories forefront in my mind, the ones I would change . . .

Jason walks across the field with a football under one arm and a letter in the other. I know what it is. It's the letter that will end us. He's gotten the scholarship he's been wanting and I've been dreading. He'll move on without me. He knows my family can't afford for me to go away to college. He knows we're barely making tuition now.

How can he leave me?

After four years, I thought we were heading for the aisle, not a breakup.

Talented. Skilled. Handsome. So ruggedly handsome. Strong. Smart. He got a scholarship to the local university for his grades. The school just lucked out that he was an amazing football player too. Guess he's not McKinney's secret weapon any longer.

He was mine.

Every girl here wanted his attention, but he only gave his time to one—me.

I should be grateful for the time we had together. I'm not, though, because I'm in love with him. As my heart shatters to the ground, I watch his team pat him on the back and the other cheerleaders congratulate him. When he's a few feet in front of me, he stops, reading my inner emotions. He's always seen me too clearly.

I'm not ready to hear the words. I'm not ready to wake up tomorrow and know he's not mine anymore. Is Cole right? Has Jason felt held back by me, but hasn't felt he could say that? I can't hold him back, and if I don't go, he'll stay. I don't want him to give up his dreams for me.

If he's decided there's no place for me in his new life, I'll not stop him from taking his chance. It will break my heart . . .

How do you ever repay someone who sacrifices their own dreams for your petty needs to be loved? You don't.

A football scholarship means that team owns him. His focus needs to be football, not me back home. The distance will kill everything we are. So many words echo around my head. I can't question myself any longer. I have to let him go so he can be everything he dreams of being.

Dropping my pom-poms into my bag, I grab the handles and lug it over my shoulder. He moves in. "I'll carry it."

"I got it," I snap at him. Without waiting, I start to leave.

"Delilah, wait. I wanted to share the good news." He catches up next to me. "I got the transfer."

"Yeah, I know." I try to sound disinterested to cover the sobs filling my chest.

"Hey!" I look back to find he stopped walking a few feet back. "What's wrong?"

The hand-delivered letter from the new coach seems too white under the bright lights of the stadium. I choose to stare at the ripped-open envelope instead of the golden-brown eyes that will weaken my knees and my resolve. Stick to what's best for him. Cole warned me. "Don't become a hindrance he'll regret one day.

He'll get rid of you as soon as he transfers anyway." Think of Jason. Protect my heart. I blurt, "I don't want to see you anymore."

"What?" The words come like a slap. "No, Delilah."

. . . More water. It pours over my head, drowning the memories with the remainder of my life. The only way to express the immense love I'll carry with me comes between coughing, "Jason."

I push one more time, putting all the strength I can muster behind the effort. Water sloshes over the side of the tub, then it hits me. Cole's muscles have softened.

"I'm sorry. I'm sorry. I'm sorry."

Falling over the side, my shoulder hits the ceramic base of the toilet. Cole reaches for a gun on top just as Jason barges in. The gun goes flying across the small room and spins on the linoleum. Jason grabs the gun and then me under my arms. He pulls me free from the room, but everything still seems fuzzy. "Are you okay? Delilah, speak to me. Say something."

Despite almost drowning, my throat feels dry. I cough. "You came for me."

He kneels down and lifts me up. I've never gripped him so tight, so desperately. Whispering rapidly, he says, "Go to Ricardo's and wait for me. Tell him what's happening."

"We'll go together."

"No. I'll handle this. Go!"

I grab my boot from the floor and take off running. Pushing through the front screen door, I run down the steps and across the lawn. I don't stop until I reach the field. Just beyond where the porch light reaches, I stop and step into my boot before taking off again.

Halfway across the field, I hear a car and stop running. It's not a cop car, nor any car I recognize. The windows are too dark to make out if anyone is inside the back. Two men get out and start looking around. I drop to my knees keeping my head hidden until I feel it's safe to take another look.

They're on the porch.

Oh no.

Jason.

They open the door and go inside.

I start running, but don't make it to the edge of the field before I hear a gunshot ring out stopping me in my tracks.

Jason.

I run as fast as I can until I reach the border of the floodlight on the side of the house.

Another shot causes me to duck.

Hiding behind a tree, I look over trying to see inside the house.

My gun.

I have to get to my gun. I have to help him.

I love him too much to lose him.

He promised me.

I'm his future.

I'm his future.

26

Jason

"HOLY SHIT." With the gun cocked and ready, I look at Cole, who's hiding in the closet. "Who's out there?" I ask the cowering bastard.

"I don't know what I'm doing."

"Shh. Keep your voice down."

"I wanted to die. I wanted to die with her."

I have a good mind to take him out of his misery. The fucker shouldn't live. He caused all of this. Our lost years. Her pain. The fucker tried to kill her. Drown her. I want to take him out so badly. But something about the two warning shots fired in the living room make me think he's not the one I need to worry about right now.

The door to the bedroom is still open, but I've turned the lights outs. I have Cole's gun, which has one bullet. *Fucker.* I'm guessing he intended to play a game of Russian roulette. My gun is in my truck but that means getting out of here undetected to retrieve it.

With the shades up on either side of the bed, enough light filters in from the lights on the side of the house outside to see Cutler wet and shivering. “Cutler,” I whisper between gritted teeth. He’s useless as he buries himself behind the clothes. Fucking coward.

My body stills when I hear the floors creaking down the hall. My mind ticks through the escape routes of this house.

Front door through the living room.

Window out onto the roof upstairs.

The backdoor in the kitchen.

I’ve become complacent. My mind rushing to the obvious instead of what I can actually get to undetected.

Two windows in either corner.

One larger one at the end of the hall.

Small horizontal window in the shower.

Fuck.

The windows in here are my only hope. I just hope there’s not a surprise waiting for me outside. When I hear another set of footsteps, I run. Needing all my strength, I set the gun on the bed, unlock the latch, and pull.

Fuck!

The window is stuck. Yanking again, it doesn’t budge. I run my finger along the seam, and that’s when I see it’s been painted closed. *Who the hell would do that?* Glancing over to the other window, I see the same thing.

Fuck.

Fuck.

I grab the gun and head to the door. Backing up to the wall, the gun is against my chest, my finger loose on the trigger.

One bullet.

One.

Delilah.

Images of her carefree and hanging out of my truck, as if there was nothing that could stop her from loving life. *She deserves that.*

She's who I'm living for, so I hope she's long gone. Please to fuck, let her have listened this one time. Ricardo will keep her safe.

I suck in a slow and steady breath that fills my chest, and then round the corner, running to the window at the end of the hall. Glad I wasn't wearing boots. The rubber of my sneakers dampens the sound of my feet as I run. The fucking wood floors give away my precise location, if you know the house as well as I do. The latch is released with one hand and I reach down pulling it open and dive out. I hit the grass and roll before maneuvering to the side and pressing against the siding of the house.

My breathing is too loud. I've let myself go, trusting I was safe. Will I ever be? Have I brought danger here? Are they here to take me out?

I eye the large trunk of an oak tree. It will give me a better vantage point of the house and get closer to my truck.

Three.

Two.

One.

Running with all my power, I grab the tree and bring myself to a stop. The house has been quiet since they called out, "Come out. Come out," and fired the two shots. I can't see any movement through the open curtains of the living room, but I stay still. Looking over to my truck, I've got a good seventy-five feet to cover to reach it. Wide open with nowhere to hide.

Fuck.

I keep to the shadowy parts of the lawn but run like I've never run before. If someone wants me dead, this is prime time. Skidding to a stop at the back of the truck, I duck down behind it and try to catch my breath while listening for any commotion outside or action inside. *What the hell are they waiting for? If it's Cutler they're actually after, they can hear him, surely.*

I hurry to the front of the truck, thankful I've disabled the internal light and that damn buzzing that comes on when I open the door. I click open the driver's door and grab my gun from inside a blanket shoved in the corner behind the passenger's seat. Dropping to the ground with both guns in hand, I regulate my breathing.

In the distance, across the field, I see the shining beacon of Ricardo and Paloma's house. My heart steadies as I take a gun in each hand ready for the battle ahead. One bullet in Cole's. Six in mine.

Seven opportunities to take down two intruders. With adrenaline pumping, my breathing sounds like water rushing through my ears. Standing up, I position myself to the side so I can't be seen from the house. I peer through the truck windshield at the brightly lit front porch, then blink.

What the hell?

I swear that's Delilah running onto the porch. *Shit.* I run to the front of the truck both guns ready to fire. "Delilah!" I whisper-yell.

But she's too determined and makes it to the front door before she hears me. I run. There's no waiting for a perfect moment to take these fuckers down.

It's them or Delilah and it better not be her.

My heart is beating a mile a minute as I hear shots fired but no screaming. *What are these fuckers after?*

I take the front porch steps by three and have the screen door swinging open by the count of four. The lights go out when I hit the floor and slide between the couch and the coffee table. Crouched down, I listen for sounds in the house besides the door screeching closed.

A tap on my ass causes me to jump, turn around, and aim both guns right into the blue eyes of my girl. Lowering my guns, I whisper, "For fuck's sake, Delilah. What are you doing?"

"I was coming in to help you."

"I told you to go to Ricardo's and wait."

"I did, but then I heard the gunshots and came back." Her eyes are glassy, and her bottom lip trembles. "I thought they were going to hurt you."

"Now they'll hurt you, too. Fuck. Why didn't you listen to me?" We can't argue about this now. I've got to get her out of here.

When we hear muffled voices we still our bodies so we can listen. Glancing back to her, she points upstairs. I mouth, "You sure?"

She nods.

"I'm going up. You go to Ricardo's and do not stop for anything. Do you understand?"

"Stay alive. For me." Nodding again, she tugs on my jeans. "I love you."

"Love you. Now go."

As soon as she's moving, I'm up covering her as she runs back out the door. I hit the wall that leads upstairs. It's going to be damn hard to not get shot if I go up there. I need to wait them out. I need to be near a door and the living room has no coverage when they come down, so I head for the kitchen. I turn and stare right into the cylinder of a silencer.

"Guess that wasn't you shooting up the place?"

"Drop the guns."

I give the gun one long look, and then I drop my guns

because unfortunately, escaping isn't an option when you're staring the Grim Reaper in the face.

"Cole Cutler, you owe my boss $57,850. You are being served a death sentence—"

"Wrong guy." As relieved I am to know they aren't here to kill me, figures that fucker is responsible for this shitstorm.

"What?"

Tilting his head to the side, his face comes into view. "I'm not Cutler."

"You're in his house."

"I'm in his ex-wife's house."

"Ex?" He sighs, but doesn't lower the gun. In fact, he nudges my nose with it.

"Well, you're in the wrong place at the wrong fucking time."

I hear the cock of the gun and hope to God Delilah is safely across that field.

"Benson, you down there?"

Saved by the sidekick. Using the distraction, I jack my knee into his groin as hard as I can. He falls as a bullet whizzes by my ear when I drop to grab my guns. Seconds feel like minutes until I find myself standing over him with both guns aimed down—one at his head and one at his dick.

"What's happening, Benson?"

He groans in response but his partner stays put with the upstairs advantage. I have the darkness as mine.

"Shut the fuck up, Brooks, and kill this fucker."

When this guy's greeted with silence, I toe him in the shoulder. "Your buddy's not too worried about you. Why does Cutler owe you money?"

"He owes my boss money. Backroom poker tournaments. He's a shit card player."

I could shoot this guy in the head right now and take out his partner, even in the dark.

But what do I do with Cole? I'm going to have to deal with him differently despite my desire to end him.

"Stand up. Slowly. Keep your hands up and visible. Tell your buddy to come down here."

"Get down here, Brooks."

"What?"

"Get the fuck down here."

He comes down the stairs and his gun is lowered to his side. I add, "Get next to your partner. Lose your gun." The guy drops his gun to the floor.

The first guy says, "Look, buddy. It was a simple mistake. Show us where Cutler is."

"You're not letting me walk out of here, so let's not pretend."

Before I can decide what to do with these guys, Cole comes barreling down the hall screaming and pounding his chest. *What the hell is he doing?* They're knocked to the ground and Brooks takes me down with him. All the guns scatter across the floor. *Fuck.*

I grab one and turn on my ass to find a gun already pointed at me. The sound of a weapon discharging echoes through the air, and for one brief second I close my eyes and wait for the hit.

27

Jason

Cole groans in pain, dragging himself to sit up. "I've been shot. You shot me."

It's going to be a bloodbath, yet my mind keeps flicking back to Delilah.

Delilah and I didn't fall in love slowly. Nothing came slow when it came to us. We fell fast and hard. I can't lose her.

. . . The door flies open and Delilah stands there in all her innocent, yet fierce beauty. My hand is steady on the gun I'm aiming right at his heart as my heart sinks. "Get out," I yell.

Out of the corner of my eyes, I see her flinch in response. Benson turns his gun on her. Fuck. His partner and I are still in a standoff. Benson yells at her, "Come here."

I say, "Run."

Benson laughs. "I'm not afraid to shoot a woman in the back."

"You shoot her and there's no reason for me to keep you alive."

"Tough guy, huh?" He moves around to Delilah and grabs her by the arm. Her body is stiff, but she's not fighting him.

What the fuck?

Fight.

I stare at her, wanting her to read my mind.

He laughs, yanking her in front of him and puts the gun to her head. His free hand dips from her neck to her breast. "Pretty girl. So this is Cutler's ex-wife?" Looking at me, he adds, "No wonder you're hanging around. Maybe I'll have a taste before we leave. Before she dies."

"You'll die before you touch her again."

"Really, pretty boy?"

The term grates my nerves, drudging memories of that gun to my head back in that alley years ago. My body tenses, and I grind the words out, "You and your partner will be dead before it registers with your brain."

Cole is moaning. "Shoot them, Koster. Shoot them." The asshole needs to shut the fuck up.

My finger twitches, causing Brooks to blink. I'll win. I can kill him and have a bullet between Benson's eyes a quarter second later. My target's coming into focus. The room starts to turn gray.

"Jason?" The sweet voice of an angel wipes the gray away and brings me back to her. My eyes slide to Delilah's. "Remember how you said it was us or them?"

I will never forget the night I killed that man. "I remember." I don't want her dead, but I don't want her left to be tortured by these guys either if I'm killed. We're stuck in this damn standoff like we have no chance at that happiness Delilah and I have talked about.

"This is one of those times," she says. Why is she referencing our conversation about why I had to kill someone? Without regret. "A situation like this is why you made the decision you did, right?" Her words are fierce. Stronger than I thought possible.

I glance back at Brooks who yells, "Shut her up." His hand is shaking. Mine is not. He doesn't want to shoot me. What kind of money collector is this clown?

When I look back at Delilah, she's not scared. She's not shaking. She's strong and almost relaxed, even though a gun is being held to her head. But I won't let her die. "Yes, just like this."

I'm just about to shoot Brooks when she says, "I understand why you did it now." Before Benson can react, she shoves her elbow into his ribs and reaches down. Pulling a gun from her boot, she spins and shoots before he can aim his gun at her.

Brooks shoots when I roll to the side. The bullet penetrates the wood, and I aim over my shoulder, shooting him in the thigh, choosing to spare his life for the time being. I'm on my feet and over him. Cole is dragging his ass into the kitchen. "Get the fuck up and call the cops."

Benson is wailing and Brooks is turning white. Standing side by side with Delilah, both of us facing in opposite directions with our guns aimed on these assholes, I say, "Nice shooting." She's going to be in shock. I need her to stay focused. Just for a little while longer.

Her hip bumps mine. "You're not the only one who used to practice shooting with a BB gun." *And amazingly, she can even find humor in this. Who is this girl?*

"It paid off." I like her cockiness, but with Cole whining on the phone in the kitchen, we're going to be here a while. This situation needs to be handled or contained. Directing them with my gun, I say, "Move over. Next to each other."

Delilah turns with her gun still aimed on them. When they slide over, she takes a step back, letting me take over. Blood is messy. "You guys look like you might bleed out. This is where I give you a choice. You can either make sure you never come back to this town and our farm or I kill you and feed you to the fishes out back before the cops arrive. Which do you choose?"

Grabbing his leg in agony, Benson replies, "Our boss will kill us, so we're already dead men. You need to let us go."

"Can't trust you."

"I swear. We won't. No one will. I've got a wife—"

Squatting down, I look him in his beady eyes. "You threatened my fiancée with bodily harm. You threatened her life. And now you beg for your life by telling me you have a wife?" He squirms under the intensity. "I have a good mind to take you out just for disrespecting her."

"Don't. Please. No trouble. For you."

I add, "And her."

"Yeah, and the broad. It's Cutler we're after."

"Right."

"We made a deal. There's no going back on a deal." *We'll see what sort of deal you get with the sheriff's department.*

I turn my attention to where it needs to be right now. Sirens sound in the distance. Red and blue lights flash across the fields and invade the living room. "You know I can't let you go, but I'll let you live. This time." *Fuck. I just want this nightmare to be over. I need to get to my girl.*

"THIS GUN IS STILL REGISTERED to your daddy, Delilah. You need to file the proper paperwork to put it in your name."

The farmhouse is shot up. Holes are in the walls, the floor, and in people. Cutler is in the ambulance on his way to the hospital, two gambling-ring criminals are also on their way to the hospital, and all Whaley's concerned about is the proper paperwork for the gun Delilah used to protect us.

"I'll take care of it this week," she says. Paloma wraps a blanket around her. Delilah's dress has dried from the warm night air, but when you're up that high, running off adrenaline, the fall is sometimes chilling.

I take her hand. "Are you okay?"

"It's just catching up with me. You don't need to worry. I'll be fine."

She's not a good liar and at times like this I appreciate that fact. Wrapping my arm around her shoulders, I hold her while we finish giving our statements.

In towns like McKinney, the whole jail staff comes out for a lookieloo, so we're grateful we don't have to go down to the station. Three hours of questioning is quite enough. We're repeating ourselves with each round. Delilah's exhausted, so I wrap this up. "We're done, Deputy. If you have more questions, you'll have to contact our lawyer and set up a formal interview."

Whaley scratches his chin. "I think we have enough to file our reports. If we don't, we'll be in touch."

"What about your men inside?"

"They'll be there all night. I suggest you find another place to stay for a few nights while we do our investigation."

Delilah walks toward the fields and stands, staring out. With her arms crossed, I can tell she's struggling and doesn't want an audience. "Thank you, officers." I walk to her, wishing I could make this all go away, like it never happened. Sometimes bad shit happens though. I hate that the outside made its way to the inside of our little piece of paradise. I don't want to startle her, so I speak before reaching her, "Whaley said we could go."

She glances back to me and then returns her eyes to the field. "Where can we go?"

"Anywhere we want."

"Paloma said we could stay with them. She has a sewing room with a foldout couch."

"Billy called. They wouldn't let him on the property, but he said we're welcome on his farm." I move next to her but keep my eyes ahead.

"Your mom called me." Taking my hand, she holds it. "She said she wants us to come over."

"Tomorrow. How about I take you to a hotel so we can decompress?" We've had a lot happen and we've told the story more times than I care to tell again. "How about a room just for us?"

"Can we treat ourselves and get one with room service? I'm hungry. By the time we reach a hotel, I'll be starved."

"You can order the whole menu if you want."

A sliver of a smile finds its way home on her pretty face. I'll spend the night coaxing the full one out, though, as she deserves to smile.

An hour and a half later, we're standing in our room and she's staring at the tub, her tone full of disappointment. "Normally I'd take a bath to wind down." Coming to sit on the bed next to me, she says, "I think I'll skip it tonight."

Almost drowning in one makes her reaction reasonable. *Fucker. He's stolen that from her too.* "Sorry I wasn't there sooner. I thought he'd run, not gone inside."

"I thought he was on drugs. Now I'm thinking he was on

a mission." Resting against my chest, her arm drapes over my middle.

My arm curves around her back, holding her to me. "He only had one bullet in his gun, Delilah." I don't mean to sound ominous, but his intentions were clear.

"He was going to drown me."

"And then kill himself."

"His life is shit. He's shit. I hate him so fucking much."

Swearing doesn't come natural to her. The words are distorted, dripping from a place that should never reside inside her heart—hate.

Sitting up, her palm presses over my heart, and she says, "What if you wouldn't have found me in time?"

Caressing her cheek, I lean forward and kiss her. "You saved yourself. I have no doubt after the courage you showed tonight that you would still be here."

"In your arms?" It's an odd question, but the whole night was odd.

"I have everything to live for now, so no one's taking me out that easily."

Her smile returns, the light in her eyes smothering the darkness that tried to win, tried to take her hostage.

A knock on the door signals our room service. I hop up and let them push the cart of food inside. After tipping, we're left alone with enough food to feed a small army. Her eyes are wide and my stomach growls. "Was the drive worth it?"

Grabbing a bowl of spaghetti, I can tell by the way she settles back on the bed and starts flicking through channels that she's content . . . for now. "It was definitely worth it."

I've been paid a shitload of money over the last few years. It gave me financial security. Something in the bank. But living within the confines of darkness, at times existing just outside the law, I didn't have this. Contentment. With her, *my* girl, I've found it. Peace, solace, that no paycheck ever provided.

I'll take this life over the last every day of the week and twice on Sundays. I reach for the steak because there's no time like the present to enjoy a few of the finer things in life.

28

Delilah

MY THROAT IS FLOODED.

Water overflows.

I can't breathe.

I savor the fiery orange on the inside of my lids. Orange means life.

Flailing my arms to find anything to hold on to that will give me the leverage to save myself is useless. I'm held under the faucet as it pours over my face, drowning me in his arms.

. . . The horror I felt in that moment has worked its way into my veins. It's attached itself in ways I can't remove. I was so close to that slice of paradise with Jason that even though we survived and still have that future, I don't think I'll be able to easily let last night go as I almost met death.

I thought I was doomed to spend eternity tangled up in Cole and death, hate, and hell.

Jason stirs and I look back. Just the sight of him, the feel of him and me alone in this room has me smiling, though.

He once told me he was a soldier, a mercenary of sorts, but when I look at him I only see my dark-haired knight. His sleep is steady, his features finding peace, as his body lies bare for me. The sheet is tangled around a leg, exposing parts of him that I'm the only one privy to these days.

How can he possibly be that hard when he's sleeping?

Men will always be a mystery to me.

It's a mystery I'm happy to solve over the next sixty or seventy, or more years. I'd love to live a long life with him. The years we were apart, when he was off doing those things he doesn't like to talk about, will pale in comparison to the years we'll spend together. One day they won't matter at all.

One day, last night won't matter.

We survived. Together. That's all that will matter when our souls leave this place.

I shut the blinds and crawl back into bed next to him. Careful not to wake him, I untangle the sheet and cover us both up. I lie there staring at him. Even in the dark he's so damn handsome. It doesn't matter that time has touched the carefree youth we once existed in.

Life has changed him.

Sighing, I let my mind go where I usually stop it from going.

Life has changed me, too.

Lying here now, I know it had to. It would have with or without my permission anyway. I need to accept it.

Is that how he sleeps so soundly tonight? Even after what could have been a horrific tragedy?

Is the peace that keeps his features softer in the moonlight his acceptance that the world has bad people in it? He's just learned to deal with it?

If he had his way, my life would remain pristine and

untouched by the outside world. It's good in theory but not realistic. I'm human, which means I'll make bad choices . . . breaking up with Jason and trusting Cole hopefully the worst. It also means I have a chance to start over, clean the slate, and move on. Move on is what I intend to do. I feel so incredibly fortunate I get to move on *with* him this time.

I run my fingers lightly over his arms, appreciating the dip and rise of the muscles beneath. After the events from earlier I shouldn't want him. Is it wrong to want to get lost in something wonderful for a while?

His eyes open. "Delilah." My name languidly rolls off his tongue as if we have more than one lifetime together. In no great hurry, his hand reaches for me.

"Make me forget for a little while."

Reaching for my top, he starts pulling it up. I raise my arms as it's taken off and tossed. When his large hands take control of my breasts—kneading and squeezing—I close my eyes and enjoy the feel of him and how my body responds to him, to his touch. Moving on top of me, I open for him, opening myself and letting him in.

I need his weight, his lips on mine, the rough tips of his fingers scratching across my skin. I want him to mark me as his. I don't need to feel pretty to the world, to wear a tiara and smile. I just want him to find me beautiful when I'm not wearing makeup and my hair is a mess. I only want to be how he sees me, the real me . . . the bare and bold me. The *me* I am with him.

His mouth moves to my neck. He kisses and sucks. My hand slides into the back of his hair, wanting this, wanting him to want me like I want him—ravaged and real, carnal and lustful.

He warms my neck as his fingers flame the fires of desire between my legs. "Yes," I whisper in his ear.

"I want all of you, baby."

"Take me. Take every last bit of me."

The stubble of his beard has grown in overnight and scrapes against my chest. My skin is left raw and stinging. I love it. It's not so pretty, fitting for how I feel. He looks at me, his eyes gently drifting back forth between mine. "Sometimes the bad helps us remember the good. Let me be that good for you." *He is so good. He knows exactly what I need, how I need to be loved.*

"Leave no part untouched."

He pushes inside me, clearly needing me like I need him. My back arches and my head goes back, leaving my neck exposed. Jason pulls back and thrusts forward while his lips find my throat again.

Wrapping his arms under me, he uses my body against his, uses me for his pleasure while heightening mine. Our bodies start to sweat, sliding with ease and creating more. The sounds of our love are the only sounds I hear. The troubles from the night drift away as I find the ecstasy in his arms instead.

"I love you," I exhale with every breath. "I love you. I love you."

Our bodies slow until our souls sigh in satisfaction. His head rests on my chest and I hold him there, never wanting to let go.

Time doesn't stand still for us. It ticks by as we lose minutes or days, like the years we lost that we'll never get back. This time there's no true loss because it's time I've spent losing with him. Allowing the ugly of the day to fade away, together we find our own safe haven. I've found solace in his arms.

Moving to lie next to me, his hand covers my cheeks. He

kisses me gently on the lips and whispers, "I didn't use protection."

With my lips against his, I kiss him back with such care for this man I love so deeply. I fall back on my pillow and twirl his hair between my fingers. "I know."

I would welcome a baby into this world if it were his, if he was there with me to prove that when lives are meant to be entwined, they twist themselves completely into eternity.

"Let's get married as soon as we can get away from here."

"Away?"

"I want to show you all the places I went looking for you."

"You didn't have to leave to find me. I was here waiting for you all along."

"I didn't know you were mine to find. I was searching for the next life. I wasn't willing to lose you twice."

Oh God. All those years he'd believed I hated him. That I didn't love him. But here he is, forgiving me when I can't forgive myself. Could I be so kind if the roles had been reversed? My heart would be too damaged to repair if I had seen him with another woman. This man. This man before me is the most generous of beings. And like he once said, maybe my true heart now can heal the broken parts of his soul once and forever. "I'm sorry."

"What are you sorry for, honeysuckle?"

"For assuming instead of trusting. I did more than break my heart. I broke yours, and that's harder to live with."

Taking my hand, he places it over his heart. "You healed this broken heart and settled my restless soul." He brings my hand to his mouth and kisses each finger. He takes my left ring finger, closes his mouth around it, and then slides it out slowly. "If you could have any ring, what kind do you dream of?"

"I don't need rings or jewelry. I have everything I need right here."

Smiling, he chuckles. "Oh no, you don't. You don't get off that easy. I want everyone in Freeland County and wherever we travel to know you're mine."

"And you'll wear one because you're mine."

"I will flash that ring every chance I get, proud to say I'm the lucky bastard who gets to go home with you every night."

Dawn peeks through the window. We slide farther under the covers. "I'm not ready to get up."

"Ricardo will manage the farm. Let's stay a few days."

"Here at the hotel?"

"Here in this bed. We'll make love. We'll eat like kings. We'll binge on bad TV—"

"And we'll fuck."

"Fuck, it's sexy when you say that."

Snuggling closer, I rest my head next to his on the pillow. I steal a quick kiss but he catches me before I sneak back to my side. "Better get used to this, honeysuckle." Slipping his arm under me, we mold to each other. "I plan to hold you like this every night for the rest of our lives."

My eyelids dip closed, my body finally heavy with sleep, or maybe it's that peace he found earlier. I turn and he spoons me, his arm wrapping over me. His breath is warm on my neck, but it's even and comforting. Cocooned against him, I feel safe. "You saved me."

"I didn't save you. You saved yourself."

"I'm not talking about last night."

No more words are needed. We both sigh in contentment and close our eyes.

Just as I'm finding sleep, he whispers, "I'm going to make

up for every minute of time we were apart. I promise I'll give you the forever you deserve."

"I'll give you the same, Jason," I whisper. My lips turn up, happiness filling me, and I tighten my hand around his as I drift asleep.

THE HOTEL WAS A NICE REPRIEVE, a little escape in the middle of chaos. Returning to the farm is difficult at first. Not because I'm scared. I'm not. This place holds way more good memories than bad, but dealing with the aftermath of physical damage is stressful. "I don't know where to start," I say, rubbing my temples.

"We just start. Pick something to fix and see it through."

Billy stands staring, inspecting the bullet hole in the living room floor. "You turned and the bullet landed here?"

Jason is standing on the other side of it with his arms crossed and nodding. "Yup. Pretty much."

"Damn, dude. Did you shit yourself?"

I laugh when Jason scrunches his nose and replies, "No."

Billy's hat is off, and he's scratching his head. "What'd you do then?"

I peek back at Jason before I enter the kitchen. "I shot the fucker."

"Whoa."

We had a cleaning crew from one town over come and clean up the blood on a referral from the police. It makes it easier to deal with a mess of broken lamps and a few holes.

Following up his astonishment, Billy asks, "What did you do while you were gone again?"

"Fishing boats in Alaska. A little time in New England. A few other cash-in-hand jobs."

I guess that's the story we're sticking with. His past doesn't matter anymore. Like he said, he doesn't have regrets. I don't either. Guess it took being in his shoes to finally understand why. I do. Us versus them. I hate that there's even the necessity to think this way, but when push comes to shove, I'll fight for us. Just like he did.

Looking out the window doesn't bother me. It should, considering that's how the beginning of that night began, but Cole's been released from the hospital straight into a rehabilitation facility. He's facing time for his alleged ties to an underground gambling ring.

He doesn't rule my mind or control my life anymore. The people of McKinney are no longer blind to who Cole Cutler really is. I doubt he'd be able to get within a mile of my farm now that they know the truth. I finally feel . . . free. *Vindicated.*

I let myself rest, leaning on the counter. Warm lips caress the back of my neck as his hands slide around my hips, coming to rest across my belly. After kissing the shell of my ear, he whispers, "You think we have a baby in there?"

I cover his hands. "I hope so."

29

Delilah

SHELBY NOELLE always stands out in a crowd. As much attention as I got for my looks growing up, I'd simply followed in her footsteps. She's two years older than me and won everything from Homecoming Queen to Miss Freeland County, prepping me for the roles. But she was always something I wasn't—outspoken.

After picking her up from the airport more than an hour away, Jason and I have been peppered with questions from the backseat of the car we borrowed from his mom. Everything on updating her on the farm to more personal questions like, "Where are you sleeping if you're not staying in the house?"

"We put a bed and a few essentials in the loft," I reply, already knowing how she's going to react.

"The loft of the barn?" she exclaims but then laughs. "Good Lord, Delilah. You two are literally rolling in the hay."

"Sort of."

Jason's adds, "Definitely."

She laughs and then adds, "I lost my virginity out there."

Jason's shaking his head. "Petey Monroe was an asshole."

"He was, but man was he good with his—"

"Eww," I say, hoping she doesn't finish that thought. "Don't even go there."

Under lots of laughter, she rubs my shoulder. "I think you're old enough to handle the truth, Delilah."

"I'm pretty sure you don't want to hear too much of my *truth*."

"Actually, I want to hear everything." Her tone turns sentimental. "You don't know how terrified I was when Jason called me and told me what happened."

I sigh, exhaling heavily. I'm still not sure I'm happy he called her. On one hand, I get it. I do. He did it because my family should know. On the other hand, I knew it would worry her unnecessarily. "I'm fine."

"Now. But that might not have been the case."

"We can play out fifty different scenarios, but the only one that exists is the one where we survived. Let's not rehash this." We can bicker about it all we want, but I don't want to spend my time with my sister like that. "We're here. All is good."

"Okay," she relents. "You haven't changed much, Jason. Charming my sister just like you always did."

He's changed so much, but those changes are hard to see when you're looking at our *hometown hero*. He's more than that. He's my savior in so many ways, the king of my heart. I won't correct her though. He's fine lying low and letting everyone else fill in the blanks. Now I understand the deep-seated reasons behind his calm demeanor, he deserves even more respect. Jason doesn't need the glory. He never did. Not when he played football and not now.

He quietly goes about putting himself on the line for others, protecting what he cares about, and loving me like there's no tomorrow. I don't mean for my swoony mewl to slip out, but it does. After grieving the loss of my parents, missing my sister, the fear of losing my home to debts, and the abuse—emotionally and physically—I survived at the hand of Cole, it feels good to feel this happy, to find happiness with this man I've loved for what feels like my whole life.

He's changed.

I've changed.

Our once naïve young love has changed, and I like us better. I'm better just from him being back. We are moving forward together with our eyes wide open. I'm finally me again, the me I've always wanted to be. And for that, I'm thankful.

Jason reaches over, his hand covering the one resting across my stomach. In this sweet moment, it's easy to remember the most valuable lesson my sister taught me: looks don't matter. It's what's in your heart that counts.

We came from a long line of beauty queens, but they all had something else in common—they loved with their whole heart, and they lived for their families. With one hand on my stomach and Jason's nestled on top, I've never felt closer to my roots, and for the first time, I truly understand what Shelby meant.

Jason Koster has good looks down to a science, but it wasn't his looks that drew me to him. It was his heart. It still is. He's given me his heart to protect and I will with all that I am. "We're getting married."

The back of my seat is grabbed and she pulls herself forward. "What? You're engaged?"

"We are."

"When? How? Oh my God. My baby sister is getting married." Her accent has lessened since she's lived in Chicago the last couple years, but every now and again, I hear it. Like now. "Delilah Rae, how could you keep this secret from me? Tell me everything, and you owe me a pie big time. You so lost that bet."

Jason's too busy laughing to get in the middle, so I reply, "Not even a week ago. I wanted to tell you in person, and I already have one cooling in the kitchen."

"Yum." She hits Jason on the arm. "Well, look at you coming back to town and sweeping my lil' sis right off her feet all over again. Took you long enough."

Turning onto our property, he says, "It's good to have you back, Shelby."

"It's good to be back. So. When's the wedding?" Sidetracked, she leans so far forward she's practically in the front seat with us. "Oh wow."

"What?" I ask.

"This place. Doesn't matter where I go, or how long I've been gone, there's no place like home. Pictures do not do this place justice." As soon as the car stops, she jumps out and heads to the side of the property to see the lake.

Jason looks at me, his hand gently rubbing my shoulder. "You okay?"

"I'm so much more than okay." His smile sends my heart soaring. "I've never felt happier."

The engine is off and he gets out to open my door, but I hop out before he can help me. It drives him nuts when I take away an opportunity for him to be chivalrous. He ribs me over it, but he also knows that sometimes I'm okay standing on my own independence. I take his hand though, because I appreciate having his support too. He allows me to feel safe and secure, which gives me the courage to be me. *The me I like.*

We reach the corner of the house. He kisses my temple and says, "I'll take her bags inside. Go spend time with your sister."

A small look is exchanged, but it says all we need to say. Love fills the gap between us, and we both smile.

When the tips of our fingers part, I walk around the house. Shelby stands with her hands clasped in front of her. I stand next to her, looking at the lake. The sunlight glistens across the water as the wind blows. "It never gets old."

She glances to me with a gentle smile on her face, and then wraps her arm around mine. "You're pregnant."

My head jerks back, my body shifting. "Why do say that?"

"I can see it. Your eyes. Your skin. Your happiness. The way you hold your stomach without even realizing you're doing it." The lake holds nothing to the glistening in her eyes. "Mom and Dad would be so happy for you, Delilah."

"What about you?"

A tear slips down her face. "I'm so happy you found a love to last a lifetime."

I embrace her as my own tears slip down my cheeks. Leaning my head on her shoulder, I sniffle. "Thank you. That means more to me than you know."

After our mother died, Shelby not only looked after me like a sister, but also a mother. It's a role she shouldn't have had to take on, but she did, putting her needs behind mine. When we look back up, we laugh—feeling a little silly and a lot sappy. "You've done so well managing this farm on your own. Maybe you should take this time for you and Jason." Pressing her hand lightly on my belly, she adds, "And for your family. The farm will always be here. Go see the world you've always wanted to explore."

"Jason has seen so much, but he says he wants to see it with me this time."

Turning back toward the lake, her arm is around mine again, her head on my shoulder. "You should. It's your turn, Delilah."

"You sacrificed a life back here to help keep this place afloat. We still have so much debt to deal with."

"Let's walk to the dock."

I follow her as she meanders, taking her time, as if she has all the time in the world. Slipping off our shoes, we sit on the edge with our legs hanging off and our toes in the water. She leans back, closes her eyes, and raises her face toward the sun. "The farm has been paid off."

I'm about to mimic her position, but instead I bolt upright from her words. "What? When? How?"

Peeking over at me through one open eye, she says, "I think that's a discussion you should have with Jason."

"Why do I need to talk to Jason?"

Patting my leg, she says, "Just talk to him and then we can talk again."

The sound of tires grinding against the gravel draws our attention to a truck parking in front of the barn. Shelby's eyes go wide, and she asks, "Good Lord. Who. Is. That?"

I burst out laughing, and turn my gaze back to Billy as he unloads some bags of feed. "*That* is Billy Langston."

Now she's upright. She might even be sticking her chest out if I'm not mistaken. "No way. That cannot be Billy."

Shrugging, I laugh again. "I told you he wasn't that lanky kid anymore."

"Yeah, but you didn't tell me he looked like *that*. Good gracious, he could be mistaken for Chris Hemsworth."

"Yeah." I nod and look back at him just as he lifts the front of his shirt and wipes his face. Shelby's jaw drops open. Nope, not lanky at all. "It's happened a time or two from what I hear." Raising my hand into the air, I yell, "Hey Billy."

A large bag goes flying onto a pile, and he looks up. Tipping the brim of his cowboy hat up, he smiles. "Hey Delilah." I can tell the moment he realizes who's sitting next to me. He walks over as Shelby stands and starts straightening the bottom of her shirt like he'll care if it has a few wrinkles.

Billy runs his hands down the front of his jeans as he comes closer. "Is that you, Shelby Noelle?"

"Sure is, Billy Langston."

My, oh my. Look whose accent has suddenly made a comeback. If you were wondering, the answer is Shelby's. Billy has a way of doing that to the ladies—you know, making them all gooey inside and flipping their worlds upside down.

Except me. My heart knows where it belongs. I've found my home with that sexy man inside the house. This second chance is one I'll never take for granted.

While they start chatting, I slip my shoes back on, and say to Billy, "Don't forget about tonight."

Shelby asks, "Are you joining us for dinner? We're making a big homemade meal with all the fixins'."

"I'd be a fool to miss it, Ms. Shelby."

I think I hear her swoon. "Well, don't go getting all dressed up for me. What you're wearing now—this T-shirt—is such a good fit. Feel free to come as you are." I definitely see her blushing before I turn and head inside, giving them some time to get reacquainted.

I find Jason sitting upstairs in my bedroom. Leaning

against the doorframe, I look around the room wondering what he's looking at. "What are you doing up here?"

His eyes find mine. "Thinking about life."

"That's heavy."

Chuckling, he looks down. "Yeah, kind of."

I go inside the pink room and sit on the bed next to him. "Shelby told me the farm is paid off."

Almost expecting him to tense up, I watch his shoulders for the subtle movement, but it doesn't come. He's relaxed, and I find comfort in that. When he finally looks at me, he says, "You would have never taken the money."

"Because it's yours."

"Don't you see, Delilah? There is no me without you. If I can do something to make your sister, Ricardo and Paloma's, and your lives easier, I will. That feels like a good way to spend money." I rub his back and nod. He adds, "I also bought my mom's house and paid off her debts."

Now I smile. "You are an amazing man, Jason Koster. Thank you for everything you've done."

"I'm only amazing because you love me."

"And I always will." We sit there a moment longer before he says, "Now that it's all paid off, Shelby said she wants to move home and into the house. I was thinking we could build one a few acres down, around the lake."

Thrown for a loop, my words get caught in my throat. "Eh. Wait. Jason."

"Yes?"

"Maybe we should talk about money like you wanted to."

"I have a lot."

"Do I want to know how much?"

"Since it's half yours, I think it would be wise for you to

know. That way we can make decisions on how to spend it together."

My mind is struggling to wrap around this massive turn of events. "You're giving me half your money?"

His arm works its way around my lower back as he teases, "You're not going to make me sign a prenup, are you?"

Rolling my eyes, I laugh. "Not likely."

"Then we share everything fifty-fifty. How's that sound?"

I stand and move in front of him. Pushing him down on the mattress, I crawl onto his lap, and straddle him. I kiss him, my body awakening from the intimacy. When our lips part, our breaths are heavy between us. "Like heaven on earth."

Pressing my mouth to his again, I will never tire of these lips on mine. He rolls us over and says, "The best is still to come."

Not a prediction.

A promise.

30

Delilah

SOME MATCHES ARE MADE in heaven. And some are made right here in our little parcel of paradise.

Billy's been here every day since Shelby arrived in town. He was here before Jason came back too, but his help hasn't been needed as much since Jason started taking on more of the upkeep and maintenance of the farm.

He's here for the second time today though, because he forgot to "check on something left in the barn." From up in the loft, I see him pacing, psyching himself up to ask her out on an official date. I smile but remain quiet. Unfortunately, Jason doesn't. "Stop fucking around and just ask her."

I whack Jason's leg. "Don't tease him," I warn while laughing. "The man is clearly head over heels for my sister."

Billy's gaze darts up. "Oh, man. What are you doing out here?"

Jason calls from his reclined position on the bed. "Making love to my woman. Ask Shelby out and get it over with. I'm tired of watching you two dance around the obvious."

I look over the edge at Billy and laugh. "Sorry. We should have told you we were here. It wasn't nice of us to eavesdrop. But since we're all here, Jason's right. I think she'll say yes, but you have to ask."

"Any advice?" he asks.

"She loves sushi."

His nose scrunches. "What the hell is sushi?"

Jason states, "Raw fish."

I glare at him. "You're being bad today."

"I am. You should punish me. With your mouth again."

"Oh my God," I whisper-yell. "Behave."

"What's the fun in that?"

I'm about to tackle him and show him how punishing my mouth can be and then let him punish me with his, but then remember Billy is still here like his whole life is depending on some tidbit of insight I can give him regarding my sister. He says, "Gross. So catch a fish out back and give it to her?"

Jason says, "Go away, man. I've got business to take care of."

"But I need help," he replies.

I peek over the edge again. "Just ask her. No gimmicks. No pretenses. No games. Just be you, Billy. She'll appreciate the sincerity."

"You're right." He appears empowered as he walks with purpose toward the house. "Wish me luck."

"Good luck," I call after him. *Shelby's about to be the second luckiest girl in Freeland County.* When he's out of sight, I turn the fan up and turn back to Jason who looks devilishly sexy and smug, lying there waiting for me. "About that punishment—"

"Punish away, baby."

I do, and then I let him reciprocate, but it's more making love and lust, punishment of the *good* kind.

~

BENSON AND BROOKS were charged with aggravated assault, attempted murder, tax evasion, and fifteen counts of illegal gambling with no bail. I'm not sad in the least.

Us versus them.

As much as I wish we hadn't experienced the nightmare of that night, it brought me to an understanding. Taking Jason's hand as we watch them be charged, I have no regrets. I would put my life on the line time and again for the ones I love.

Cole Cutler is asked to stand. His assigned lawyer stands behind the defendant's table with him. My hands don't shake. Anger is stronger than the fear he used to instill in me. The judge reads the charges, and then asks if he understands what he's being charged with. With his head down, he replies, "Yes."

The judge asks, "What do you plead?"

Cole's lawyer whispers in his ear while we all anxiously await his answer. Cole nods, looks at me, and then to the judge. "Guilty."

The gavel strikes, causing me to jump. I whisper to Jason, "Did he really plead guilty?"

"Yes." This is what we wanted when we walked into the courthouse this morning, but the shock of it happening is staggering. Jason's chest deflates and he exhales his relief. However, there's something in his body language that surprises me. Grabbing the bench in front of us, he drops his head. "He was my best friend." When his eyes land on mine, he asks, "How could a person I once trusted be so intent to destroy our lives?"

That is a question I have given much thought to, but avoided thinking about in the aftermath of kicking him out and our divorce. I think I was still so shell-shocked about what I'd been through and doubtful that he'd ever really be gone from my life. *And now I know that fear was well founded.*

There's no obvious reason for his actions. Greed? Hate? Sadness? "Jealousy?"

My marriage to Cole never felt real, not in the ways that count. Marriage is love and beauty, support, and friendship. I was betrayed, tricked into believing I deserved less in life.

Jason nods silently and then moves to leave, taking me with him. His mother catches us in the hall. She hugs me and then him. "Is it over?"

"They were charged," he says, assessing the courthouse exits. I wonder when he'll truly be home and not need to know how to escape if necessary. "Not sentenced. They pled not guilty so they'll go to trial."

She looks from him to me and back to him. "What about Cole?"

"Cutler will go straight to sentencing. We have to wait."

Meredith replies with a smile, "Well then, how about dinner tonight?"

We've had dinner with her at least once a week, when she's not busy with her boyfriend, Fred Carver. Jason starts grumbling, but I place an arm on him and reply, "We'd be happy to. Will Fred be there?"

"Yes. I think it's time for my guys to spend some time together."

"You're killing me, Ma."

"Oh, you'll live. I have needs too—"

"No." He rolls on his heel, turning his back to us. "I do

not want to hear about your needs when it comes to stuff like this."

"Maybe we'll have a double wedding," she teases. I love that she gives him a hard time. It's good for him.

I joke, "Our girl is all grown up."

"Don't you start in too." Walking backward toward the doors, he says to her, "We'll see you tonight."

"Love you, Jase."

"Love ya, Ma."

I catch up to him laughing and smacking his ass as I pass. He's quick though. And good with his hands. Correction: *great* with his hands. I'm scooped up in his arms outside the courthouse, kissed, and carried to the truck. When I'm set down, my back rests against the truck, and he cages me in. As always, I'm ready to make out right here on the sidewalk, but it seems he has other plans. "I want to take you somewhere."

With how he's looking at me right now, he can take me anywhere.

I DIDN'T EXPECT to be sitting across from Sabrina Smith inside McKinney National Bank, but here we are. Cole's name has been removed from all the paperwork. The farm is in Shelby's and my name. "It's surreal," I say to Jason, who's sitting next to me.

Rubbing my leg, he nods. "It's how it should be."

Sabrina, in all her snooty flair, stands abruptly and taps the papers on the desk. "I'll need to get my manager to handle your paperwork, Jason."

When she leaves the cubicle, I whisper, "What is she talking about?"

Matching my tone, he replies, "Wait for it."

The bank manager, Worley Hiccolms, comes in and heartily shakes our hands. "Mr. Koster. Ms. Noelle. Good to see you today." He glares at Sabrina. "If you'll excuse us."

"Sure," she says, like she's not totally wanting in on whatever this is.

He smiles like a Cheshire cat and pushes a piece of paper across the desk toward us. "Ms. Noelle has been added. We can update name changes after the nuptials. If you could both sign here, she'll be granted full access to the safety-deposit box and the two bank accounts."

I bump my knee against Jason's. He says, "Life is unpredictable. I thought it was a good idea to get you added sooner rather than later."

The bank manager says, "It's good to take precautions. Now, if you'll sign here and here, you can be on your way, and we'll take care of the rest." Jason has me sign first and then he signs on the line beneath mine. Worley stands eagerly. "I want to personally thank you for trusting your financial interests with our fine establishment."

They shake hands. "Thank you. Don't get robbed."

"Eh, we're insured."

We all laugh politely through a round of goodbyes until we reach the sidewalk. I ask, "What was that about?"

"I guess he's just happy to be working with us."

"Jason?" My hand goes to my hip. "Be open with me. How much money are we talking about? Worley doesn't treat everybody like that, so I'm assuming a lot. Twenty? Fifty? A hundred thousand?"

We reach the truck. He opens the door and says, "We can go inside and get a statement if you'd like."

"No." I climb into the cab. "Just tell me."

He shuts my door and drags this out, adding to the

drama, while he walks around to the driver's side. When he slips into the truck next to me, he starts the engine.

"Jason, tell me."

"You sure?"

His arm is on the back of the bench while he reverses. "Well, after paying off the farm and Mom's house, one point eight million in the accounts.

"What?" I shout. My throat tightens and I start coughing.

Patting me on the back, he looks over, but I see the smile on his face. "Are you okay, baby?"

I clear my throat, my hands on my chest. "One point eight million dollars?"

"No, Oreos. Yes, dollars."

Leaning back, I can't even fathom that amount of money. "From jobs?"

"Yes. I was paid well."

"That much is more than well, Jason."

He shrugs as he pulls out and starts driving. "I was very good at what I did."

"I would say so."

"This is a lot to take in. I get it. Every penny I earned was for this life, for us. I know that sounds unbelievable. You were married. I shouldn't have thought of you as more than someone else's wife. I think deep down my heart knew where it belonged. I knew. This is where I belong. Right here with you. Call it kismet or luck, great timing, or great fortune. Doesn't matter as long as I have you."

Our hands reach out and find each other in the middle.

This is love.

Pure.

Soul-enriching, life-affirming, deep-seated, raw, and real love.

Getting a second chance to be with this generous and kind man is more than kismet or great timing.

It's destiny.

I WALK into the barn and climb the ladder to the loft. We can't live up here forever, and definitely not through winter, but it's been fun. It's been the escape from the house we needed after that night we were attacked.

When I reach the top, I spot a gift box in the middle of the mattress. Sitting down next to it, I take it and lift the lid, smiling. I don't understand it, but maybe the note will explain. I pull the card from the envelope and read:

Dear Delilah,

For old times' sake, please wear this uniform and meet me at that stadium one more time, for me. I'll be waiting for you at 8 p.m.

Love you,
Jason

HOLDING the note to my chest, I swallow down the emotions he's stirred inside and blink back tears. It's hard though, when you read the sweetest letter you've ever received.

I set the note aside and reach for the uniform. Laughing, I stand up and hold the skirt to my hips. Not sure if this will still fit, but I'm willing to squeeze into it for Jason. With the top and bottom part of the uniform in hand, I rush back down the ladder and into the house.

"Shelby?" I run to the hall and call upstairs, "Shelby? Where are you?"

"Stop yelling, Delilah. I'm in here," she calls from the other room. It's been great having my sister home. Working remotely is allowing her to rediscover her love for country life. With the farm paid off, she gets to decide her future and whether she returns or stays. I'm hoping she stays.

I rush into the kitchen, my boots coming to a halt against the linoleum. Holding up the outfit, I ask, "Will you help me get ready?" A smile already sits on her face when she turns around with an iced tea in hand. "Uh, you know, don't you?"

"Maybe." She shrugs before setting her glass on the table and taking me by the arm. "Come on. Let's get you ready for the big game."

31

Jason

BILLY DRIVES his fists down on my shoulders. "All done."

All suited up in my old football uniform, I say, "It's been a long damn time since I wore pads."

"You're a big dude, you know that?"

Chuckling, I bend down to tie my shoes. "Yeah. I'm aware." When I stand up, the cleats add some height. "Shorty."

"At six one, I'm not usually considered short."

"Eh, don't worry. We're not playing football anymore. What time you got?"

"Ten till eight."

"Okay. I'm gonna head out there."

We shake hands, but I bring him in for a chest press. He asks, "Are you hugging me, man?"

"Maybe. Just go with it." He remains and I inwardly laugh. "Thanks for everything you've done to take care of Delilah through the years." We step back and I grab the football helmet. Holding it under my arm, I make sure I have everything else I need. "Thank you for tonight too." *I want everything just right for her.*

Giving me a middle-finger salute, he replies, "Aye. Aye, Captain." Some things never change. The smartass. When we enter the tunnel that leads to the field, he stops. "Good luck out there."

"Thanks, but I never need luck." I just need her. We walk in opposite directions. By the time I reach the field, the sun is starting to set. I scan the field and then the bleachers.

Six field exits.

Three on the far side.

Three behind me.

Ten exits up the bleachers.

Five on each side.

I make my way to the fifty-yard line, put my helmet on, and take a knee to wait. This afternoon, the rest of the pieces of my life fell together . . .

The paperwork has been signed. I'm here to pick it up. Delilah and the farm are free from Cutler forever. It didn't take much to get him to sign. I recommended it might be safer for him in jail than roaming free if he didn't. I simply rubbed my neck and bam, he signed that afternoon. I don't need to see him again, but apparently he wants to see me again, so here I am.

Sitting across from Cutler, I don't say anything. I'm not sure what to say anyway. But he says, "You were a good friend to me, Jason."

I scrub a hand over my jaw. "I was."

"I'm sorry." The fucker knows nothing about love. Never has.

"What you did to me was nothing compared to how you hurt Delilah."

"I loved her."

"No, you didn't. If you did, you wouldn't have laid a finger on

her. If you truly loved her, you would have wanted to see her happy, which she was with me."

"Guess the best man won." Idiot.

"It was never a game with her. There weren't winners or losers until you made it into a competition."

"I'll tell her I'm sorry."

"Don't." I stand. "Don't ever contact her again. This paperwork is all she needs from you."

I push the button. It buzzes as I wait for the door to open. The guard releases the door and I walk out. With glass dividing us, he yells, "I'm sorry."

He will be sorry. He will be sorry. Where he goes exists with no hope, no friendships, alone, no future or direction. He will understand a little of what I went through. Then maybe, he'll be sorry. But right now, the asshole doesn't have a clue.

. . . The lights flick on, lighting up the stadium and surrounding area. The scoreboard comes on next. The final score from that night years ago lights up the board. I spy Billy looking over the field from the announcer's booth and give him a thumbs up.

When he returns it, I know he's seen Delilah. The second she comes through that tunnel, it's as if the night became brighter.

Shelby was supposed to coach her about the setup. When Delilah sees me, she stops, a wide smile seen clear across this field. As much as I want to greet her, I don't. It has to be perfect. For her. So I stay. When she heads to the spot she used to cheer for the team, I know the plan is coming together. I continue to wait on my knee, and she keeps peeking my way.

I take a deep breath when she stands on the sidelines

with her pom-poms in hand and exhale. I'm nervous. This isn't about second chances. We already have that. Tonight is about righting wrongs.

Dragging my tongue over my bottom lip, I fix my eyes on her, get up, and start walking. I glance up to see Shelby next to Billy in that booth. She's clapping, and it's great to have their support.

When I look back at Delilah, she shifts her weight between her feet. She's nervous too. For some reason that makes me feel better knowing we're both invested as deeply in each other. Then I focus on my target—a strawberry blonde with big blue eyes, wearing her heart on her sleeve.

I take the helmet off and carry it by the face guard at my side. Just ten feet separate us when the world comes back in color—vivid and electric. And there in the center of my universe stands the only girl I ever loved. She's as gorgeous as she always was. That uniform is a fantasy come to life. Damn, she knows how to work her assets to her advantage. My mind goes blank just seeing her. I had prepared a speech, but fuck it. I walk right to her and pick her up by the waist. Her legs wrap around my middle and her laughter echoes around us. She bends down and kisses me.

"You're all I ever wanted, Delilah Rae Noelle."

Setting her down, her laughter is replaced with glassy eyes as she struggles to hold back her tears. "Me too. You're all I've ever wanted, Jason."

I drop down to my knee and take her hand. "Three thousand fans crowded into this stadium every Friday night to watch our team play and hopefully win. We usually did. I was named MVP all four years at school, but it's not the trophies or accolades I remember. It was great to be held on the shoulders of my teammates in high praise after winning state. But when I look back on my life thus far, my highlights reel plays our love story.

"The first time I ever saw you, you were wearing a purple shirt, a denim miniskirt, little socks that had frills, and blinding-white sneakers. You walked into the school with your sister, and I was dumbstruck.

"You were the prettiest thing I'd ever seen. Prettier than any flower I'd picked for my mom or picture of any model in a magazine.

"You may not have realized that every time our team scored or I won any kind of award, I looked for you. Nothing really mattered like your approval, your support, your love.

"Life may have taken us in different directions. We may have taken a few detours knocking us off course, but it carried me right back to you. This is the redo you wanted. This is our chance to put things back the way they were always supposed to be. Delilah Rae Noelle, marry me. Travel the world with me. Have babies with me. Hold my hand even when you're mad at me. And I promise I'll kiss you even after we fight. I'll take the middle-of-the-night feedings so you can sleep. I'll protect you. Always. But . . ."

I get choked up. I take a deep breath and exhale. "I'll love you more with each passing day. I'll love you until we're old and gray. I'll love you in this life and the next. I'll give you the world and the universe, the stars above, and will make love to your body and heart. Will you marry me?"

Throwing her arms around my neck, she sits on my bended knee. Her head is tucked between my head and shoulder pads, her shoulders shaking with sobs. When she wipes her face, she lifts up and I hear her.

Loud and clear . . . "Yes. A thousand yeses, Jason."

Jumping up, I bring her with me and turn around with her in my arms. We kiss again and when our lips part this time, Billy and Shelby are cheering over the loud speakers and shout in unison. "Congratulations!"

The song, "Someone to Stay" by the band, Vancouver Sleep Clinic, starts playing through the speakers. I set Delilah down, still holding her hand, and say, "C'mere."

Moving into my arms, we start a slow dance. "You went to a lot of trouble for a girl who already said yes."

"You once asked for a redo. I want to make all your dreams come true."

She tilts her head to the side with a sweet smile on her face. "You always did look good in a uniform."

"You look amazing."

Spinning from me, she shows me the back. "It's all rigged with safety pins. This skirt is way too tight."

I laugh seeing how she's pinned the back zipper together. There's at least two inches keeping the sides from meeting. "You're sexy as hell anyway."

"I've put on a little weight since you've returned, a few love pounds. I'm not worried, but it will be more."

"More?"

She grabs one of her pom-poms and bends over, flashing me her fine ass. Man, I'm getting hard looking at her. She's going to have to bring this ensemble into the bedroom for a little role play later.

When she turns back, she comes over and says, "Yes. More."

I'm so confused until I see the stick. A white stick in her hand between us. A white stick with two pink lines that she's holding out for me. I take it, my thoughts fumbling to register what this is, even though I know exactly what it is. "Jason?"

"Yeah," I reply, glancing to her and down to the stick again.

"We're having a baby."

It wasn't just one time we didn't use condoms. We stopped using them altogether, because we wanted this. We want this. I drop my head, but keep my eyes on her. "You're pregnant?"

"Yes." Her smile is even prettier than seconds before.

"We're having a baby." I take a knee before her again. "We're having a baby."

She laughs. "Yes, we're having a baby."

"What about the wedding? Do you want to get married sooner?"

"It doesn't matter when. It only matters that we're together."

Sitting on my leg, she cups my face and looks me in the eyes. "I was in town earlier, and I overheard Karen Taylor spreading gossip at the pharmacy."

"And what gossip was she spreading?"

"Well," she starts, raising one eyebrow, "rumor has it that you're bad for me."

"Shouldn't believe everything you hear. Sometimes a little bad can be good for a girl."

"I'd say." She kisses me and I kiss her with all the love she deserves.

"You know they're going to gossip about me knocking you up before marriage?"

"Let 'em. They don't matter. Only we do. And this baby. We're going to give this baby the best life ever."

Standing her up, I lean forward and kiss her bare midriff. "Hey baby, it's your daddy." Delilah's fingers run through my hair, holding me there. "Do you know how much I love your mama?" Looking at her, I confess the last of my secrets. "I have more money than what's in McKinney National Bank. Your name is on all four accounts. I was going to give it to you as a gift when the paperwork came in, but I guess we should figure out how to manage it together to make sure our family is always taken care of, and we can re-file all the paperwork."

"More money?"

"I don't really have a lot of faith in small-town banks. I was protecting our financial interests by spreading it out across the U.S. and one account in Switzerland."

"Wait, your name is on the accounts too, right?"

"Yes, but you have full access. No more secrets. That's it. You know everything now."

"I guess I should confess my final secret to you, too."

I stand, suddenly shaken. "What secret?"

"You know my tattoo?"

"My number eight that's nowhere close to twenty-two?"

"Yes, that's the one."

"What about it?"

"I wasn't drunk."

A grin grows across my face. "Have I ever told you how sexy that tattoo is?"

"Nope." A little hip wiggle punctuates her reply.

"How about I show you?"

I do. I show her three times before the rooster crows.

32

Jason

I SHIFT for like the tenth or twentieth time in the five minutes I've been sitting here. Maybe there's still time to bolt. The door opens. Guess not. I stand, unsure what I'm supposed to do or what I should say.

"Jason, good to see you." We greet each other with a handshake.

"You too, sir." I sit back down as he sits in his chair on the other side of the desk.

"Stephen is fine."

"Yes, sir."

"Look, son, I'm glad you finally came by. It's been a while since we've had a chance to talk."

"Yeah, I think maybe the last time was when I was fifteen. It was a warning about masturbation and the dangers of it."

Stephen starts laughing. "Yeah, for the parents' sake, we

give all the boys around that age the same warning. If not, imagine the mess on their hands."

I think the minister just made a joke. Am I allowed to laugh or was that a slip-up? "So we don't go to hell for it?"

Leaning forward, he lowers his voice. "Look, masturbation is natural, but you don't want it to control your life. Do you have a masturbation problem you'd like to discuss?"

Shaking my head, I'm horrified and squeak, "No." Clearing my throat, I finish by saying, "That's not why I'm here at all."

"Why are you here?" He leans back in his chair and studies me.

"You might have heard the rumors."

"I was happy to hear that the angels played a hand in bringing you and Delilah together again."

I'm not sure how to say what I want versus what I should with him. "Is everything between us confidential?"

"Yes. Unless it's illegal. I can help you repent to the Lord, but not keep you out of jail. What is it, son?"

"I'm seeking forgiveness."

"Forgiveness from God?"

"I've done things I'm not proud of, but I don't regret them either. But I also want to spend eternity with Delilah, so I'm coming to you for help."

"Hmm. Interesting quandary. Can you elaborate?"

"Not really. I can tell you that I didn't carry God with me while I was gone. I'd lost faith and left to find if there was still good in the world."

"Did you find any?"

Sitting back, I cross my ankle over my knee and think about his question. "A little, and in that little good, I realized I needed faith to find the rest."

"Ironic, isn't it?"

"I had nowhere to go, but my motorcycle led me back to McKinney."

"To McKinney or to the Noelle farm?"

"To Delilah."

"And what did you find once you were there?"

"Myself."

He nods with an all-knowing smile. "You don't need to seek forgiveness. You needed to find faith, and you did. It will always lead you exactly where you're supposed to be."

~

I BLAME the sun for shining in my eyes and causing them to water. Not the gorgeous woman walking on the arm of her sister down a pink rose-petal aisle. I'll never admit otherwise.

Yup, the sun.

That's my story and I'm sticking to it.

Billy nudges me. "Are you crying?"

"Are you?" I snap back.

"Maybe. A little."

"My soon-to-be wife is beautiful."

"I like Shelby."

"Yeah, I know."

"Really?"

"Yes, it's obvious. Apparently to everyone but you. Now can we get back to *my* wedding?"

He nods. "Yeah, sure. Sorry."

"It's okay. Shh."

The music wafts through the air from the trio playing by the barn. My eyes stay fixed on my pretty Delilah, her shoulders exposed as the lace hangs down on the sides. The dress flows around her and the flowers circling her head make her look like a goddess. My goddess.

"Do you think Shelby likes me? She flirts with me, and we hung out a few times, but—"

"Shut up, Billy." I laugh. Right before the girls reach us, I whisper to him. "She likes you, or she wouldn't give you the time of day. You guys need to seal this deal, once and for all. Make your move at the reception. Chicks love weddings." I turn back in time to take the hands of my sweet girl. "Hi."

She whispers, "Hi."

Her hands aren't shaking and her voice is steady. She's confident like the girl I always knew her to be. The difference is, she's not *that* girl. She's a woman who acknowledges the challenges of her past and is choosing to focus on the future. She's as kind as she is beautiful, accepting me with open arms despite my past. I begin to tell her all the reasons I love her, but it's the last one that means the most to me. "When I think of love, I think of you, Delilah. Home is where the heart is and my heart is wherever you are, my soul mate, my lover, my wife, the mother of my children. You gave me a reason to stay, and in return, I pledge to you my love in this lifetime and every life after."

"You showed up here on a motorcycle in the pouring rain. If that wasn't a love song in the making, I don't know what is. There you were, Jason Koster, looking at me with eyes that carried the burden of years of a broken heart. What you didn't know was when you took a chance and came out to the farm to see me, I had a broken heart, too. You carried half with you all those miles you traveled and all the seas you sailed. We didn't have to be together to know we were no good apart. Two halves only make a whole when the puzzle pieces fit, and we fit. Forevermore, our souls will be whole because we found our way back to each other."

"I always did enjoy a good love song. Care to finish this melody together?"

"I do."

CHAPTER 33

Three Months Later . . .

"Then what did he say?" Delilah asks, drawing figure eights in the sand.

How am I expected to finish a story about a minister when she's dressed in a skimpy bikini? She's way too distracting, and some guys were eyeing her earlier. I almost kicked their asses for ogling my wife like that.

I've discovered it doesn't matter what she's wearing though. Whether she's wearing a fancy dress in Paris or she's mostly naked on the beaches of California, they stare everywhere she goes.

Makes me miss the privacy of the farm where I'm the only one who gets to stare at her.

Lounging back on the sand, her baby belly is barely a pooch. I actually think that's from the hot dog she had at lunch, along with the salad, the large glass of water, and the two scoops of ice cream. I don't argue though. She's insisting it's what our baby boy needs.

I'm kind of hoping for a girl. She'll be a badass like her

mom and learn to throw a football like her dad. Guess we'll find out in about five more months. In the meantime, it's been one long honeymoon. Shelby's taken over the farm, with the help of Billy. Ricardo and Paloma also manage the fields like they always have. They are going to love the vacation to Hawaii we've booked for them when we return. They've been not only employees, but friends and parent figures to Delilah and me for years.

The floor plan for our home on the other side of the lake is approved and should be built before the baby comes.

There's a lot to be grateful for, and I owe it all to the woman next to me. "Who?"

"The minister, Jason."

"He said I'm where I'm meant to be."

Waggling her finger at me, she says, "Come over here."

She's irresistible. I kneel down between her legs and then drop my hands on either side of her head. I've traveled the world with this woman and nothing compares to her natural beauty.

"What is it, sweetheart of mine?"

"I've been thinking even though we've both been to hell and back, we are finally living the life planned for us all along."

"I have no doubt."

Lowering myself down, I'm careful about putting too much weight on her. I kiss her lips, and she moans into my mouth. I'm hard from the sound. "Want to go back to the hotel?"

"Can we order room service?"

"Anything you want."

"Anything?"

"Any. Thing."

"I have a few ideas."

"Do they include me or food?" Jumping to my feet, I offer her a hand. "What are you craving?"

When I help her to her feet, she presses against me. "You. Let's go play. I brought your jersey with us."

"You want me to put it on?"

"No." She winks. "I'm going to wear it for you . . . with nothing else underneath." She grabs her bag and walks through the sand, kicking it up with her feet. My mouth is still hanging open when she stops and looks back. "Well, don't keep me waiting. I have a new cheer I want to show you."

"Does it include you being naked?"

"It does. C'mon, MVP, show me how you earned that title. Maybe with a few tackles and first downs."

Jogging, I catch up with her. "I was thinking of a touchdown *there* to kick things off."

"As long as you drive it home, Quarterback, I'm in this game."

"You're very good with the football talk, but how about I show you my best moves, baby?" Taking her hand, I stop my beautiful wife. "Hey."

She smiles at me. "Hey."

Feeling much like the shy kid I was once around her, I hesitate, but then I step into her warmth and touch her cheek. "After the adventures we've had, traveling to all these places these past few months, have your dreams come true?"

"Don't you know, sweet man? I didn't have to travel the world to make my dreams come true. I just needed to be with you." She leans into my hand. "Do you think the farm can give you the peace to calm your restless soul?"

"It's never about the farm, or the lake, though both are peaceful places. It's always been about you." I kiss her forehead and whisper, "I'd lost myself, but I found my way home because you gave me a reason to stay."

She takes my hand from her cheek and lowers it to her belly. "Now you'll have two reasons."

"How do you feel about three?"

Though her eyes go wide, she doesn't say no. "Is that why we're building a five-bedroom house?"

Moving my hands to the sides of her waist, I wiggle her just a little. "No, that's for the fourth baby I was going to beg you to have down the road. That's why we're building five bedrooms."

"You want four kids, Jason?"

"I want a big family, sweetness." I sneak in a kiss attack on her neck, making her giggle.

"You keep that up and we might end up with a football team."

"That's the plan."

With her hand on the back of my head, she tilts to give me more access. "Oh Lord, help me. You are my complete undoing."

When I lean back to get a good look at my girl, she tilts her head, her ponytail swinging to the side, looking just as beautiful as she was that day we first began. Taking her hand, I kiss her palm, and the side of her mouth before whispering, "I was undone the moment I laid eyes on you, so we'll call it even."

~

I thought I knew what love was. It was all tied up in a pretty package of silky hair and soft skin, a smile that warmed me, and a soul that cared for me. Delilah held every emotion I'd ever felt—happiness, heartbreak, protectiveness, possessiveness, caring, and an emotion I've not been able to identify with a single word, but a bundle of things I feel when I look at her.

It's overwhelming and soft, rounded on the corners, but sharp-tongued, fiery and passionate, pure and comfort, desire and lust, kindness and genuine . . . safe. Complicated to describe. Easy to feel. Perhaps sanctuary is the best word for it.

That changes the day I meet my daughter. My head clears and things aren't so complicated after all. All these feelings—jumbled inside my heart in a mass of emotion—become clear when I look at Delilah with tears in my eyes. I still need more than one word to describe what my wife gives me that day:

Love.

Hope.

Faith.

Faith Noelle Koster is born on a Sunday morning in early spring. She comes into this world screaming, but as soon as I hold her in my arms, she stops and coos. This little human might be small, but she is mighty. When her tiny fingers wrap around one of mine, she does more than hold my hand, she steals my heart.

Two days after we arrive home with our little bundle of joy, I wake up before five in the morning to find the bed next to me empty. I go down the hall and find my wife sitting in a rocking chair holding our newborn. Watching her in this sweet moment, I'm reminded how I once thought I didn't deserve this life. I didn't believe that a sinner like myself deserved solace from the wrongs committed.

But here I am, living proof that sometimes bad guys simply need to find their purpose to be good. Sometimes their souls aren't completely black, just a little singed around the edges. Sometimes it just takes seeing the light to make it all right.

I walk into the room and catch Delilah's eyes. Her early morning smile is one of my favorites, though she argues she's tired and has dark circles. "How'd I get so lucky to be your husband and Faith's father?"

Reaching for my hand, I kneel next to her chair and take it. "It was never about luck, babe. It was destiny."

Destiny.

JASON KOSTER

If you'd like to spend more time with Jason Koster, you can meet him in SAVAGE, where he was first introduced. SAVAGE is now available.

SAVAGE

Welcome to the mysterious world of the rich and the damned in this gritty, modern day fairy tale. Two star-crossed lovers will either find their destiny or meet their fate in a world where demons come in the form of familiar faces and pawns aren't just players, but deadly.

She was my destiny.

I was her downfall.

We were a match made in hell.

But when we were together, that hell was pure heaven.

The moment I laid eyes on her, I knew she would pay the price for my sins. I wasn't much older than she was, but old enough to know better. Old enough to know she would be good for me and I was bad for her. But I pursued her anyway. Back then I had hope that maybe she could change my future.

Maybe together we could change our fate . . .

PROLOGUE

The sun shouldn't be shining

Considering the pain I'm feeling, it's too bright.

Too happy.

Too blue.

The periwinkle sky reminds me of the only blue I want to see. Brilliant blue eyes, not found in the heavens, but here on earth.

The world dims momentarily. "Where's your boyfriend?" the man asks.

How did I end up here? *Like this?*

I know. I just don't want to admit the truth. *Even now.*

Closing my eyes to block him out, I search my mind for the answer. "He'll come for us," I whisper.

Us.

A sharp slap to my face sends my head to the right. I'm too stubborn to scream, to give him any further satisfaction, even as the taste of copper coats my mouth. Curling to the side, I hold my stomach, attempting to protect the only thing that matters. I haven't told Alexander. I haven't had the chance. I was going to, but an unforeseen detour brought me here.

Grief begins to envelop me, but I try to hold on, just a little longer. Reaching out, I touch the red pooled in front of me, wondering if that's someone else's blood. *It can't be mine.* There's too much to be mine. I'm alive, but now I'm wondering for how long.

"Where's King?" is shouted, but I'm too tired to answer. Even if I could, I don't know where he is.

He didn't answer his phone. I allowed him to ride away, and the memory of his face causes my breath to stutter in my throat. As I cough, and blood splatters my present, I wish I could change the past. I wish I could go back to the beginning and relive our love from the start.

I would do so many things differently. Despite how we ended, I wouldn't change *us*. I wouldn't change our love.

His life is full of lies—the kind he tells and the ones he lives. Lies that have become mine and will haunt me as I learn to live without him. Those lies still haunt me as if they are mine to survive.

He once told me he would give me the life I dreamed about—the ending I deserved—a happy ending—but with rocks cutting into my skin and a stranger kicking the life from me, I start to wonder if all hope is lost.

Until I hear that familiar sound—the distinctive sound of a Harley's exhaust foreshadowing my knight in leather armor.

It doesn't matter how long it's been since I've seen him.

It won't matter what bad has happened between us.

Our love will never die, even if I do.

"I told you he'd come for us."

Knowing he'll be here soon, I close my eyes, and dream of the fairy tale we once had . . .

CHAPTER 1

Alexander Kingwood IV

This is my favorite way to wake up.

Often pretending to be asleep, I spy on her as she climbs out of bed, finding peace watching her day begin. Life is better with her around.

Simpler.

Happier.

A kiss to my face. Location varies from the tip of my nose to forehead, the occasional closed eyelid before she sneaks out of bed, tiptoeing into the bathroom and then back out. I struggle to stay still this morning, needing her in ways that aren't quiet. The night clogs my throat, my voice still gruff. "Come back to bed."

Standing at the dresser, digging through the top drawer where she keeps some of her things, Sara Jane looks back at me with a smile at play on her lips, simultaneously giving me a peek at some side tit. "I thought you were asleep."

I stretch my arms up and grab hold of the top of the headboard behind me. "I'm up." Her back is smooth. The curve from her waist to her hips defined more with each year that passes. Her ass sits high and tight above her legs. Her body caught at the other end of transitioning from a girl's into a woman's. Giving her a solid once-over, she knows what's on my mind. "Come back to bed," I repeat the request without a plea. She'll come. She always does for me.

Sara Jane is not just good to me. She's good *for* me. She's kept me from burying myself or being buried more than a few times. My pretty firefly has seen me through my highs and lows and now stands by my side as the one constant in my life, the only person I can truly count on.

Her lace panties slide down her thighs and she returns. She knows what I want. She wants it too, so I don't have to put on a big production or sweet talk her back into bed. Settling on top of me, she slides down over my cock, ready for me, slick with desire. Slow and steady feels like a good idea this morning. I hold her hips, keeping my grip light as she fucks me.

Her hands press to my chest and she leans down to kiss me. Before she has a chance to pull back, I grab her face, making sure our eyes meet, and I hold her gaze. "You know how much I love you, right?"

Softness covers her expression as she smiles. "As much as I love you, Alexander."

Alexander. Hearing her say my name keeps me grounded to her and planted in reality. She's the only one who calls me that, the only one I *allow* to call me by my full name.

When she sits up, she begins to rock, her head dropping back, her hair long, the tips running over my thighs. Her tits are amazing, full with weight to them. For someone so small, she was blessed in all the right places. My pretty little firefly has changed a lot since we first met. If possible, she has become even more stunning.

The first time I saw her, I knew she would be mine. Nothing would keep me from her. Something wild and untamed stirred deep inside just from the sight of her.

Cruise hadn't understood. He'd been busy talking about some cheerleader he scored with the night before, but my mind had drifted, which had been standard anytime the chicks from school were brought up. I'd lost interest in the easies by tenth grade. But after what happened two weeks before, I'd struggled to find pleasure in anything. My taste buds had dulled, and life lacked color.

Except for that damn blue polka-dot umbrella and the girl standing beneath it, who stole my world from under me. She was sunshine on a rainy day, a rainbow against gray clouds, hope in a Catholic school uniform. She was why poetry was written and art created. I could deny I became a fool for love the second I saw her, but it would be a lie. She made me want to be a better man, a better person in life. She made me think twice about the direction I was heading. But we both knew better. Our course was already set, our love a sweeping storm that would brew for years before raging.

Her hair hung down, darker because it was wet, soaked as if the umbrella hadn't protected her. Her eyes were wide with innocence as she ate a candy bar like it was the best treat she'd ever tasted. Her skirt . . . damn that short skirt. I saw the man in the car next to me staring at her and I wanted to beat the shit out of him for looking at her like she could be his next tasty treat. That fucking pervert was around my dad's age. *Fucking asshole.* She couldn't be more than seventeen.

I was tempted to go over and cover her bare legs with my jacket. The girl was oblivious to the attention she attracted, and I almost felt I should become her protective knight in shining armor. I wanted to kick my own ass for that thought. So fucking lame. Until she looked my way. My throat went dry and my lips parted. The humid air wouldn't save me. I was lost to this girl from that moment on.

She looked away, and the sweetest of pinks colored her cheeks. *Damn.* Her purity shined like a beacon. I've never been one with a need to take a V-card to feed some locker room pride. Nah, I didn't need to prove anything to anyone, least of all some jock-asses who bragged about every girl they bagged. But when she dared to look my way again, a deep-seated desire stirred. I wanted her.

It was a carnal reaction I felt in my gut, but it had nothing to do with sex. Sure, sex crossed my mind, but its images were blurred like visions of déjà vu.

With no justifiable reason, right there at a busy intersection in the suburbs north of downtown, I became determined to be everything she would ever need. I would risk it all just to talk to her. If she'd never been kissed, I'd kiss her so she never desired to kiss another man. If she was still innocent in other ways, I would earn her trust and not just make love to her, but create it, a bond so strong she'd never need anyone else. I would be her first *and* last love. That day as the rain came down, I made sweet Sara Jane Grayson my mission. With nothing left to lose, I vowed to steal her heart and own her soul.

As I watch her moving on top of me, buried deep inside her, I hope I've changed her for the better. Three years ago, when our worlds collided, she changed me.

She collapses on my chest and I hold her tight as our bodies relax after the intense release. Fingertips tap across the tattoo that honors her, the one she hates. To be fair, she doesn't want me to have any, but she calls this one an ugly bug. There's nothing ugly about the firefly. Just like her, its strength is illuminated in the darkest of times.

Lifting up, she rests her chin on my chest, and asks, "What are you doing today?"

In any other room, in any other house, with any other couple, this question would be so easy to answer. But it's not in another place and we're not just any other couple. We're complicated and my life is twisted. I try hard to spare her from getting caught up in my tornado. My self-destructive ways have become worse, but I don't mention most of that to her anymore. Instead, I respond like we are one of those other couples, where answers are easy, and life is simple. "I'm going into the office, and have a meeting with my father. I'll pick you up on campus later."

Sitting up, she maneuvers away, but I'm quick and grab her wrist. When her sweet, soulful eyes—that melt me like butter—reach me, I add, "More."

"More?"

"I love you more."

A smile slips into place and she pokes me in the chest. "You're not so tough, Mr. Kingwood." It's a game she likes to play, to pretend that some of my bad isn't as bad as her mind imagines.

I play along because despite the light she brings into my world, I only bring darkness into hers. The smile she evokes from me comes naturally though. "Nah, I'm not so tough."

Leaning back down, she kisses my cheek and then gets up to shower. I watch that ass I'm so fond of until she disappears into the bathroom. My phone vibrates on the nightstand. It's been going off for at least an hour. We both ignored it, but I can't any longer. Reaching over, I grab it and glance at the messages.

The sigh is automatic as soon as I see the text.

Cruise: *When are you coming in? Your dad is flipping out.*

Me: *I'll be in shortly.*

Cruise: *Fucker.*

Me: *You know it, Sucker.*

I toss the phone on the bed and head into the bathroom. I open the shower door and look in, eyeing her. "Perfect timing."

Sara Jane laughs and her hands go up. "Oh no, you stay back. I can't be late again or I'll be counted absent."

Taking the soap from her hands, I step in and run the bar over the silky skin of her breasts and down farther until the bar is dropped and my fingers are between her legs. "If that's the worst that can happen . . ."

"Damn you."

"You love it, baby. So much. Just like you love me."

Her eyelids dip closed when her shoulder blades hit the white tile wall. I lean over her and kiss her breath away when my mouth covers that little O her lips are forming. Hands press against my chest then slide up to grab hold of my shoulders, pulling me closer.

Soap and sex covers her as I glide my tongue up until it's discovering every curve and alcove of her mouth. I want to fuck her. *Again.* So fucking hard that she forgets she has classes altogether. She forgets the outside world. She forgets everything else, everything but me. Pressing my cock against her hip, I push as my fingers fuck her pussy. I'm trying to be good, trying to make it about her. Only about her, but she makes it damn hard when she grabs my cock with both hands and starts to get me off.

"I want to fuck you." My words are minced under the water's spray as I lean my head against the wall and take the shell of her ear between my teeth.

"God, Alexander." Her body folds against mine, her

orgasm close enough to feel her tightening around me. "Why do you do this to me?" Her question is loaded, and I'm not sure it only concerns our sexual deviancy.

"It's what you do to me. Turn around." I take her by the ribs and spin her toward the wall. Her hands go against the wall in front of her and she parts for me. Such a good girl.

My dick is big and she's small, so I bend down until I feel her wet heat with my tip. I bite her shoulder lightly then thrust hard. Her cry echoes off the walls with her hands braced higher up. I take her hips and fuck, lost in her, lost in the sensations of her sweet little pussy.

My fingers dig deeper as our bodies gyrate together, slicker by the second. I close my eyes and let the water rain down over me as movements become erratic, compromised by the slipperiness. Close. So close. I will never have enough of her, never satisfy the heavier urges my heart craves. So I stake claims for her, but more for me. "You're mine. You know that?"

"I always have been." Her words are strained and then sucked back in as she takes another deep breath.

"Mine. Fucking mine. Always. Say it."

"Always yours, Alexander."

"King," I demand, fucking her harder. She knows what I want. It's something she only gives me when I'm at my best, in my opinion, *worst* in hers.

She won't say it. I know her too well to know she won't play into that game. And I'm coming too fast. "Fuck," I shout and pull out, my cum covering her lower back and dripping lower. Backing away to the corner, my breathing is harsh as I stare at my painting with pride. I shrug. "What can I say? You feel too good." She rinses her body and steps out of the shower without a word.

She's pissed off.

I won't make apologies just yet. She felt too good to be sorry. Lazily, I clean up and shut the water off. I step out and grab a towel from the rack. "Come on. Don't be mad."

"Easy for you to say. You came."

Her feistiness is a turn-on. If I didn't just fuck her, I'd try again. This time I'd fuck that damn sexy mouth of hers. "I'll make it up to you."

"I think you've done enough. Now I'm late for class and wound up."

I take the ends of the towel wrapped around her and tug her to me. "Don't be mad." I kiss her on the head, and then give her the smirk that will win her over, easing her irritation. "I'll make it up to you tonight. I promise."

"I have a group project to work on tonight. I'm going to stay on campus." She backs away, not looking at me while running the towel over her hair.

My brow cinches as I watch her. "Hey, are you really upset?"

"I'm not happy."

When she still doesn't look at me, I nudge her. "Don't be like that."

That gets her attention. She stands straight up, throws her hand on her hip, and narrows her eyes. "Like what, Alexander? What am I being like?"

"I know where this is going, and I'm not doing it. Don't start a fight where there is none."

"I learned from the best. It's what you do every day."

"Not with you." When she turns her back on me, I lose it. "I'm warning yo—"

Spinning on her heels, she points at me. "You're warning me? I'm not one of your lackeys, Alexander. Stop trying to make King happen. I don't call you King, and I never will. So don't you dare warn me about anything."

If she were one of my *so-called* lackeys, she'd be knocked right the fuck out for that. Seeing her with wet, messed-up hair, a towel wrapped around her, and her finger poking my chest, I stand down, deciding to give her the respect she demands. "Fuck, you're scary, Firefly."

Her hand falls to her side, and she rolls her eyes, but the smile I wanted to see is there and brings one to my mouth. When the tension in her muscles loses its momentum, she says, "You're ridiculous. Get dressed. We're both late."

Thirty minutes later, I kiss her before we open the door. I straighten the backpack on her shoulder and wrap my other arm around her. She whispers, "Be civil with your father."

"It will be a struggle, but I'll try. For you, I'll try." Stepping back, I hold a few fingers up pledge style, not sure if it's supposed to be two or three. "Scout's honor."

"You were never a scout," she corrects and laughs, stepping into the hall. "But try. Okay?"

After slapping her ass, I wink. "I always do."

If you would like to continue reading about Alexander and Sara Jane, SAVAGE is now available.

EVEREST

Make sure to look for EVEREST, my new romantic suspense releasing November 2017.

Add to your Goodreads To Be Read Shelf.

ON A PERSONAL NOTE

Thank you to my family. You are amazing and patient, supportive, and my always in my corner. Thank you!

To my friends: Adriana, Andrea, Anthony, Heather M., Irene, Jennifer S., Jessica H., Kerri, Kirsten, Lynsey, and Serena. You are awesome and inspiring.

Amy Bosica, Andrea Johnston, Kristen Johnson, Lynsey Johnson, and Melissa Krehley for beta reading my books. They are better because you read them.

Thank you to my Scottie Girls: Annette, Kristen, Lynsey, and every member who make that group one of the best places to hang out <3

Thank you to my editors for all their hard work.

ALSO BY S.L. SCOTT

The Kingwood Duet

SAVAGE

SAVIOR

Hard to Resist Series

The Resistance

The Reckoning

The Redemption

The Revolution

The Rebellion

Talk to Me Duet

Sweet Talk

Dirty Talk

Welcome to Paradise Series

Good Vibrations

Good Intentions

Good Sensations

Happy Endings

Welcome to Paradise Series Set

From the Inside Out Series

Scorned

Jealousy

Dylan

Austin

From the Inside Out Compilation

Stand Alone Books

Missing Grace

Until I Met You

Drunk on Love

Naturally, Charlie

A Prior Engagement

Lost in Translation

Sleeping with Mr. Sexy

Morning Glory

To keep up to date with her writing and more, her website is www.slscottauthor.com to receive her newsletter with all of her publishing adventures and giveaways, sign up for her newsletter: http://bit.ly/SLSNewsletter

Join S.L.'s Facebook group here: S.L. Scott Books